CW01500168

To *Kenneth Pitchford*
Friend, poet, novelist and prominent gay
activist who fought the brave fight for most of
his ninety years.

And to *Steven Pasternack*
Authority on media law, ethics and the international press who died as a result of a blood
infection contracted in Rwanda.

And to *Shane Hoover*
Journalist, freelance writer and podcast
producer who generously shared with me
his extensive research on the burlesque star
Busty Russell, on whom my own Busty is based.

And to *Barbara Griffel* and *Holly Druckman*
First readers who provided helpful comments
and suggestions.

And, finally, to *Stephen Games*
My editor, guide and conscience, who was
determined to get the very best from me
at all times.

SECRETS OF THE
FOUR-CHAMBERED HEART

ABOUT THE AUTHOR

Steven Jay Griffel has been a novelist for the last twenty years, after thirty years in corporate publishing, initially with McGraw-Hill and then as a writer and freelance editor.

His first novel, *Forty Years Later*, became an Amazon Number One bestseller and was followed by four other titles centred around the character of David Grossman, a middle-aged publishing executive. *Secrets of the Four-Chambered Heart* is his eighth novel.

He studied at Queens College, CUNY, where he registered as a Creative Writing major, going on to gain an MA in American Literature from Fordham University.

He lives in New York City, where he was born and raised, is married and has daughters and grandsons.

SECRETS OF THE
FOUR-CHAMBERED HEART

A Novel

Steven Jay Griffel

24

ENVELOPEBOOKS

Published 2025 in Great Britain and the USA by
EnvelopeBooks
12 Wellfield Avenue, London N10 2EA
116 West 73rd Street, New York, NY 10023
www.envelopebooks.co.uk
A New Premises venture in association with Booklaunch

Cover design by Stephen Games | Booklaunch

A CIP catalogue record for this title is available from the
British Library and the Library of Congress Cataloging-in-
Publication Data

Edited and designed by Booklaunch
EnvelopeBooks 24
ISBN 9781915023520

NOTHING COOLER THAN THAT

Mark Goldstone

Back in the early nineties, James Andersen and Francine Rose lived off campus as husband and wife. At the time, I doubted they were actually married, as I never saw a jot of suggestive proof: no marriage bands, no wedding pictures, no intimate connection of any kind. In fact, I saw them together only once and never in their home, which I visited occasionally as a grad student and much more often after I had met their daughter, Molly: a sylph — a sparkplug — a compassionate, flame-throwing firebrand who walked with a limp, the rhythmic thump of which made me initially suspect that she had a wooden leg.

I was visiting Professor Andersen in his home, a strangely cramped, labyrinthine apartment on the corner of Tenth and Lexington, right above Thielsson's (an old-style diner with red-topped counter stools and booth jukeboxes), when I heard, coming up the ancient wooden stairs, that loud repeated clomp that might otherwise have been made by a drunkard. But it was Molly, a freshman at The New School, where (according to her father) she intended to major in Journalism and minor in Women's Studies. I knew she'd also applied to the John Jay College of Criminal Justice but had withdrawn her application on learning that her criminal misdemeanors would likely scotch her candidacy; and to NYU's Institute of Human Development and Social Change as a pathway to helping her ethically challenged friends in Washington Square Park; and to the Jewish Theological Seminary, in the slim but fervent hope of finding a God — or Goddess — to guide her Wonder-Woman yearning to fight social injustice. Ultimately, she'd been persuaded by her parents to accept the four-year, no-strings-attached scholarship offered by The New School, which underpaid her parents but gave them a platform to teach their popular, ground-breaking courses in journalistic ethics, gay rights and feminism.

Knowing of all the various colleges and curricula she'd considered, it appeared to me that Molly had been influenced equally by her father and mother, though she was then living exclusively with her dad. Two months earlier, her mom (riding a wave of sudden celebrity and having had enough of her husband's domestic laxity and existential hypocrisy) had left the family abode and moved into her partner's home. I say *partner* as in business associate, not a publicly acknowledged, monogamous lover of the same sex (as the word is often used today), though the latter meaning would also prove to be true.

Anyway, I was at Molly's home because her father, Prof. James Andersen, was my academic advisor and had asked me over, presumably to discuss the progress of my dissertation (*Journalism as Activism: The Ethics and the Law*). I later discovered that he had conspired to bring Molly and me together, in the vague hope that we'd hit it off and that my studious and responsible ways might blunt or redirect her increasing rebelliousness.

Molly X

Bullshit! Having to write *Molly Jean Andersen* on all those college applications was pure, paternalistic bullshit. I loved my dad but bristled at the idea of being branded with his patronymic. Having recently read *The Autobiography of Malcolm X*, I decided that I should break all my binding shackles and declare myself free — hence my new moniker, *Molly X*.

That was my mindset when I arrived home earlier than expected to meet Mark Goldstone, A1 mensch and grad student extraordinaire, according to my dad, Jimmy, who'd been talking him up for the past month. Weeks before that, when Jimmy asked if I was making new friends at school, I'd slipped up and said, "You know, same-old, same-old." Big mistake: not what he wanted to hear. He must have imagined me backsliding into the funky shadows of Washington Square Park, where my old friends — a merry band of hip-hop wannabes and dreadlocked Rastafarians — smoked dope like it was a contest and sold it like a Wall Street commodity.

But that life was mostly behind me. I mean, I still smoked dope but I was no longer childishly cavalier. I knew who my parents were. I knew I'd been gifted with an amazing opportunity to learn from them and others. I knew I had a responsibility to save the world.

But I also knew I wasn't quite ready. I knew this to be true because every time I went alone to a campus meeting or to some political outpost I had the jitters. Deep in my gut I felt like I needed to share the experience with a partner: someone to play Smith to my Pocahontas; perhaps a Vita to my Virginia. (I was just then beginning to explore what is now referred to as my *sexual fluidity*.) In any case, knowing I must remain authentically me in any relationship, I announced my arrival home with a thumping climb up the stairs, putting my worst foot forward, half-hoping my dad's choice of Dudley Do-Right would betray his inappropriateness by saying something weak or stupid.

Mark Goldstone

Prof. Andersen (who'd asked me to call him *Jim* when we were in off-campus, social situations) had left five minutes before to bring back sandwiches from the diner below, leaving me alone in the strange apartment, stuffed with books, homosexual and lesbian art, and large floor plants whose vines sprawled and spiraled like monstrous tentacles. I was already unnerved when I heard a pounding on the stairs that grew louder and louder, suggesting that someone (or some*thing*) was fast approaching. Suddenly (while I cowered on the couch), the apartment door slammed inward and there on the threshold stood a smallish young woman: her hip cocked, her hair cut short, like Joan at Orléans.

Molly X

His face blanched; his mouth was a silent rictus. I don't think he expected a pretty cripple to kick open the door.

Mark Goldstone

Thinking she must be Jim's daughter, I moved quickly to greet her, only to have my right ankle ensnared by one of the creeping floor vines, tripping me and sending me headlong into her arms.

"So much for small talk," she said, disentangling.

"I'm so sorry. How embarrassing!"

"Don't be," she said, separating from me. "The room isn't well lighted. The windows haven't been washed in my lifetime. And the floor plants are a health hazard. Welcome to my world."

I shook her extended hand, noting its surprising strength.

"Mark Goldstone. I'm one of your father's students."

"I know who you are. I'm Molly."

Molly X

"Let's go into the kitchen," I said, leading the way, knowing he'd have a clear view of my lame gait and wondering if he'd dare mention it.

Mark Goldstone

I saw what I saw but didn't know what to say. I have an easy sense of humor but this was such a personal thing — and Jim was my professor and advisor.

Molly X

I would have let any other guy squirm but I already liked

him. His clumsiness was adorable. His old-school manners were so comically uncool, I thought he might actually be cool. Then I recalled what Jimmy had said about his intelligence and dedication, his interest in journalistic ethics and social politics and I knew there was nothing cooler than that.

THE CAGED BIRD SINGS

Molly X

My mother's parents died when I was quite little and she rarely mentioned them, other than to criticize their criticisms of her rebelliousness.

In my earliest memories she worked at home on a portable typewriter; later, on a small Wang computer whose phosphorescent green screen mesmerized me, like the hovering head of Oz the All-Powerful.

Over time I learned that she was an editorial freelancer, writing and editing language arts materials for high school students and their teachers. Often, when playing with my trains or toy soldiers, I'd hear her speaking with an editor on the telephone, decrying the under-representation and mischaracterization of strong females ... or how young girls' opportunities seemed too narrowly prescribed ... or how single women were depicted as overly preoccupied with getting married ... or how married women all too often lost themselves in the dutiful service of their families. When my parents spoke of these issues, my father always seemed to agree with her, even adding his own vehemence. He was an enlightened journalist and I was proud they got along so well; seemingly so copacetic and evenly matched.

I wasn't yet born when the first issue of *Ms.* magazine launched but apparently Frankie, my mom, was rapturous, yelling for all to hear: "Finally, the caged bird sings!"

According to family legend, she had taken a copy of the

magazine to a local printer and asked about getting the cover enlarged and framed. Two weeks later, the now three-by-five-foot cover was hung on the main wall of our living room, between a pair of antique sconces.

After the giant magazine cover was installed, my mother would sit on the living room floor like an acolyte before a shrine, staring up at the image of an attractive, eight-armed woman, blue-skinned like a Hindu goddess, each hand holding an object that defined her multi-tasked life: a blaring phone; an analog clock; a rake; an egg-frying skillet; a black typewriter; a steaming iron; a steering wheel; a hand-held mirror. Other aspects of the goddess were also revealing: Her long dark hair was splotched with the curse of early graying. Her blue legs were shapely and her feet were shod with red pumps. Her left foot was raised as if dancing a jig. There were tears in her eyes; vermillion on her lips; and her see-through womb revealed a demanding male homunculus.

Inspired by the magazine and its cover, Frankie started writing feminist articles. Because many women's magazines had been moving in that direction for years (away from the pap of fashion trends, holiday recipes, craft ideas and ways to rejuvenate through exercise), there was no shortage of outlets interested in what she had to say. Over time, her articles appeared in influential publications like *Rolling Stone*, *The Village Voice* and even *Ms.* magazine.

My father seemed to be a big supporter, reading her early drafts and making suggestions, when solicited. For his part, Jimmy's own professional area of expertise, journalistic ethics, was becoming increasingly focused on the gay liberation movement. Jimmy first became interested twenty years earlier, when it seemed to him that many gays were having their Constitutional protections violently abridged. Many journalists and their editors seemed unsure how to depict the injured parties, some of whom seemed shyly innocent (the guy next door who just happened to proposition an undercover cop at a gay bar) ... and others (who performed lewd acts onstage or in a public pine barren) who were more flamboyantly anarchic.

By the time of my dad's early professional interest, the issue of gay rights had become a national conversation and while some progressive journalists regarded social ethics as a mutable thing, conservative journalists usually saw it as sacrosanct and inviolable. Debates related to Constitutional protections, especially as they related to gray areas of government reach and personal choice, seemed destined for the Supreme Court.

SEPARATE, BUT NOT QUITE EQUAL

Lawrence Schielding

In the early 1970s, Jimmy and I were undergrads at New York's Columbia University, majoring in Journalism, while Frankie studied Education across the street at Barnard College. Columbia, the older, better-known Ivy League school, had a *Males Only* admission policy.

The official word was that the two schools were separate but equal but there were inequities, beginning with the fact that Barnard was generally referred to Columbia's sister school. Such slights (and more) bothered some members of the Barnard community more than others. It bothered the fuck out of Frankie. While she loved studying and dorming with her brilliant scholastic sisters, she despised the implicit segregation. "It's just another Jim Crow law. Another way of restricting women. Another way of keeping us down."

The three of us were best buds but I can't say any of us would have taken the Musketeer oath of one for all and all for one. We loved ourselves as a trio but each of us loved ourselves best and secretly plotted personal pairings within the group: Jim plotted with Frankie, Frankie plotted with me, I plotted with Jim. We were young and unaware of our truest motives. Somehow the relationships survived, though they would morph considerably with the years.

Francine Rose

I met James and Larry at a Christmas concert at St. John the Divine, the great cathedral on Amsterdam Avenue and 112th Street, just a few blocks south of Barnard and Columbia. As classes had ended for winter recess and the concert was free, lots of students had showed up and the place was packed.

For ten minutes I walked up and down the aisles but could not find an empty seat. There were dozens piled high with coats but I didn't then have the balls to make a scene — and the concert was about to start. Wavering wildly between determined and defeated, I gave myself one last chance: a half-hearted sprint up and down the aisles — but there was nothing. Finally, I stopped in the middle of nowhere, all alone, feeling all eyes on me — the only person who didn't belong. The forlorn and outcast Jew.

Disappointed and with stupid tears in my eyes, I'd started walking back to the main entrance when I noticed two hands flash up, apparently meant to catch my attention: two guys around my age — both students, I assumed — each waving a hand while adjusting their positions and piled coats to accommodate me.

James Andersen

Though elegant in her outfit of alternating black and white, there was nothing festive about her attire ... not a thread of holiday red or green ... nothing to suggest Christmas cheer. But she did look beautiful.

Lawrence Schielding

I tried to maneuver so she'd sit to my left and Jim to my right — the best of both worlds, as far as I was concerned.

But she insinuated herself between us, which was fair, I supposed. In hindsight, that moment altered the arc of our personal histories.

James Andersen

I hadn't dated much — was still trying to figure things out — but when she slowly removed her black hat ... her white muffler ... her black coat ... to reveal the impressive bosom of her feathery white sweater, I couldn't help but think of Busty Evans, burlesque queen and siren of my dreams.

My obsession with Busty began on a sultry Saturday night in late August, 1954. Larry and I, both fourteen, were crouched outside an imperfectly blacked-out window of a bungalow colony casino, which afforded us a passable view of the small stage on which Busty Evans (and her Twin Fifties) would shimmy and fan-dance to the hooting pleasure of all the males and some few of their wives.

No one under twenty-one was permitted to attend. The rule was strictly enforced. Trespassers would be severely admonished.

Having weighed the consequences, Larry and I swore a blood oath to defy the law and live the dream.

A CRUSHED TIBIA

Molly X

"You walk with a limp."

I let his comment hang in the air, unanswered.

We were in the kitchen. I was busy laying out plates, glasses, napkins ... spoons, forks, knives ... ketchup, mustard ... salt, pepper ... all the necessities for a simple lunch, none of which my father would have considered laying out himself, however quickly he'd become enraged if they weren't in place when he was ready to play host. This shortsightedness, this kind of selfish, paternalistic shite had driven my mother out the door.

Mark Goldstone

I didn't ask what I could do to help. I just did what made sense and my helpful actions passed without comment.

"Bike accident," she said, eventually.

I thought I deserved more but didn't say so. I let silence reign while she pulled two seltzer bottles from the fridge and set them on the table with a double thud. Finally (after removing an ice tray from the freezer and noisily dumping its cubes into a pretty porcelain bowl) she continued speaking.

"When I was twelve there was this local biker dude named Billy, always tinkering with his bike, always smiling when I walked by but never saying a word. One day I stopped and asked, 'What kind of bike is that?' Not that I cared. It was just something to say. But he replied like he'd been waiting all his life for that moment."

"Sixty-one Triumph TR6 Trophy."

"Oh," I said and left it at that.

He looked disappointed.

"Steven McQueen rode one in *The Great Escape*," he added.

"Nice," I said, already bored, ready to continue on my way.

"Wanna go for a ride?"

Molly X

I opened my belt, popped a brass button, unzipped and dropped my pants. I wanted to show Mark my scar and gauge his reaction. You can learn a lot about a person by seeing how they respond in heightened circumstances.

Mark Goldstone

She began undoing her belt, stretching the unbuckled end slowly, revealing one empty notch after another. When the prong popped, her fingers began wrestling with the brass fastener. When that too popped, the sides of her waistband flew open like two welcoming arms and her pants dropped with a plop.

Molly X

The doctors — all men — examined me every few hours, always managing to open my hospital gown a little more than was strictly necessary to see what was left of my repaired left leg: pins and plates holding together all but the four inches of tibia that had been crushed and removed.

But I didn't make it easy for them. I wasn't there for their leering. I'd willed my spirit to hover nearby, depriving them of their truest voyeuristic pleasure. Let them gander at my reconstructed tibia and whatever else they might glimpse of my erstwhile privates — but they wouldn't have *me*.

Mark Goldstone

The expectant thrill of seeing her crotch-defining panty evaporated as soon as she stood before me, relaxed and carefree, in an old pair of boxer shorts. The unsexy garment would have made it easier for me to focus on her misshapen and scarred lower leg had her father not suddenly barged through the door, carrying a cinched white plastic bag, heavy with our three lunches.

James Andersen

Seeing Molly exhibit herself while wearing a pair of my old underpants didn't fluster me. She often acted out her anger-management issues for my benefit.

She blamed me for forcing her mother from our home — the only home she had ever known. She blamed me for not going after her. She blamed me because her mother had left her for another woman. She blamed me for keeping company with so many men.

It was in the hospital room that our family life really began to unravel, with Molly looking desperately helpless, her bandaged right leg in traction, her left arm attached to an IV stanchion, and electronic data flashing her vital signs impersonally on two display boards.

I'd arrived first, having heard from the police what had happened and where Molly had been taken. There had been no way for me to contact Frankie. She'd been out running errands, so she'd said. We didn't yet have cell phones. I'd had no choice but to leave a large, conspicuous note, which she'd be sure to see when she finally arrived home.

Francine Rose

The night before the accident, Jim and I had yet another argument, this time about our record albums. He liked jazz. I liked opera and musicals. Over time we'd developed a taste for each other's music; except that I respected his records while he treated mine — and his own — like shit. I'd tried keeping them all on two shelves, arranged alphabetically — just like our many books — but his music listening was like an orgy: album covers, paper sleeves, the records themselves strewn all over the place, like the spent shells of a crazed gunman. It was beyond carelessness. There was real anger there. Real disrespect.

My favorite album — *The Barry Sisters Sing Yiddish Favorites* — was the only thing my mother ever gave me that I cared about and he'd left it naked on the radiator, where I found it the following morning. I approached it warily and saw that it was warped and spotted with steam drops. It looked dead. To make sure, I placed it on the stereo (like placing a mirror before an unbreathing mouth) but its only response was a lurching, deathly hiss.

Oy, Mama, I moaned, over and over, invoking my mother's spirit ... and all the other mothers I'd known who'd married stupidly selfish men.

That was my mood when I went to sleep that night — alone — in the guest room. That was my mood the next morning, staring at my untouched breakfast cereal, gone to mush. That was my mood when I left an hour later, tossing "Errands" over my shoulder when Molly meekly asked where I was going. That was still my mood hours later when I returned (having failed to walk off my anger) and learned that my only child — my beautiful little Molly — had been taken to the hospital.

James Andersen

It was my fault for putting Molly in harm's way. That's the way Frankie saw it. And all I did was give the girl a little break, some calculated freedom for having finished her homework and a book report not due for another week. I say *calculated* because the neighborhood was already improved (new co-ops having replaced the worst of the old tenements) and it had been a surprisingly lovely day, the last of winter melting away, only rare patches of ice on the sidewalks.

Francine Rose

I couldn't believe what I was hearing. She'd done her homework. It was a nice day. She needed some fresh air. She knew where the pharmacy was. ... Who was this man? It couldn't be my husband. He wasn't that stupid. She was twelve!

James Andersen

I explained that Molly was feverish to be outdoors ... that I'd given her express instructions to the pharmacy (detailing the exact route I expected her to follow) and had told her she must be back in an hour. Hell, having grown up on a farm outside a Minnesota town, I'd had license to roam wherever I pleased by the time I turned eight. At twelve, Molly was smart, plucky and mature — and still, because we lived in the city, we took reasonable precautions.

Francine Rose

She'd barely escaped death, was forever maimed and might never walk normally again, and he was trying to sound *reasonable* — like Father of the Year! I could have killed him.

James Andersen

I didn't tell Frankie the whole story. I spared her the excruciating details: how when an hour had passed and Molly hadn't returned, I thought, *Okay, she's bending the rules, stretching her wings ... all good ...* and how after two hours I'd called the pharmacy and learned that my prescription was still ready to be picked up and I started to panic ... and how when the police had called after three hours, informing me that my daughter had been in an accident and was at Mercy Hospital, I swore on my mother's soul that I'd be in all ways a better husband and father if Molly were okay ... and how when I'd written Frankie a hasty message and posted it where I knew she would hang her key, I knew my scribbled news would rock our marriage.

Francine Rose

I didn't look at James when I entered the hospital room. For the moment, he was dead to me. I simply kneeled beside Molly's bed, stretching my arms so my hands touched hers.

James Andersen

Frankie arrived breathless and hurried to her side, dropping to her knees to bring her face closer to Molly's. Or maybe her knees just buckled at the sight of her maimed baby girl. We didn't speak to each other. Molly was asleep or feigning sleep.

Dr. Kamen (old, white-haired) arrived, busy and authoritative. Frankie and I remained apart and he seemed to sense that our separation was necessary. He told us, looking from one to the other, that we were all very lucky. That Molly might have been killed. As it was, she had a shattered leg and bruised ribs and would walk with a pronounced limp. At this news, I thought I saw Molly shudder and her eyes squeeze a little tighter.

Dr. Kamen said she'd remain in the hospital for at least two weeks. As soon as he left the room, Frankie stood suddenly and pounced on me, throwing a wild slap that caught me flush on the cheek.

That, as they say, was the beginning of the end. Somehow, we stayed together another seven years. There were times I thought we'd patched things up pretty well but when she came a successful writer, she was out the door, leaving behind her wedding ring and all the photos that included me.

As to Molly standing before Mark in a pair of my old boxers, let's just say I still hoped the young man would have a positive influence on her, but I wasn't betting the house on it.

IN THE SHADOWS OF THE ARCH

Molly X

I was standing still as Pygmalion's statue in a pair of my dad's old underwear when Jimmy appeared suddenly, looking like a middle-aged delivery boy, trying hard not to flinch at the sight of me exhibiting my faded but still hideous scar.

As usual, Mark kept his cool. (I'd learn that he had a great practical talent for removing his subjective self from such situations; meaning, he could distance his personal feelings and judgmental views so that he might observe newsworthy events more clearly and thus remember them more accurately: a skill not unlike my own ability to separate my consciousness from my body in order to avoid feeling demeaned or objectified.)

After lunch, I told Jimmy I would accompany Mark to The New School library, knowing he might not believe me but could hardly object. In fact, I had other plans.

Mark Goldstone

Compared to all the discomforting things I'd experienced in Molly's home, it was no great shakes to accommodate myself to her unusual gait: a quick ambling that included a compensatory skip, like a child might make in order to keep pace with a long-striding parent.

Molly X

I led Mark south on Fifth Avenue, crossing a row of ritzy, nineteenth-century townhouses on Eighth Street, before standing in the shadow of Washington Square Park's iconic arch — a great marble wonder, seventy-seven feet high, featuring sculpted eagles, giant laurels and a pair of George Washingtons: the courageous general in his cape and tricorn, on the left; the indomitable and judicious president, bewigged and stockinged, on the right. To me, the two Washingtons epitomized the virtues of strength, sacrifice and service. I wanted Mark to see Washington Square Park as I saw it, with all those ideals in mind — and so much else besides.

Mark Goldstone

Compared to Molly's, my family was rock-solid sane. My father was in finance, specializing in asset depreciation. Mom and I had no idea how he spent his workday — and cared less. It was enough that he was a good provider; a loving, punctual man who rooted for the Yankees and read all he could about the Civil War battles of Vicksburg and Gettysburg.

I was more like my mom, who had a strong and active social conscience. She'd worked ten years as a high school guidance counselor before joining the HR division of New York City's Department of Parks and Recreation, where she worked in the sector of Professional Development that oversaw the volunteer and intern programs, which is how she came to know Felix Kwizera, a young refugee from Rwanda, before he began using the alias *Philippe du Jour*.

"I'm not a rookie. I've been here before," I told Molly.

"Yes, but you've never lived around here. When you call it home, as I do, you see it with different eyes."

"How so?" I pressed her.

"Places are like people. Get to know them and you learn their secrets."

She took my hand (which shocked me) but as she seemed so guileless, I went with the flow.

Molly X

I wasn't guileless. We were in a public place and I wanted to test Mark's response because I already liked him. I liked that he was taller than me and good-looking enough not to care. I liked his subtle humor and what I knew of his social politics. If he pulled his hand from mine or showed the slightest nervousness, I had a ready script of plausible deniability. That was my fallback plan. Every physical freak has handy fallback plans.

Mark Goldstone

On second thoughts, I figured she might be testing me. It didn't matter. I already trusted her and I already liked her. I liked her Joan of Arc feistiness. I liked the way she compensated for her lame leg with what seemed unselfconscious fortitude. I liked that her hair looked roughly shorn and I liked her natural, unenhanced prettiness.

Holding hands, we circled the central fountain, whose jetted waters spumed in the breeze. Completing our orbit, we picked up speed and shot off to explore the outer spaces of the park.

In Molly's company, everything seemed clear and profound: boys playing catch with a red rubber football ... a baby tossing a red rattle ... old men reading newspapers; women reading books, crossing and uncrossing their legs ... chess players facing off ... sunbathers facing up ... guitars strumming ... hip-hop blaring ... the earthy scent of marijuana.

Felix Kwizera

Washington Square Park was my second home and my office. Not common for a Rwandan orphan. It was like this: Having arrived at the Church of St. Francis Xavier at age twelve (I was housed in an adjacent barracks building, also on West Fifteenth Street), I was grateful for the safety, the food and the roof. But it was hard, you know? I didn't like going to church every day or being indoors so much. Even on cold days, I preferred outdoors, where I tried hard to imagine the great buildings and wide avenues as my old hills and valleys.

Inside my barracks home, my homeland was dead to me. Many things were dead to me. My father was dead, hacked down in the street by hooligan teens while I watched from my window. That night my mother went for help to her home village but never returned. I was left alone and hungry. I think I was eight or nine.

I was glad to be in New York, where I was safe and well fed. Still, as my memories grew faint with distance and time, my heart yearned for some knowledge of my homeland and its peoples, for it had not always been bad. There were years when people worked on their farms and in shops in peace. But then the government would change (it was always changing) and the land would fill again with angry mobs, stirring others to blood violence. Young boys, barely older than me, were forced to fight for competing armies and militias: the Rwanda Patriotic Front, the National Resistance Army, the Rebellion Alliance — all killing machines. But unlike America, where each military has its own fancy uniform, a Rwandan fighting boy was lucky to get matching shoes or a belt. Guns were even rarer, though everyone had some killing weapon: a knife, a scythe, some shank of sharp metal.

My young eyes saw terrible carnage. The boys who slashed my father's neck used to sell us mangoes; my history teacher bloodied my father's ear before driving a knife into his heart.

So tragic, especially as Rwandans are so alike. We're almost all rural and speak Kinyarwanda — a Bantu language — and almost all are poor and hungry. My family were Twa, a tiny population among the millions of Tutsi and Hutu: maybe one in a hundred. Perhaps because we were the poor of the poor and so relatively few, and maybe because I'd learned some French from missionary Catholics and a little of their Bible, the nice people of Jesuit Refugee Services took note of my orphan status and removed me to France ... and then to England ... and finally to America, to New York.

But I did not like living in a barracks next to the church. We had tutors to help us learn but some of those tutors were so zealous they'd invite us to their homes for free private lessons, suggesting we would graduate more quickly and be more likely to go to college.

I sensed what would happen at a tutor's private apartment — and didn't want that to happen to me. Also, I didn't want to go to college. I liked to read but didn't want to be locked in classrooms. I was ready to work. Ready to make money. I wanted to be important so thugs could not hurt me. And I wanted to save Rwandan children, like I was saved.

These were my thoughts when I wandered one Saturday into Washington Square Park for the first time. The park was crowded in a way that suggested a common interest or focus, so I moved with the moving crowd until we reached a great circular fountain. Behind it I saw something strange, like a great elephant standing on its rear legs and covered with bandages, as if it had grievous wounds.

Skinny and intrepid, I moved through the crowd until I saw more clearly a great arch on two wide columns, all wrapped in gauzy bandages. So, no elephant. Just an elaborate illusion, like so many things in America.

Mark Goldstone

Leading up to the event, my mother (as a representative of the NYC Department of Parks and Recreation) had met community residents to consider ways of raising money for the renovation of the deteriorated arch and surrounding park. Working with co-sponsor New York University, it was finally agreed that the proposal by West Village artist Francis Hines to wrap the arch in 8,000 yards of polyester gauze (symbolizing its wounded status) was the way to go.

It was a great success. Hines's transformation became one of the most memorable public art installations in the city's history and the necessary funds were raised to improve the arch and park. Further, NYC park representatives had collected the names and phone numbers of several dozen prospective park volunteers, including one enthusiastic young man from Rwanda named Felix Kwizera.

Felix Kwizera

When I wasn't in church or with my tutors, I was at the park, sweeping bathrooms, raking leaves, cleaning the fountain. I always did my best and always with a smile. But I was still only a volunteer, not yet paid for my work. I needed to be paid: only wives work for free. I thought of contacting the woman who had first invited me to become a volunteer. She was a very nice white woman. I knew she had worked with teen boys and girls for many years as a high school counselor and that she had one son, not so many years older than me. I also knew she had the power to give me a better job with pay. In a twist of fate, I received a letter from her before my second spring in the park. It began: "I trust you are doing well," and ended with "I'd like you to meet my son, Mark."

Mark Goldstone

My mother worried about him. The park was a well-known marketplace for drugs: mostly marijuana and hashish but also pills and tablets that could make your mind soar — or stop your heart with a single spasm.

To help keep Felix alive and on the straight and narrow, she asked me to meet him ... offer friendly advice ... be a role model of sorts. I thought I'd be useless but I agreed: the park scene, the drug scene, the black teen scene were all outside my experience. Still, the idea of helping Felix appealed to me.

I met him at the park on a Saturday, right after his work shift. He was friendly and greatly appreciative that someone as important and wonderful as my mother should take an interest in him. He seemed like such a good kid, though a little naïve. I told him I was in college, studying journalism. He asked me what that meant. I told him I wanted to write newspaper stories that would help people get justice. He seemed impressed. I told him if he ever needed someone to talk to, he could call me. I gave him my phone number.

I thought we'd hit it off but he did not call and it was several years before we saw each other again. Not long after our first meeting, he accepted my mother's offer to become a full-time, salaried employee. He wrote her a lovely note of gratitude, shyly inquiring if he might be allowed to continue working at Washington Square Park, claiming it was an easy walk from his home (the barracks beside the church) and the convenience would allow him more time to study and practice his English.

Felix Kwizera

I had many reasons for wanting to work at Washington Square Park. My first impressions (seeing the great monument wrapped in bandages) made me think of it as a healing place. Later, I would learn of the unseen river that flows below the park (like the deep aquifers of my old village) and the early African-Americans buried there (along with the poor and unknown): in all, 20,000 souls buried beneath the fountain, benches, chess tables (like the numberless

Rwandan bodies buried without consecration), broken bones and tortured meat left to rot.

For these reasons, Washington Square Park called to me. But the best reason, as it seemed to me then, were how many young boys like me were happily hanging around, laughing, listening to music, occasionally handing someone a tiny bag and getting an envelope in return, which they handed to someone else, who paid them good cash, so I heard.

Molly X

I knew him by sight when he was just a kid, a park volunteer who loved cleaning up and helping people. And then one day I saw that he'd been promoted from volunteer to staff and soon after that I noticed him setting up meets and drops for the Pope and walking around with a brand-new swagger.

Felix Kwizera

Pope thought he was like God because he had the best bud on the planet, though I couldn't see what was so special about it. (To me it looked like the sorghum my father and his brothers harvested on their half-hectare lot — after the green sheaves had dried and turned tan.)

Moby3, a skinny skateboarder who played bongos (and who boasted African heritage by way of Cleveland) was a park regular and friend. Many times I watched him hand out small plastic bags and accept an envelope in return. But I never mentioned it until the day he showed up with a gold neck chain and designer skateboard, things so extravagant I could not resist asking how he came by them.

Molly X

After my recovery, I watched with my own eyes how the park drug trade evolved: sly word-of-mouth inquiries ➔ barely covert exchanges ➔ use of public pay phones and bicycle messengers ➔ use of beeper messaging to arrange private drops.

During that time (and in that place) Felix Kwizera self-styled himself *Philippe du Jour*. Having criminally monetized his status as an official park employee, his uniform served as both his calling card and his cover.

SECRET PLEASURES

James Andersen

In the beginning, Frankie and I were secretly proud that Molly was something of a wild child. Having raised her on a very liberal set of behavioral strictures (especially as they related to gender identity), we'd both encouraged her natural, uninhibited expression ... until we couldn't control her at all. The motorcycle accident changed everything. In addition to shattering her tibia, it shattered her fear of shame and convention. She'd been only twelve but once that genie was out of the bottle, there was no luring it back in.

Had the eighties been a time of calm and social sobriety, we might have been able to keep Molly in check. But all hell had broken loose. Facing bankruptcy, New York City public services had been severely reduced, with cuts to police and firefighters. Without those protective stalwarts to ensure safety, order and comfort, chaos ensued. Murder, rape, burglary, car theft — all hit record levels. The emergence of crack cocaine, extremely cheap and highly-addictive, brought a wave of city-wide violence and a pandemic interest in getting high. Most infamously, Central Park, Bryant Park and Washington Square Park became trendy marketplaces of drug dealing. Many Rastafarian brothers gathered there to smoke ganga and groove to their reggae, reminding at least one young Rwandan of his old friends and family who'd also loved music and dancing in the streets. In addition to the parks, other famous neighborhoods fell derelict to the times, perhaps none worse than Times Square.

With its dying breath (before the addicts and hookers and homeless took over; before prostitution, peep shows and crime ruined the nabe), the formerly upscale theaters of Times Square hosted burlesque shows, tawdry swansongs of faded glories. One day, walking streets that had become my after-hours beat, I saw a marquee advertising my queen: "Busty Evans and Her Twin Fifties".

At fifteen, I did not know that we would connect again and again. I did not foresee that a few years later I'd have a driver's license, a second-hand car and the screwy devotion to travel as far west as Detroit, Michigan and as far north as Toronto, Canada to see her spectacular shows. Later, when college and grad school kept me to a tighter circuit, I saw her whenever I could in Jersey and in eastern Pennsylvania. And when she came to New York City, often for weeks at a time, I saw her every show at the Folly, the Lyric and the Mayfield — theaters whose wine-red velvet seats had been worn to a dirty nap and whose bathrooms were dank, acrid and always out of paper. I cherished those times but I never shared them with Larry.

Lawrence Schielding

We were best friends and shared everything, other than the deepest secrets of our truest selves. Early on it was easy to dissemble, as neither of us fully recognized the telltale signs of our burgeoning homosexuality.

For our separate reasons we'd both been gaga the night we spied on Busty Evans. For me, the tumult had more to do with the trespass, the shadows and Jimmy's pressing physicality than with the spectacle of a giant pair of tits, which (if I'm being truthful) reminded me painfully of my Aunt Yetta's pendulous breasts, espied once (and only once, thank God) through a partially opened bathroom door.

Jimmy and I never discussed that night, each of us instinctively avoiding where the conversation might lead.

Instead, we talked baseball, books and even about girls. That pathetic dodge carried through our college days when our palpable desires always proved less powerful than our respective terrors.

Francine Rose

During the second half of Handel's *Messiah*, James's right thigh and Larry's left pressed against my own. When the concert ended, we were all jazzed and unwilling to separate. One of us suggested the West End Bar (with its Beat Generation vibe) and we all agreed. We were all hip and daring.

The walk wasn't nearly long enough to take the edge off our energy. Because it was Christmas break and an odd, late-afternoon hour, the bar was uncrowded and we were able to find a small round table in the back, where we sat, equidistant from each other.

Both guys were intelligent and attractive. As far as looks, Lawrence was like my comfort food, resembling most every nice-looking Jewish boy I'd ever liked: dark, smoldering, bordering on craven intensity. Good looking as he was, I had a *been-there, done-that* reaction to his romantic possibility — no fault of his own, I should note. But James had a very different look. He reminded me of the gorgeous hunk-in-profile on the cover of my edition of A.E. Housman's *A Shropshire Lad:* beautiful Byronic eyes and a farm boy's strapping frame. His innocent freshness promised new and exciting possibilities.

James Andersen

Reading *Ivanhoe* as a young teen had been an awakening. You see, my Midwestern boyhood had been full of light-haired, good-hearted Rowenas, uninspiring in their relative sameness. But Francine was something new: a fierce, raven-haired Rebecca; an exotic Jewess. And she wasn't Larry.

Ironically, my courtship with James did not eclipse Larry from our lives. He may have been a third wheel but he was the lead on our tricycle. After graduation (Columbia for them, Barnard for me), he was the first of us to get a job. With unemployment high and entry jobs in related fields almost nonexistent, Larry still managed to get a job at *The New York Times*, albeit as a copy boy. Over the years, Larry's responsibilities grew. Eventually he became Jack Rosenzweig's Associate Managing Editor, helping Jack oversee the newsroom's stylebook and provide advice to staff, especially as it related to journalistic standards and ethics. The latter was key, as it would influence both James's interest in the gay liberation movement and mine in the women's movement.

MENTOR, MONEY, MILITANCY

Mark Goldstone

I learned a lot from my parents. From my mother (the former high-school guidance counselor) I learned that young students' frailties, pains, confusions could be alleviated through professional advice and shifted toward socially approved dreams. From my father, a successful asset appraiser, I learned the difference between inherent and contextual value and that both were variable and susceptible to influence. Essentially, I learned that life was complicated, unpredictable and impossible to assess in terms of price. Eventually, I saw in journalism — the public, rigorous assessment of general life — an opportunity to improve society. But early on I realized that journalism was no perfect prism. Far from offering honest objectivity, its reporters, editors, managers — and certainly its owners — could be biased, venal, even corruptible. The idea that journalism might be cleansed of bias and made more rigorously ethical appealed to me. So when I learned of the writings and teachings of James Andersen, I sought him out as a possible mentor.

James Andersen

To be honest, I had reasons for connecting Mark and Molly besides wanting him to redirect her wayward ways. Sadly, they were all about money. You see, my main employer, The New School, contrived to keep me poor. Instead of a fixed salary, I was given compensation according to the number of classes I taught, the number of students in each class, the number of committees I joined, the number I chaired and so on. In short, I was made to hustle. In such an arrangement I found it almost impossible to pursue my research and writing.

I thought Mark might be a big help. He was a brilliant student and likeminded in his passion for journalistic ethics. I enjoyed his company and found him attractive. I also knew that he spent a fortune renting an apartment near the school and that if he paid me half as much to share my apartment, I wouldn't have to hustle myself breathless.

Though the idea of inviting him to live with me and my teenage daughter made me feel vaguely pimpish, the upside was too strong for me to ignore. Besides, I knew Molly was intractably principled and would never do anything she didn't want to do. And I trusted Mark, who had some surprisingly old-fashioned and fastidious ideas.

Basically, I figured the idea was cool. A win-win-win. And I really did need the money. When Francine and I lived together, we'd made a go of it financially. But as soon as she tasted big success, she flew the coop, moving in with her partner and new best friend, Gloria.

Gloria Applebaum

I was older and placidly doughy, having already greeted middle age with calm acceptance. I was single but not unattached. I had a great many friends, even a few men. I lived in a Village brownstone on Minetta Street, sang in the Lavender Ladies choir, played the flute and cared for two aging and unspayed cats, Eve and Lilith.

Financially speaking, I was somewhere between "very comfortable" and "well-to-do", depending on who was knocking and why. My father had developed a booming *shmata* business for delicately proportioned women and juniors. When he passed, my three younger brothers took over the thriving business and gave me a twenty-five percent stake, so long as I remained an inactive and silent partner. The offer was both generous and insultingly exclusionary but (as an older woman with many skills and too few opportunities) I took their money and used it as I pleased, donating to charities and seeding various businesses that interested me. That's how I met Francine.

Francine Rose

Professionally, I'd been soaring. My feisty feminist articles had skyrocketed my profile and landed me a teaching position at The New School, just like Jimmy. Except I was paid more. Which pissed the hell out of him. He wouldn't admit it but the dishes he placed in the drying rack, still smeared with grease and ketchup, the untrimmed floor vines that had grown like a nest of barbed wire and (perhaps worst of all) our shared record collection, scratched and warped beyond repair — all these screamed his resentment. And there was more: an even deeper rage (deeper than any professional jealousy) because he knew that I knew what really stirred him.

No surprise, I started spending more and more time away from our apartment. Lucky for me, we lived on the edge of Greenwich Village, home of a hundred exotic diversions: vintage boutiques; ethnic eateries; second-hand bookshops; foreign film cinemas; French and Italian cafes. One day, strolling on West Tenth Street, I noticed the cutest little terrier sitting expectantly upright outside a half-opened white door, on either side of which was a visually impressive book display. Right above the door (set on worn brickface the color of indigenous mud) was a simple black sign with white lettering: DJUNA BOOKS / *a bookstore for women.*

Gloria Applebaum

I didn't need labels. I knew who I was. I've always known. I never needed to pretend. I've always liked dolls and babies and clothing ... things soft and scented. Nothing Butch or Tomboy about me.

But when I became an adult and saw what was what, I didn't like what I saw. Things weren't fair — and I hated that. They weren't fair for my mother and they weren't fair for me.

It wasn't until my thirties, however, that I saw with my own eyes how the world was full of mean fathers and brothers, all too willing to take advantage of their accommodating mothers, sisters and wives. It was then that I began talking with other women and learning how they'd also been prevented from realizing their fullest potentials. If I'd been a stronger, braver version of myself, I think I might've tried to unionize them. They needed a voice. They needed advocacy; not because they were weak (they weren't) but because the laws and social conventions (made by men) were stacked against them, making progress so incrementally slow, it sometimes seemed impossible to envision a time when things would be better.

I nearly swooned the day *Ms.* magazine launched. It was everything I had prayed for.

Alas, our progress was too haltingly slow to suit me. After ten years there were many more successful, self-empowered women but we still had too many daughters withering in an unfair system. Things needed to improve fast.

Francine Rose

I loved Djuna Books as much for its inventory as for its omnipresent doyenne and part owner, Gloria Applebaum, who slinked about like a fat house cat, looking to be petted into conversation. On my first visit, we toured the women- and lesbian-oriented books, especially those from the small presses. Next, we admired the archly feminized posters and calendars ... flipped through handsomely bound, achingly blank journals ... tried on wool hats labeled "DYKE" and buttons that read "WE ARE EVERYWHERE."

After my second visit, Gloria and I knew each other's backstories. After my second week, I was greeted with a cup of coffee and led to a chair beside the register. After my second month, Gloria and I would close the store together and continue our conversation at a local restaurant. After my third month, I visited her in her home on Minetta Street and stayed the night. After my fourth month, we began serious discussions to launch a magazine that would be an edgier, more militant platform than *Ms.* "A feminist maga- zine with balls" was how Gloria put it. After five months I left James and my apartment on Tenth and Lexington and moved in with Gloria, her cushiony warmth providing levels of relief and realization I'd only dimly suspected.

Francine Rose

Ms. had been created to make women's voices heard; to help women see how they might stand up for themselves against social norms designed to subjugate them by keeping them satisfied with being "the fairer sex" and "the second sex." But ten years later, even while *Ms.* remained current and popular, a new rumbling was heard from a substratum of neglected, disaffected women who believed that *more* must be done and *now* was the time. Like underground moles moving towards the light (a tropism so powerfully innate it could not be denied), these women were ready to pursue a new degree of self-empowered independence with an unabashed, unapologetic militancy. *Take us seriously or seriously regret it* was not their formal mantra — but that message might have served.

Gloria and I heeded that message and worked hard to conceptualize a new magazine to compete with *Ms*. It took us a long while to decide on the title. Eventually, with the help of a female-only focus group, ages eighteen to sixty, we narrowed the list to: *Lysistrata, Athena, Bitch, Virago*. We chose *Virago* because it was the most daringly on point: "VIRAGO: a brave, warlike woman who demonstrates exemplary and heroic qualities." We loved it. It wasn't shrewish; it wasn't merely oppositional. It suggested honorable, daring militancy — exactly what was needed.

REVELATORY SIGNS

Molly X

Spouses say *I left my husband* or *I left my wife* … but no one says *I left my son* or *I left my daughter* — but that's what it feels like for the child not invited to join the departing parent. Not that I wanted to go. I mean, I just wanted to meet this Gloria person. I wanted to see what she brought to the table that Jimmy was lacking.

You see, I wasn't blindly loyal to either parent. I knew all their arguments by broken heart. I knew Jimmy was domestically lazy and unfair. I knew Frankie could be explosively critical and unforgiving. But I also knew that the muddy rift between them was not about floor plants and warped records but the ill-concealed secrets each had nurtured since their first meeting. Within our own home, there were revelatory signs all over the place. Had my parents scribbled their confessions on our walls and in their own blood, their situations would have been only marginally more obvious to me.

For example, I clearly remember my mother's home office covered with classic prints of female nudes. When I was twelve, I asked her why and she said, "There is nothing more naturally beautiful than the human body, especially the female's." Though only twelve, I decided to test that interesting theory, which led me to ride off with the Steve McQueen motorcycle guy ... which resulted in an icy accident ... which resulted in the maiming of my right leg ... which led me to conclude: it's okay to leap before you look — but be prepared to pay a steep price.

Anyway, while I don't remember all the beautiful female nudes that covered the walls of my mother's lair, I vividly recall *The Large Bathers* by Auguste Renoir; several nude sketches by Mary Cassatt; two paintings of fleshy nudes by Peter Paul Rubens; and several by Picasso — not the sharply fractured Cubist ones but several Abstract nudes of soft curves and overlapping, enveloping shapes.

The wall decor of Dad's study was similarly revealing. But instead of beautiful art prints, it was covered with newspaper articles (mostly yellowed) and photos (mostly black and white). It wasn't a pretty room, like Mom's. It was like one of those rooms seen on a TV crime show, the sanctum of a maniacal criminal — usually a terrorist, a pedophile or a crazed stalker. Of course, my dad was none of those things. But he did have powerful obsessions.

One of the newspaper photos showed a melee at Sixth Ave. and Tenth Street. Jimmy appeared shown center-right, near the bearer of a poled Gay Activist Alliance flag. On the other side of him was a long-haired young man, a placard hung from his neck, reading: GAYS UNITE and showing the intersected symbols for male and female, suggesting a partnership or shared vision.

One of my favorite black-and-white photos showed a group of men being dragged by the police during the Stonewall riots, their heads bashed and bloodied. One head had been red-circled, presumably Dad's or a friend's. I never asked.

My favorite photo was taken outside St. Marks Church in-the-Bowery. Across its bottom border, annotated in Jimmy's recognizable handwriting, were the words "St. Marks Political Poetry Workshop." The photo showed ten Caucasians, male and female, in summery dishabille. Jimmy wore a floppy sunhat, tank top, belted shorts and sandals. Nine of the ten gazes were looking straight ahead at the camera; only Jimmy was caught looking away, to his right — the viewer's left. It was at this Political Poetry Workshop that Jimmy first heard of the bloody troubles in Rwanda. Unlike most political calamities, he didn't initially pick a side; instead, he and Frankie remained passively abreast of the news for many years, until they both felt the need to engage.

Mark Goldstone

I was honored — and excited — when Prof. Andersen invited me to move into an available room in his apartment. He told me — briefly and vaguely — that his wife had moved in with her business partner as a matter of convenience. Molly didn't offer much more on that front. I sensed husband and daughter had been blindsided by the event and were still working out their feelings.

As a full-time resident, I had quite enough time to inspect Mrs. Andersen's collection of classic nude prints and Jim's collection of photos and ephemera related to the Gay Alliance. As open as Molly was, she did not confide her thoughts regarding her parents' separation.

Over time, though, I connected some of the dots and, when I was ready, I asked her specific questions:"Do you think your dad is gay or just passionately connected to the movement as an ethical journalist?" ... "What is The Beholding? Your Dad has alluded to it several times." ... "Is your mother's business partner also her personal partner?"

I didn't ask Molly how she felt about these issues, as I didn't want to risk having to answer similar questions.

Molly X

That he asked direct questions about my parents wasn't surprising. Mark was a born journalist. But I wasn't sure what to make of the fact that he didn't ask me personal questions about myself. Right or wrong, I figured his reluctance (or reserve) was tied to the fact that he really liked me and didn't want to appear pushy or intrusive. Such sensitivity and tact made me think he might become my first boyfriend, perhaps even my first lover, which scared the crap out of me.

Bold as I might have appeared, I was a terrible fraud. My own big secret: After puberty, I became uncomfortable with my body. I mean, we got along great, when we were alone, but the idea of sharing it with someone else — male or female — terrified me for a long time.

Quite aside from my shortened leg (most noticeable when I walked; I never ran or danced, which broke my parents' hearts), I hated my small breasts that pointed in different directions like they were cockeyed. Worse, my right areola was small and dark but my left was light and puffy: like the breasts of two different women, neither of them me. And I hated my teeth. They were too small; a child's teeth.

When I was younger, older boys took notice of my friends but never seemed to notice puny me. But the motorcycle boy saw something he liked. Young as I was, I sensed a come-hither look when I saw one. On three previous occasions I'd passed him without a word, though I always felt his hungry eyes on my retreating back. One day, a warmish winter day following an ice storm, my dad mentioned in passing that he had a filled prescription waiting to be picked up at a local drugstore. Sensing that motorcycle boy would advantage of the pleasant weather to shine his bike, I connived to pick up my dad's prescription, promising to come right back.

Well, that didn't go as planned. I never did pick up that prescription. But my stupid, thoughtless egoism did ruin my leg and my parents' marriage: for without my tragedy to focus on, I believe my parents might never have separated — and I carry that terrible secret to this day.

Mark Goldstone

During the first two weeks of living in Jim's apartment he never even alluded to the possibility of a relationship between me and Molly. I just assumed there were house rules that should guide my behavior.

But one day, fully three weeks after I'd moved in and several days since Molly and I had begun spending long hours talking to each other in our respective bedrooms, he took me aside and led me into the kitchen. Molly wasn't home and I thought he was going to read me the fatherly riot act. Instead, after laying out two cups of steaming coffee and some cookies, he calmly confided the details of Molly's wayward past, citing her several criminal misdemeanors and known associations with local druggies. He said (with a deep sigh) that it wasn't easy being a parent, especially of such a strong-willed person as Molly. He then repeated the old chestnut about a child always being a parent's child, no matter their age and adult experience. Suddenly, gathering himself to his real purpose, he looked me dead in the eye and asked if I would do my best to curb his daughter's outlaw tendencies (which had almost killed her; as witness her lame leg) by exampling my own impressively mature and moderate behaviors. Though he said I'd be doing him a personal favor, it felt like a direct order. I shook his hand and said I'd do what I could. What else could I have done?

PINK PUSSYCAT BOUTIQUE

Molly X

We talked endlessly in the kitchen and living room and even in our bedrooms when Jimmy was out and about. I'd thought we'd been getting closer and closer, Mark seemingly attuned to my every nuance of expression. But one day, he suddenly seemed distant. Like we'd hit a brick wall.

Why the problem? I knew he liked me. He knew I liked him. We'd even had a few dates. At least, I thought they were dates: lunches at Thielsson's diner, a Friday-night movie at the Angelika where we held hands in the dark. But after that he seemed standoffish, over-polite. I needed to loosen him up.

Mark Goldstone

Molly was such a complex wonder. Even her certitudes conflicted. "I look at clouds from both sides now," was how she explained herself, paraphrasing her favorite line from her favorite song.

I loved her complexity and unpredictability but could have easily done without the danger and drama she seemed to attract. But Molly had an irrepressible need to balance on the razor's edge, the resulting frisson infusing her body with edgy energy — like a junky's fix. I didn't think it was my place to reign that in but I'd promised her father I'd try.

Molly X

Just a block from the Waverly, opposite the West 4th basketball court, the Pink PussyCat Boutique was impossible to miss, its crassly bright storefront spotlighting a pair of mannequins, clad in leather and lace and standing among a vast array of fetishist toys and tools. The Pink PussyCat was a place for dommes and submissives and anyone else who dared stretch their sexual IQ. I took Mark there on our fourth date.

Mark Goldstone

Everywhere I looked there were whips, collars, restraints, inflatable sex partners, vibrators and dildoes of every crazy shape and dimension, objects I had no idea how to hold or where to insert.

"Come here often?"

She smiled at my quick wit, which was more credit than I deserved, for with each passing second, I felt myself nervously tumbling down the rabbit hole.

Molly X

He looked a little green around the gills and I wasn't a bit sorry. Though politically and socially passionate, he'd been emotionally reticent the past couple of weeks. I don't do reticent.

I'd brought him to the Pink PussyCat to shake him up. My next step was to get him high.

Felix Kwizera

In my business, being quietly cool was a necessity. Some dealers were better at it than others and the ones who weren't so good — who were flashy and loud — got pinched and went to jail. I was afraid of jail. Some of the older guys weren't, or pretended not to be. They had friends or brothers or cousins who'd been jailed and saw the experience as a mark of toughness, like a battle ribbon. But where I came from — Rwanda — when they took you away, you stayed away — because you were dead. I had a dead father and dead uncles and dead cousins. My mother left the night my father was killed. She had no choice but to fly to her home village to find help. But she never returned. The nice Jesuits took pity on me. I was a sweet and bright boy. Presumed to be an orphan, they clothed me, fed me, taught me some polite French, then sent me to America to save my soul.

Here in New York, in Washington Square, I worked for

the Parks Department. It was a good job but didn't pay very much. Because I chose not to go to college, I had aged out of the dormitory barracks near the church and needed a place to live — at least, a place to sleep. For a while I found places to sleep in other men's apartments but that was not a life I cared to pursue. I decided to become friends with some of the older boys who were park regulars but who never seemed hungry or worried about where they would spend the night. I soon learned that they also worked in the park but, like subcontractors, quietly selling fresh, unrolled marijuana (which reminded me of our sorghum back home) to nice customers — young and old, mostly white and male.

That's how I met Moby3. He was one of those who sold marijuana from little plastic bags in his coat pockets. He was a good friend but very flashy with his fancy skateboards and new clothes. I suppose he was too loud and flashy because the police arrested him and took him away. A few days later a man approached me while I was raking fallen leaves into plastic garbage bags. He was dressed nicely but quietly. He said I was a good worker but did not earn as much money as I deserved. I did not ask how he knew this. When he said he'd seen me speaking with Moby, I had a sense who he was but still I didn't ask any questions. He then said that Moby had worked for him but had lost his job because he was careless. He said I could have Moby's job. He said it was relatively simple. He said he could train me in fifteen minutes and I would make a lot of money, so long as I was honest and quiet. He said it would not interfere with my park work. All I had to do was take my breaks in a certain area of the park every day. I said I didn't want to take my friend's job. But the man said that Moby would not be back for a long while. He even promised to find Moby another job if he returned to the park. In the meantime, he said he would spread the word that I had taken Moby's place.

For several years I kept both jobs. I used to joke (to

myself): *What a life! I pull weed from the lawns and sell weed to my customers. God bless America!*

With my pockets full of cash, I rented a one-bedroom apartment in Hell's Kitchen. The neighborhood was rough but I minded my own business. I even opened a savings account a few blocks north, where the neighborhood was safer.

Molly X

Moby3 was the only park dealer willing to sell me a nickel bag, which was all I could afford at the time. But that wasn't the only reason I liked him. He was funny, sassy and I liked chatting with him — though I was always aware he was working and didn't want him to lose any sale on my account.

One day, I asked him what else he liked to do and he said he liked to read but when I asked what books he liked, he said he couldn't remember. A week or so later, before returning to the park, I picked up a used copy of *Native Son* at the Strand and gave it to him. It was Christmas Eve and his eyes watered at the sight of the gift. He then gave me my usual nickel bag but refused to take my five-dollar bill.

I was very sad when I heard he'd been arrested. I tried to find out where he'd been taken but no one would tell me anything, partly because I'd never learned his real name and partly because I myself looked like a weedy street urchin.

Sometime later, I saw a young park attendant named Felix (with whom I'd become friendly) spending a lot of time in the shade of the Hangman's Elm in the northwest corner of the park, where Moby used to hang.

"Hey, Felix. How's it hanging?"

He didn't catch my joke, so I changed tack.

"Any word about Moby?"

He shook his head.

I asked a few more friendly questions and then hazarded:

"Moby and I used to do a little business."

"How little?"

"Nickel."

"That's very little."

"I know, but we were friends." I told him about the book I gave him for Christmas and how he cried. "I miss him."

Felix seemed to like that.

"Next time you see me, I'll have a nickel bag for you. But I am no longer Felix to you. I am now Philippe du Jour."

Mark Goldstone

"Let's get some fresh air."

Molly led me out the Pink PussyCat Boutique. Following her lead, we crossed Sixth Avenue and walked east on Eighth Street towards the park. With each step away from the Pink PussyCat, I felt a little better.

Molly X

"Since you bought lunch, dessert is on me," I said.

"That works. What are we having?"

"Trust me?"

Mark Goldstone

I did ... and I didn't. But what could I say?

We walked to a shady corner of the park. In the near distance I saw a uniformed park employee standing under a mighty elm. Molly's pace quickened as if she wanted to arrive there first. I gave her the space she seemed to need, reducing my own pace to a crawl. At a distance of twenty yards, I recognized Felix Kwizera, the young boy I'd met near the arch a half-dozen years before and subsequently referred to my mother.

"Come here, slowpoke," Molly called to me. "I want to introduce you to a friend. Mark Goldstone, this is Philippe du Jour."

I knew he recognized me. He knew I recognized him. After an exchange of curt hellos, we both dropped our eyes to avoid embarrassment. I don't think Molly noticed. For the moment, Felix and I kept our secrets. We did not address each other while Molly purchased two loose joints. One for me, one for her.

OPPOSITES DETRACT

James Andersen

Despite our years at Columbia and Barnard that had shaped our revolutionary politics and social views; despite our twenty years as husband and wife; despite having conceived and raised Molly together, Frankie and I separated.

My take: Frankie was free-spirited when out in the world but at home she was a menacing hausfrau, always tormenting me with rules and regulations. Things had to be cooked a certain way. Things had to be cleaned a certain way. I even had to fuck her a certain way.

We'd had decent sex in our early years but over time my tastes had changed. The time came when I preferred taking her only from behind — truly from behind — so her breasts and vagina didn't distract. For a while she complied uncomplainingly. Eventually, she wanted to talk about it — and I didn't. Finally, she demanded that we talk about it and when I refused, she protested, pulling a Lysistrata-like sex strike, which was fine with me, as I'd already found that I didn't miss sex with her. When I realized that it was actually a relief, I knew our marriage was untenable. What I didn't know was that she'd already reached the same conclusion.

Francine Rose

While I freely admit that I'd never forgiven him for Molly's accident, I'd moved on from it to face the real battle of our marriage — Jim's callous disregard of my reasonable requests for his fair participation in a working partnership.

How many times had I complained about the toilet seat, the unwashed dishes, the dirty laundry in the hamper? These may seem like petty complaints but they're the politics of housework. If he'd only learned to take decent criticism I wouldn't have had to rail until there was a clot of rage in my throat and a boiling bile in my gut. And I wasn't hardass. I wasn't intractable. I would have accepted less than enormous changes at the last minute — had he ever indicated a willingness, a conscientiousness to share the labors of an equal marriage. But I never saw any evidence of his desire for fairness and equality. Make no mistake: he wasn't taming a shrew; he was creating one!

I stopped fighting when I finally understood the crux of our real problem: Jim should have married a man and I should have married a woman. Then again, we had Molly.

James Andersen

Frankie convinced herself that I was a closet homosexual to explain why I fell out of love with her. She wasn't entirely wrong but she was far from entirely right. Recalling my early teen feelings for Larry, I knew I was capable of man love. But I also knew I was capable of loving a woman.

Before Frankie there had been Shoshana from Ashkelon. While still a Columbia undergraduate, I'd met her at the Horn & Hardart automat on Broadway and Forty-second Street. She was tall and slender and had a great volume of unrestrained red hair. I approached her as if magnetically drawn. From three feet away I saw a book bag hung from her shoulder that bore the name and insignia of Stern College for Women, one of Yeshiva University's undergraduate schools. I assumed she was Jewish. Unlike me.

Sensing my wonder-struck presence, she turned to me. "I'm looking for something kosher," she said.

"Sorry. That wouldn't be me."

"You don't understand *kosher?*"

"I understand fine. I spent five summers with my friend's family at a Jewish bungalow colony in the Catskills."

"So, you understand a little Yiddish?"

"I know you're a beautiful Jewish girl and I'm *treif*."

She extended her right hand to shake mine, seemingly unafraid of any taint.

"Nice to meet you, Mr. Treif. I am Shoshana Avraham."

We fired on all cylinders and, who knows, might have married had another war not exploded in Israel, recalling Shoshana with its Zionist plea for support. For several years we kept in touch but she remained in Israel and eventually married a cardiologist.

I returned many times to the automat on Broadway and 42nd Street to think of her. One day, passing a row of XXX movie theaters and burlesque houses, I saw a marquee: *LIVE SHOWS ... BUSTY EVANS AND HER FABULOUS 50s.*

It was an amazing coincidence: having never forgotten my private pledge to see her perform again and having only weeks before bought my first car (a used Toyota Celica, red and rusty), I never imagined that our first reconnection would take place in my own backyard, so to speak.

The show was everything I'd imagined — and more. The dark and dank theater reprised the steamy August night in the Catskills; the stupefied, heavy-breathing men recalled me and Larry watching lustily in the shadows.

I credited Busty with my own slow reckoning of self. Strange as it may seem, I saw her as a kindred spirit, some-one who struggled with her own outlier status. While I grappled with my sexual identity (failing in my romantic youth to identify with one side more than the other, thus failing to belong entirely to either), Busty was outcast by many women as something worse than a whore, something freakish.

With these thoughts in mind, I started sketching ideas for a book. I had no clear sense of the narrative, other than it must be about my life — real and imagined — and that I must write it as I lived it, in quasi real time. I saw myself as sculptor, sculpture and spectator and my work-in-progress as a sequential unveiling. As to the title, I wavered between *The Beholding* and *Ecce Homo*, both with the subtitle: *A Tale of Modern Liberation.* Eventually, I would decide on *Ecce Homo / The Beholding.*

Francine Rose

The world had no idea how sickeningly hypocritical he was. How he wrote impassioned praise of the Women's Movement for the reciprocation he hoped would advance the Gay Movement. How he lived for feminists' curtseyed praise while raging at their political incompetence. How two-faced! How disgustingly deceitful! When I learned that he was writing *Ecce Homo / The Beholding*, I began working on my own treatise, a recounting of historical feminine warriors (including the arc of my own personal revelations): *Athena to Zelda, Women of Wonder.*

STRATEGIC ADVANCES

James Andersen

I saw Busty's every show in New York and when she left to continue her tour, I regretted her absence. When possible, I pursued solo road trips to reconnect with her, always sitting midway back in the audience, just beyond the farthest reach of the stage lights and the beginning of the darkness.

Using my new journalism chops, I arranged to interview her at the Folly Burlesk in Canton. She never asked what newspaper or magazine I represented. Had she asked, I would have said I was planning to write a book.

On arriving, I was directed to her dressing room, where I found her seated at a scarred dressing table, facing a formerly fancy mirror, now tarnished with black and silver blotches.

"Be right with you. Pick a chair."

I settled in and awaited her further instruction. It was my first interview and I was nervous.

"What's your name?" she asked.

I wavered. I didn't expect a give and take. I expected the anonymity of the shadows.

"James Andersen," I said, reluctantly.

"Nice to meet you. Lots of Andersons in the Midwest. May I call you Jim?"

"Sure. Please do."

"Thank you. You can call me Sandy."

"Thank you. Is that your real name?"

"No. My real name is Sondra. Sondra Lou Churcher. When I was getting started, a theater manager suggested *Busty*."

I resisted the obvious.

"Where did *Evans* come from, if you don't mind my asking?"

"We both thought *Churcher* sent the wrong message."

Pause.

"Just so we're clear, I'm not a bit ashamed of what I do. I make a good, honest living."

"I'm sure."

"I had to take a stage name. I come from a small town and belong to a Mennonite church."

"Mennonite?"

She nodded, resolute.

"People think we're the same as the Amish but we're not."

"Explain, please."

"Well, our faiths are pretty much the same but we live differently. We have cars, electricity, phones ... and while we mostly stick to ourselves, you can find Mennonite neighborhoods in big cities."

"Is there a language? Do you speak Mennonite?"

"I speak English. Mennonite is a dialect called *Plaut-dietsch*. It's some German and Dutch mixed together. I learned it in church and spoke it with the Elders and teachers and my classmates. My grandparents speak it a lot better than I do."

I wanted to get back to her name. "So, where did the name *Evans* come from?"

"The same theater manager suggested the last name *Morgan* but there was another dancer called *Chesty Morgan*, so I wanted something else." She smiled. "In the fourth grade I knew a boy named *Evan*. He was cute and sweet ... my first crush. So, there you have it: *Busty Evans*."

I pushed forward, daringly: "Who came up with the tag, *Her Twin 50s*?"

She shrugged.

"Don't recall exactly. But it's easy to remember, so it's good for business."

"Your booking agent, Dave Cohn, says you have a terrible memory for numbers. He says the only two numbers you remember are 50 and 50."

She laughed; a tinkling laugh, almost like a child's.

"Well, catchy names sell tickets," I went on.

"True. But it don't keep you in business. You need some personality. Plain strippin' is boring, no matter what you look like. But I can joke some. And I can dance. That's how I started. As a dancer."

"Really? Where'd you learn to dance?"

"In high school we had a nice teacher named Miss Vera who taught Music, Art and Dance. I sang and danced in all the Christmas and Easter shows."

"That led to burlesque?"

"Of course not! I wanted a proper job as a dancer. Thing is, I'm not tall and willowy. I'm built altogether different."

I let that go too.

"In high school I never practiced my secretarial skills

'cause I only ever wanted to dance, but it made finding a job near impossible. Six months after graduation and still jobless, I took a bus to Canton 'cause I heard they had real burlesk there — with dancing and singing."

"You dreamed of being a star?"

"Never. I never even expected to be on stage by myself. I just wanted to dance, like in a chorus line. But it just wasn't meant to be. I saw seven theater managers in Canton and not one took me seriously. I'd come all the way from Dayton and didn't get a single audition. I was so disappointed I just sat down and cried."

Her shoulders collapsed, recalling her pain.

"What happened?"

The last theater manager saw me crying like a baby and says to me: here, take this card and hands me this red velvet card with raised gold lettering. *Rose LaRose / Talent Agent / Toledo, Ohio.* That's what it said…. I still have it."

"I guess Rose LaRose played a big part in your success."

"Taught me everything I know. And not just the traditional bumps and grinds, but how to flirt … how to put on a show … and, most important, how to save the best for last. Rose used to say, 'The audience buys the tickets — and you're the show they pay to see.'"

I applauded.

"You see, you did become a star. When you're onstage, all eyes are on you."

She smiled. "I like that. Thank you. What did you say your name was?"

JUST A CALL AWAY

Molly X

With the launching of *Virago*, my mother was thrust into the vanguard of the Women's Movement. Frankie Rose was everywhere — radio, television, conferences — always speaking about the rights of wives, mothers and daughters.

But at home, on the corner of Tenth and Lexington, the words *wife* and *mother* were rarely spoken. Jimmy and I were still a family — the way an amputated body is still a body.

Jimmy and I continued living in our strangely cramped apartment right above Thielsson's diner. Somehow, Mark's presence intensified the sense of my mother's absence, perhaps because he'd moved into her old room.

I had mixed feelings about Frankie. On the one hand, I hated her for leaving us so completely and coldly. On the other hand, I loved her more than ever and wanted to live with her. I cried in my room, face down on my childhood bed, wondering why she no longer wanted to live with me.

Still, I was happy enough with Jimmy and Mark, though I'd already begun to feel insecure, thinking Mark would likely leave as soon as he finished school and got his first job. I also knew that a replacement boarder would not be easy to find and that the loss of Mark's rental share, along with the previous loss of my mother's contributing income, would force my dad to move. I knew we might lose our family home — the only home I'd ever known — although it hadn't felt like home since Mom had left and it didn't help much when she'd say to me, "I'm just a phone call away."

Francine Rose

I'd moved into Gloria's townhouse on Minetta Street, bringing only my clothes, typewriter and essential papers. Whatever I left behind, including my daughter, I figured I could retrieve later.

I wasn't heartless. I did what was best for me. Consider my history: I was the only child of old parents who'd seen me as the only egg in their basket. Rather than weave around me a protective nest, they trained me to fly successfully in the adult world, which they saw as a man's world. They were great pragmatists. Having read Ayn Rand, they taught me self-reliance and independence so I could create for myself a defensible eyrie from which I could visit the male world and return to shelter, as necessary.

Their training proved useful. I learned to think for myself, to lead fearlessly from the front. Ironically, their lessons were skewed, having failed to allow for any strong feminine perspective. Intuiting this lack, I chose Barnard College (a women's school) to round out my character. Sadly, rather than learn from the sisters of that society, I wasted time and energy regretting what I couldn't have, while recruiting the company of willing male students from Columbia. Eventually my social circle shrank to two strange young men, one of whom I would marry.

It took twenty years of conjugal frustration, the success of *Ms.* magazine and the launch of *Virago* to ready me for the salvation of an immersive feminine experience.

Gloria Applebaum

As a chubby young girl (following three winning brothers) I'd been discouraged from studying ballet (no one wanted to see me in a tutu) and was pushed into playing the piano, which proved tough for my thick, stubby fingers. For much of my life, I was a fat peg pushed into slim holes. I only began to succeed when I took control and looked for the right holes.

As an adult, I enjoyed some small successes but never strode triumphant. So when beautiful Francine Rose walked into Djuna Books and made herself increasingly familiar, I resisted the hopes of an intimate friendship ... until the day she snagged my fingers and pulled me close, kissing me hard on the mouth, happily surprising the hell out of me.

Francine Rose

I kissed her because I wanted to. I kissed her because I couldn't stop myself, her great womanly warmth drawing me like a beacon in a raging night. Her blessings were bountiful. She was strong and pliant. Selflessly giving, endlessly needy. She was the most honest, whole, genuine person I'd ever met. So different from my craven, conflicted ex-husband, which is how I thought of James after I'd fallen in real love for the first time.

Molly X

Mark had stolen a few kisses at home. Furtive forays followed by sudden retreats. I figured a hovering sense of my disapproving father was stunting his ardor, which is why I took him to the Pink PussyCat and then to Washington Square Park. But even after sharing a fat blunt and leading him by hand into a dark wooded area, I still couldn't spark him to decisive action. Damn! Having fought off the pawing advances of so many drunk and stoned guys, it was ironic (and frustrating) to work so hard to lose my virginity. Still, I figured it'd be worth it. I respected Mark as much as I respected my parents.

WHAT'S IN A NAME?

Dativa Natukunda

I am short, which is not surprising as I have mostly Batwa blood. My people are usually called the Twa, or the Forest People, which is much nicer than Pygmy, once meant to convey diminutive stature but now considered insulting.

When people ask where I'm from, I say Africa. If they ask where, I say Central Africa. If they ask where in Central Africa, I say east of the Congo. If they ask east of the Republic of the Congo or the Democratic Republic of the Congo, I say the Democratic Republic of the Congo is now Zaire. Actually, I come from Rwanda.

It is painfully difficult to talk about this and the bloody

history of my nation, so I avoid it, unless I meet another Rwandan and then I am most eager to share. One of the other black nannies I'd met in the park pointed out a nice-looking young man and said, "I heard he's from a village in northern Rwanda."

Felix Kwizera

Several times I saw her pushing a deluxe baby carriage whose ribbed canopy was like a fancy sedan and whose hinges and wheels shone like polished silver.

She was short but her extreme posture made her seem regal. I thought Caribbean — but I hoped African.

For the first time I was ashamed of my Parks Department uniform. I did not want to her to think I had come all this way just to mow grass and empty trash. I wanted her to know that I was a successful entrepreneur — although I did not want her to know the nature of my business.

One day she approached me, pushing the handsome carriage. I think she must have thought I was an idiot, because when she asked, "Ubwiherero burihe?" (Where is the bathroom?), I could only smile at the sound of her two-tone Kinyarwanda, which revealed not only that she was Rwandan, but Twa, like me.

Dativa Natukunda

When he found his tongue (more elegant than mine because he'd had more schooling and even some French), he pointed and said, "*Binyuze muri urwo rugi, iburyo.*" (Through that door, to the right.)

I knew he watched my swishing bottom as I walked by. I also knew he'd seen my white baby.

When I returned, about ten minutes later, he was standing in the same spot. I was happy he'd waited for me but I did not smile. This was America and I wanted to appear strong, though I wasn't ready to explain my white baby.

I said, "*Ubwiherero ntabwo bwari bufite isuku.*" (The bathroom was not clean and there were no paper towels.)

He appeared momentarily embarrassed but quickly regained his professional composure.

"Thank you," he said in accented English. "I will have someone take care of it. It will be clean next time you are here."

He returned my smile and I saw that he had good teeth.

"What is your name?" I asked.

He hesitated and then said, "I am called Philippe du Jour."

I am used to exotic names but I knew this was made up.

"Nice to meet you. You may call me Plain Jane."

He seemed puzzled how to respond.

"Or," I said, "you can call me Hiraly ... or Frolence ... or whatever you like."

After a pause, he replied, "I am sorry for my mistake. Please, call me Felix. Felix Kwizera."

"Nice to meet you, Mr. Felix Kwizera. You will please call me Dativa Natukunda."

A PLUM ASSIGNMENT

James Andersen

I had my obsession with Busty, my friendship with Larry, my haranguing with Frankie, my connection to Molly, my mentoring of Mark ... but still a large part of my heart went unclaimed. I had more to share, more to express. But as to romance, my prospects were bleak. I was done with woman love (other than Busty, a peculiar outlier) and unwilling to consider an openly gay relationship. My queer trysts were quick and anonymous.

I began to think that my deepest fulfilment might come from my literary effort or from some daring political involvement that would give my life purposeful meaning.

Lawrence Schielding

When Jim first referred to *Ecce Homo | The Beholding* as his magnum opus, I was dubious but strongly encouraging. Three years later, when he announced he'd finished the first draft, I feigned keen interest in reading it. Curbing my enthusiasm was my certainty that Jim would ask me (his lifelong friend, fellow wordsmith and professionally well-connected associate) to help him get it published.

Thing is (and sad to say), I did not want to be publicly involved with a book that was sure to be associated with the Gay Movement. Call me coward but back in the day I socialized strictly from the confines of my cozy closet. As managing editor of *The New York Times,* I didn't want my private life made public. I couldn't afford to become part of the news. I didn't want people challenging my objectivity, second-guessing my sympathies. I wanted to keep my personal life a private affair — or affairs, to be accurate.

So, I perused the novel and then flattered Jim with half-truths, emphasizing the book's obvious Jamesian qualities. That's all it took. Jim went on and on about his mimetic tribute, sparing me the plight of having to discuss in depth a mammothly long manuscript that I had mostly skimmed.

Long story short, I told Jim that his writing was uniquely expressive without mentioning his stilted styling, excessively long sentences and heavy-handed psychological symbolism.

I might have said the book would be twice as good had it been half as long, but I didn't. Instead, I told him I knew a couple of agents and publishers, but not to get his hopes up; that his book was revolutionary and would take a while to find its proper path to publication. Meanwhile, feeling a need to make up for my feckless support (and knowing that Frankie had left him, that he was strapped for cash, and that he could use a plum assignment better suited to his unquestioned talents as a journalist), I said to him, "You still belong to that Political Poetry Workshop involved with Rwanda?"

Some years earlier, I'd begun working with *The New York Times* art director Ron Silverman to modernize our dowdy-looking newspaper, nicknamed "The Gray Lady" because of its dense gray pillars of copy. Through our lobbying we were able to reduce the eight-column format to six columns, making each column wider and more readable. I also backed Ron's emphasis on new graphic-design elements, with more white space, bigger photos and more infographics. On my end, we added new sections, such as *Weekend Arts* and *Home,* to keep up with the changing times. In 1993 I supported an initiative to improve the navigation and use more color. The next year I introduced *Circuits,* to reflect the growing public interest in the internet and digital technology.

I knew these changes had been positive as we'd increased readership and fattened our bottom line. Still, there were some who took me to task for lowering the seriousness of our journalistic mission to provide "All the News That's Fit to Print." One evening, at an in-house cocktail party, Bill Carter, our executive editor emeritus, greeted me. "Larry, you're a great newsman. You know how to mobilize a reporting team to cover every angle of a story so nothing important is missed. You know how to motivate and inspire. So, what's with all the bells and whistles? How about you take all this glorious chaos" (the sweep of his hand seemed to indicate the entire *Times* operation) "and give the world its next Nuremberg or Watergate? Give us something truly worthy of our great paper."

After shaking hands, I headed straight for the men's room and locked myself in a cubicle in order to think without distraction. In my heart, I knew Bill was right. Under my stewardship the *Times* had grown relatively soft in terms of its investigative reporting. Despite my successes with our bean counters and investors, I needed to refocus my influence — which is to say, direct my staff to pursue the most potentially explosive stories and hotbed issues.

I would like to have led from the front but I'm no Stephen Crane (who covered the Spanish-American War) or Joseph Pulitzer (who explored New York's fetid and overcrowded tenements). Those guys were real journalists. I was a devout coward who used his wide desk as a bulwark against the dangerous real world. It had always been that way with me. Which is why, in large part, I'd begged my family to have James live with us during our summers in the Catskills. He was a big boy, with wide shoulders and large hands with scarred knuckles. With James as my wingman, no one picked on me.

James Andersen

I was among the core faithful who still visited St. Marks Church in-the-Bowery every Wednesday evening at seven. Strictly speaking, we no longer limited ourselves to poetry, because our group had morphed with the times, and its members looked for ever-wider expressions of form while maintaining their passion for political justice.

Our members hailed from different social and ethnic groups and were divided about equally by gender. As the only journalist and a published ethicist to boot, many of them deferred to me on matters of doctrine. I took much satisfaction from being the occasional center of attention but always pooh-pooed my cherished authority.

Over the years we had discussed and written about Viet Nam, civil rights, women's rights, gay rights, the environment, Native American rights and world issues like Russian aggression, Chinese transgression and American imperialism. The reported atrocities in Rwanda were a recurring topic. Larry's offer to write a series of articles on the ongoing crisis came at a propitious time, as far as I was concerned. Of course, a great many details would have to be worked out, financial considerations high among them but I really did need a change and I really did need the money.

I called Larry and told him I was still a member of the St. Marks Church in-the-Bowery but that we'd moved beyond poetry to wider forms of expression. "Perfect," he said. "Just what I'd hoped to hear. When can you come in?"

I'd never visited a live battlefield or even a dangerous tenement. As an essayist, teacher and expert in journalistic ethics, my work took me to offices, libraries and lecture halls — perhaps the occasional late-night interview. My work explored conflicts of law and conscience.

Though Larry had no more actual experience as an investigative reporter than I did, he at least was part of a great network of investigative journalists, a band of brothers who sought unpredictable stories, unfolding in real time, in the very live and dangerous present tense.

With my wife vamoosed, my daughter in college and no real love interest to tie me down, I thought it might be a good time to throw caution to the winds. What did I have to lose?

I met Larry the next day in his office, a glass perch overlooking the newsroom: smallish humans below, the clacking of their typing and the babble of their conversations muted by distance and the glass-sealed walls.

When I'd visited in the past, we'd always exchanged details of our personal lives before we talked shop. But this day was different. We immediately dove into the state of affairs in Rwanda, and discussed geopolitics, foreign support, alliances. We assessed the relevance of the United Nations and the Organization of African Unity, and agreed that those organizations mostly represented the interests of stakeholders and industry, rarely than mass populations.

Having reviewed the latest reports and communiques from Rwanda together, we were unable to easily distinguish the moderates from the extremists. Even when this was possible, we could not say with certainty that the distinctions would hold the following month. In Rwanda, political instability had become the norm; today's oppressed might be tomorrow's ruling elite.

So, what was the assignment? To discover changing truths? Identify the players? Assign roles of good and evil? Keep score of the body count?

One big story seemed to be the numbers. People were being killed and tortured by the thousands. Or tens of thousands. Or maybe more. Words like *holocaust* and *genocide* were being used. It didn't take long for us both to feel the pressing call of journalistic duty, albeit in our separate ways.

"This is what I'm thinking," said Larry. "At this point, I see this as more of a human-interest story than anything else. Fact is, there have been tribal atrocities in Africa for over a century and no one has ever interceded. Outside of Christian relief organizations no one really cares, and those who do are mostly Jesuits and foreigners."

"Nothing's being done?" I asked.

"In fairness, someone in our State Department occasionally issues a nicely worded statement like, 'The United States supports Rwandan efforts to increase democratic participation, enhance respect for civil and political rights and improve the quality and outcome of health care, social security and basic education.'"

"Doesn't say anything. Empty whitewash."

"Right. Political blather to cover uncommitted support."

"You think our response would be different if the atrocities involved Blacks and Whites?"

"I think we both know the answer to that."

There was an uncomfortable pause.

"Look," said Larry, "it's not our job to continually assail our government, or even our political parties, for not responding to the crisis. We're not referees and this isn't a game of football, where both sides keep punting. It may be the essential truth — but it doesn't inspire compelling journalism."

"Then where's the story?"

Larry nodded before speaking, as if sanctioning what he was about to say. "I see this as a tribal drama with a universal message."

"I agree," I said. "A family tragedy. The American Civil War fought out in the hills and jungles of Central Africa."

"I like that."

Pause.

"But is it enough?" I asked. "Will your readers care about native Blacks killing each other? An article, sure. But a series? What's the draw?"

Larry shook his heady sadly. "The draw is the revelation of modern barbarism. Gender violence has been added to the menu."

"What exactly does that mean?" I asked.

"In America, gender battles mostly involve cases of unfair representation and inequality. There is rarely any actual bloodletting. But in Rwanda, the divided populace often torture each other with sexual violence: women are mutilated to prevent procreation; men are castrated and left for dead."

"Good God!"

"Each side is guilty. Each side feels justified. Each side sees sexual violence as an effective messaging campaign."

A breathless pause.

"Ironically, the two sides are historically close," said Larry.

"Civil War, brother versus brother," I added.

"Nothing says hatred like close family."

"Everyone has a grudge. Everyone wants revenge."

"An eye for an eye."

"And worse — much worse. Grotesque sexual interest as a teaser. That's horrible."

Another pause.

"Still," I said, "That's just background. I don't have a story."

"Of course not. You're not there," said Larry. "You haven't yet interviewed the maimed, the survivors, the witnesses.

How could you know their stories? You haven't met the butchers either: those in power who ordered the horrors."

"I suppose."

"By the way," said Larry, leaning back as if for an official declaration. "You are uniquely qualified for this assignment — this mission."

I heard *mission* as a prop to my manhood and sense of professionalism.

"How am I uniquely qualified?"

I knew what he meant but I wanted to hear him say it. I wanted the managing editor of *The New York Times* to name my gifts.

"James Larson Andersen: Journalist. Novelist. Ethicist. Protector of men's rights. Vocal supporter of women's rights. You are the man for the job. You're the man to run point."

"A team affair?"

"Of course, but a small team. You'll need a guide and assistants. People to translate, photograph, even video-record. We'll set you up with contacts and papers."

"Given the situation, I expect to earn hazard pay."

"That's a given. But I'll be honest, the assignment is not without risk."

"Big risk?"

Larry took a deep breath. "Look, I don't know how closely you and Frankie have been following the situation, but in the past year it's been an absolute shitstorm — if you'll excuse my French. Massacres have taken place just about everywhere: in hospitals, in factories, at the National University, in Catholic refuges, in fields, in villages, in people's homes — you name it. An untold number of casualties: maybe a million people killed, and God knows how many brutalized and dismembered. Supposedly the worst is now over. The United Nations Assistance Mission for Rwanda and other international forces are working to stabilize the country and things have certainly settled down, but there are still reports of sporadic violence. We think some agreements will be in place by end of November, and that might allow us to launch shortly thereafter. In short, it's not without danger, but we'll do our best to keep you safe. All I can say is: hope for the best; prepare for the worst. And try and come back alive."

Lawrence Schielding

Jim and Frankie were the only two persons I ever really loved — and I betrayed them both. Jim was my first love — my friend, my protector, my everything. And Frankie? How exciting it was when she came into our lives! How we both adored her! How we competed for her attention and affection! Of course, Jim won because he always did ... because he was strong and handsome and brave ... and I wasn't any of those things, so I never won. Always second place and third wheel for me.

At the time, I did not understand the depths of my anger and regret. If I had, I never would have concocted the terrible arrangements that took Jim and Frankie to Rwanda.

Francine Rose

Gloria had warned me of the unsustainability of *Virago*'s meteoric rise, predicting that our success would continue only so long as we remained the feisty alternative to *Ms*.

We could not afford to pull our punches. But finding the right battles proved harder than we'd thought. Eventually, we found it necessary to up the rhetoric simply to throw down the gauntlet. Unfortunately, this made the magazine seem unnecessarily antagonistic, which turned off some readers and eventually hurt our bottom line.

We then tried dialing back our feistiness but that didn't work either. It just made us less distinguishable from *Ms*. With our editorial positioning seemingly indecisive, our sales sunk and we faced possible ruin.

What we needed was a glorious cause to champion, something so indisputably honorable and inherently dangerous that both *The New York Times* and *Virago* would see as fit to print.

Larry Schielding

I decided there would have to be two stories, as there were two basic enmities, Tutsi and Hutu, each of which owned that their truth was preeminent and rightful.

Ironically, as far as my preliminary research went, there were no important physical or racial differences separating the two groups; nothing religious or linguistic either. The two sides were more alike than not. I learnt that the minority Tutsi were mostly cattle ranchers (more respected than the Hutu farmers) and that it had been the dastardly European colonials (first the Germans, then the Belgians) who had instituted and perpetuated the deep divisions between them.

In post-colonial times, the two groups had taken turns wielding power over the other. Each had waged war; each had committed atrocities. At the time I was developing my idea for a dual series of articles on the subject, the Hutu were more likely to mutilate the Tutsi women; the Tutsi were more likely to castrate the Hutu men. Based on these few understandings and little more, I was ready to designate two teams, one representing each tribe. It then occurred to me that American readers would have more of a rooting interest if the teams (and the stories they wrote) were divided by sex. Men writing about men. Women writing about women. No more accusations of inauthenticity.

Francine Rose

The feisty spirit that defined *Virago*'s ascent had been hard to maintain and the magazine's fortunes subsequently suffered. Around the same time, my relationship with Gloria (which had enjoyed its own rocket-like ascendancy) began to sputter. For the most part, I blamed myself. In our early days I mistook Gloria's receptiveness for pliancy, which I saw as a kind of softness, which is another way of saying I saw Gloria as a lump of loving weakness. I was wrong. While receptive in bed, receptive to my business ideas and receptive to our living together, she was a clawed demon whenever opposed.

She revealed her sharply critical side soon after I was fully installed in her beautiful townhouse on Minetta Street. As it turned out, she was so stubbornly intolerant, so unwilling to compromise on domestic issues, I was soon reminded of my soul-deadening arguments with Jim. My relations with Gloria were already like a tired marriage.

I was also going through a difficult patch with Molly. She wouldn't call for days, then she'd call all the time — in the middle of the night, at the office — sometimes calm, sometimes panicked.

I had a cell phone but I didn't always have it with me, which Molly refused to believe, accusing me of ignoring her ... leaving her ... implying I was a bad and unloving mother ... often reminding me of her deformity — and blaming me.

With *Virago*, Gloria and Molly all bearing down on me, I received a call from Larry. I can't say it was a coincidence as he'd been calling me at least a once a week for years, having (it seemed to me) a sixth sense of when I was most needful of his sage and impartial advice.

Larry Schielding

Despite being the best man at their wedding, I never felt — not for one minute of my sorry life — that I was the best man anywhere, or to anyone. Still, I gave a rousing, best man's speech, full of warmth and wit, betraying not a jot of my seething jealousy.

Years later, when Molly was born and I was named her godfather, I used the honorific to stay deeply connected to all three of them, always up-to-date on their family dramas and politics. For nearly twenty years I played the role of trust-worthy pal, confidante and loving uncle (so to speak), carefully choosing whom to call and when in order to maximize my influence. I was the go-to guy, the one person each of them could trust to offer seemingly selfless, supportive and well-intentioned advice.

In my perverse way, I took pleasure when Jim and Frankie split, thinking I would commiserate with each of them separately, before choosing one of them to be my life partner, for better or worse, 'til death do us part. Oddly, it didn't really matter to me which one I chose. I imagined scenarios in which I was perfectly happy living with either of them.

But it didn't work out that way. When they separated, Jim became even more engrossed in his work on behalf of gay rights and even more likely to pursue anonymous gay trysts. Frankie worked harder than ever as a feminist freedom fighter, before leaping into the fat arms of that sow on Minetta Street. Neither of them gave me a chance.

It was then I began imagining what it might be like if one or the other of them died in an accident or from cancer ... or by some other violent means.

It's not that I wanted that to happen, exactly, but if it did ... if fate intervened and claimed one of them, either one, suddenly, prematurely, might the other — after a suitable period of grieving — take comfort in my arms?

EAST OF ZAIRE

Mark Goldstone

Jim told me about the assignment from *The New York Times,* speculating on what the experience might be like. Though he didn't mention my participation or even allude to its possibility, I expected to be included in his plans. Hoping to solidify my position, I queried him indirectly.

"What about Molly? Are you taking her too?"

I worried about Molly going on such a perilous journey. I worried even more that she might not be invited. It's safe to say that I'd begun to care for her.

Francine Rose

As I'd been invited to Larry's office only once before, I wondered what was behind the invitation.

"C'mon, Larry," I said into the phone on my bedroom nightstand. "Why the invite?"

"Hey, we're good friends. Besides, I'm going to proposition you."

"In your office?"

"A business proposition."

I imagined his sly smile.

Somehow I'd forgotten the staggering fact of his glass office, overhanging the newsroom. It struck me then as perfectly Larry: distant, imperious, watchful, covetous and yet unconnected.

Having not seen him for some months, he looked good, having (apparently) maintained his health and scrupulous grooming. I, on the other hand, had put on a few lazy pounds and proudly wore gray streaks in my hair like warrior pelts.

After inquiring about Gloria and Molly (as one slyly in the know), he talked generally about the *Times* before getting down to business. We were standing by the glass wall (with Olympian aloofness) when he proposed that I undertake a daring adventure of investigative journalism. Only, he didn't phrase it that way. Instead, seemingly out of nowhere, he asked, "How would you like to help Rwandan women who've suffered horrible sexual trauma?"

I remained calm, despite the red-meat challenge.

"What are you proposing?"

He smiled at that. "I propose you lead an investigative

group of women to a specific destination in Rwanda to report on the atrocities being perpetrated against Rwandan women. I propose that you interview, record, photograph, videotape and then write a series of articles for publication in *The New York Times*. After you fulfil your obligation, I'm happy for you to use your acquired content and experiences in *Virago* — or elsewhere — no strings attached."

I'd arrived with an open mind but hadn't expected anything like what I'd just heard. Before I could respond, he added, "You're the best woman for the job."

I thought so too but I really wanted to hear him say it. And he did.

"You're fearless. You're a trailblazer. You're politically savvy but independent. You can take care of yourself and manage others. Most importantly, you'll get the women to open up to you ... and you will write their stories with poetic empathy — however violent and savage the details."

And I just might save *Virago*.

And maybe Molly too. My poor baby was hurting. She felt abandoned and needed mommy love. This was my opportunity to treat her fairly; to embrace her strong-willed independence; to show that I trusted her.

James Andersen

I felt a little like Sophie on her arrival at Auschwitz, having to choose which of her two children to save, her son or her daughter.

Mark, who lived with me as a sort of son, was more qualified, deserving and mature than Molly. He would serve me well in Rwanda.

Molly, on the other hand, though of my own flesh and blood, had a history of eschewing authority and might be a liability in a small, top-down organization, where I was the unquestioned top and she was the indisputable down. Also, she was still young and reckless ... still growing into her womanhood … and forever lame because of my lazy indulgence. Could I risk indulging her again?

I chose to save Molly, which meant I'd invite Mark to go with me.

Molly X

I'd never worried about finding a job as a journalist. I mean, my parents were well known in the field and my uncle (as I liked to think of Larry) was *The New York Times*'s managing editor. So, when my mother made me the extraordinary offer to join her Rwanda-bound team as her assistant, I played it cool, as if I had other offers to consider — as if we weren't quite squared away.

"What do you want?" she asked me plainly.

I was ready.

"I want to know why you abandoned me."

Mom looked me in the eyes. "Really, is that what you think? Then I was wrong about your readiness. You're still a little girl."

She paused. I guess she wanted her remark to sink in.

"It not like I left you on the steps of a firehouse. I left you in your own home, in the care of your father. And it's not like I skulked away in the middle of the night. I moved ten blocks away to share a home with someone who respects me more than your father does. I left home knowing you're in college and ready to experience life on your own terms. Was I so wrong?"

Surprised (and impressed) by the reasonableness of her reasoning, I forgave her. Still, I thought she owed me.

"I want at least one shared byline with you. And at least one other that's mine alone."

My mother seemed to give my request some serious consideration.

"I can't promise the *Times* — in fact, I strongly doubt it — but I can promise *Virago*. You want it in writing?"

"No, I trust you," I said, feeling more mature than ever before.

"Good. Thank you, Love. Now, I have to make some phone calls. I'll call you soon for lunch."

Mark Goldstone

Molly and I were lunching in Thielsson's, in a far corner booth that we had chosen to avoid being overheard. We weren't exactly going off to war but (we supposed) we'd both face grave danger, and even the possibility of death.

"I don't want to worry about you," I said to Molly, hiding the fact that I was even more knock-kneed about my own safety.

"My parents aren't lunatics. I'm sure they're taking all reasonable precautions."

She must have read my budding terror.

"Look," she said to me gently, as if speaking to a little boy. "There has to be risk. Without risk, there's no reward. Without risk, there's no glory. And without risk, there's no story."

It was like lunching with Joan of Arc.

"Still," I said, "it won't be a walk in the park."

"That reminds me," she said, breaking into a sly smile. "Who do we know from Rwanda who might be able to help us?"

I returned a smile.

"Exactly."

"And who do we know from Rwanda who could use our help?"

I smiled again.

"Exactly."

A SPECIAL DEAL

Felix Kwizera

Dativa's disapproval of my drug business was fierce and made me ashamed of myself. I could not bear to lose her, nor could I easily walk away from my lucrative dealing. You see, I wasn't a citizen. I had no Social Security number. I could not expect to find another job that would pay me even half what I was making as a weed dealer. But she had given me an ultimatum: stop selling drugs or she'd find another park.

Dativa Natukunda

Already I loved him. He was smart and beautiful. And when I strolled my white baby around the park in its high-canopied pram, I imagined the three of us as a happy family. A happy American family!

But his drug dealing was a dead end, so my torment was keen.

I did not have many choices. I did not have romantic options. There was no other man in my life.

I worked every day but Sunday. On Sunday I went to church. There, I did not stand out among the other single women. In fact, my head barely peeped over the pew, so I was not easily noticed. And when I was noticed, it was obvious that I was short and poor and had a strong accent.

I worried that I wasn't any man's cup of tea. But I'd told Felix where I went to church and he came one Sunday and noticed me right away. The next week he came again; following the service, he asked me to lunch. He continued coming to church on Sundays and we continued dating. Sometimes we would meet in the park. We had much in common, as we both had been orphaned from our families and our nation. After some few months, he said that he loved me. He said it twice; once in English and once in our two-tone Kinyarwanda.

Molly X

Jimmy wasn't angry on learning that Larry had offered Frankie a similar assignment and that Frankie had chosen me as her assistant. The fact that Frankie and I would also be working in Rwanda seemed to add importance and attention to his own mission — and, of course, he no longer had to concern himself with my disappointment.

As to that, I was cool with Jimmy's decision to choose Mark over me. Personally, I thought it was a no-brainer, as Mark was his professional protégé. Not only was I not as qualified but I was his daughter, which might have raised some sneers of nepotism, which ethical Jimmy couldn't abide. Frankie didn't suffer from the same scruples. She had her own shit, but helping another sister — even if that sister happened to be her daughter — was just another plus in her mind.

Much more complicated was my suggestion that Felix and Dativa join our respective groups in Rwanda — in exchange for promises of U.S. citizenship. My parents liked the idea and turned to Larry for help. Drawing on his contacts at INS (Immigration and Naturalization Service), Larry was able to get in writing a pair of official promises to fast track Felix's and Dativa's applications. All this was done before Felix and Dativa had even been propositioned.

Felix Kwizera

Mark and Molly spoke with me together, outside the main park building (where the bathrooms were), not under the Hangman's Elm, where I did most of my drug business. I think they must have rehearsed because they made a very efficient presentation, each doing an equal amount of talking.

Molly said something that clinched the argument. "Look, Philippe," she said, using my street name for the last time, "every dealer gets pinched eventually. Most get a first-time warning. Thing is, you can't afford a single strike. Just one arrest could ruin forever your chance of citizenship. You're a smart guy. You know this is a special deal. Not only will you be doing a great thing for your future and Dativa's, you'll also be helping to save and protect innocent Rwandans."

I knew the argument was good; even so, I had to say what I had to say.

"Dativa and I are Twa. We have no special love for the others. The others have treated our people with disrespect — and heartlessness."

Molly nodded sympathetically. "I don't pretend to understand any Rwandan's experience. It's like talking about Americans. We're all different. Well then, all Rwandans are different too — and so many need help."

I'm a selfish man. I didn't care about the others. Let them kill each other dead for all I cared. I wanted only to help myself — and Dativa. But Molly had made a very special offer.

"You can get citizenship papers for us both?"

"Yes. It will take time, but it will go as fast as possible."

This was a big thing. As citizens, we could live as real Americans. Still, something was missing. Something in the back of my mind. I took my chance. I knew I might not have another.

"After my father was killed, my mother went back to her village for help. I waited a long time but she never returned. When the Jesuits said they would send me to America — to New York — I asked about my mother. They said if she lived, she would want me to be well and safe. I saw the sense of these words, so I let them take me away. But the shame of leaving her behind has always pained me. If I return to Rwanda, I want to know if my mother lives. If she lives, I want to see her."

Mark Goldstone

Some journalists are born to write great stories, some uncover great stories through investigative diligence and some have great stories thrust upon them.

The story of Felix and his mother felt like the latter kind. In fact, its dramatic potential felt so much like a divine gift, I thanked my vague Jewish god for my potential inheritance.

The next day I began my preliminary research, taking copious notes. When I was ready, I had a dozen questions for Felix about his mother and his mother's home village and another two dozen about Rwandan culture and customs. For the time being, I decided not to share this sidelight with Jim. I asked Felix to likewise keep mum and he agreed. I did, however, share my plan with Molly, who told me her lips were sealed ... but then immediately unsealed them and kissed me, hard.

Felix Kwizera

Mark and Molly wanted to speak with Dativa to propose the same offer they had made me.

"We will be in different groups?" I asked.

"Yes," Mark answered. "You will be in a male group, dealing with maimed men. Dativa will be in a female group, dealing with maimed women."

"We will be able to speak to each other?"

"Perhaps, occasionally."

I nodded.

"The groups will be working in the same region but not together," said Mark. "The work will be hard: possibly dangerous."

I spoke to Dativa the next day and explained the situation as best I could. She said she would miss her beautiful white baby, but if I needed to return to Rwanda, she would go too.

"Only," she said. "I want a promise. I do not need a cow for my bride price, but I want an engagement ring before we go. I want a symbol from your heart to wear on my hand. You will be my promised man. I will be your promised woman."

Dativa Natukunda

At first, I did not want to go. Yes, there were things and people I missed in Rwanda, but it was a dreadfully danger-ous place and I was blessed to be in America — and in New York, of all places. But I also saw the plan as an opportunity for Felix to leave the park and the drugs. And when I learned (first from Felix and then from his friends Mark and Molly) that we both would be awarded American citizenship for our work as translators and assistants, I knew a return to Rwanda was necessary to make our American dream come true.

Mark Goldstone

We'd left Thielsson's to continue our conversation in the apartment upstairs.

"You're braver than I am," I said to Molly. "Smarter too."

"I'm not brave. I've just seen so much bad shit happen to good people, nothing much scares or surprises me. And, for the record, I'm not smarter than you. You know a lot more than I do."

She saw me smile.

"But I do know myself better than you know yourself," she said. "I think that counts for something."

"I think it counts for a lot."

"That shows how smart you really are."

"I think we're a good match," I said, moving closer.

"That's the smartest thing you've said yet."

And then we kissed — more passionately than ever before — and the other stuff proceeded naturally and beautifully. When it was over, she stroked my sweaty forehead while I stroked her beautiful lame leg.

Molly X

Mark was a good guy who believed in doing good works. He believed in the power of journalism and the positivity of ethics. He believed in me. That was the biggest thing.

After my accident, my parents had been inconsistent in my upbringing: sometimes over-indulgent, sometimes over-protective. Early on I recognized this inconsistency and played it to my advantage. Over time, this behavior shaped my general outlook. I became more interested in beating the system than doing what was right or what was best, even for myself. At the same time, I could not help but observe how my parents lived their lives as alpha altruists and this also shaped my values.

But it was Mark who helped make me comfortable in my own skin. He was the first to look at me clearly, entirely, and to accept what he saw. With Mark, I shared all — even the scarred and lame part — and he adored it, kissing it tenderly.

Felix Kwizera

Dativa never knew her parents. She was an orphan ... good, beautiful and devoted to me. As a promise of something finer, I would give her my mother's own simple wedding ring, a circlet of bone and shell.

At first, I thought to present it in a fancy box but I feared she might think I was making a joke or a bit of irony. I wanted her to know that my love was a serious business.

Luckily, I soon found the perfect container: a simple, lidded bamboo box for tea bags. Inside were five compartments, four of which I filled with bags of Tangawizi tea, her favorite Rwandan blend. In the center compartment, hidden in a crumple of lavender tissue, I laid my mother's wedding ring, which (I surmised) she'd left in my care, lest anyone steal it during her dangerous journey home.

I was very nervous when he removed the giftwrapped package from his satchel and presented it with such a serious face. It was not my birthday or any anniversary I could remember.

"For you," was all he said.

I could not remove the wrapping with his eyes locked on mine, so I dropped my gaze, the better to concentrate.

Having removed the wrapping, I opened the lidded bamboo box. Seeing my favorite Rwandan teas, I was pleased — and disappointed. The disappointment was sharp but unfocused, as if I would not admit to myself the root of my feeling. Just then I noticed that one of the five little cubbies contained something other than a tea bag. Something small and wrapped in fine lavender tissue.

"Open it," he said.

I couldn't. My brain and fingers refused to communicate.

"Allow me," he said.

With a surgeon's finesse and patience, he removed the folded paper, as if peeling an onion, one layer at a time.

STRANGELY COINCIDENTAL

Molly X

I was nineteen when I found Dad's secret cache of Busty Evans photos and news clippings on the top shelf of his closet, in an office envelope marked RECEIPTS. I'd been looking for reasons to explain why Mom had left us and thought I'd found the smoking gun: the stark evidence of Dad's infidelity. But on closer inspection I was both relieved and weirded out. Relieved because I saw no evidence that my father had a personal relationship with Ms. Evans; weirded out because my super serious father, the admired journalist and ethicist, had such an intense interest in a frowsy, old burlesque performer, with a dull pasty face and spectacularly huge boobs.

Busty Evans

I liked that young fellow who drove all the way from New York to Canton to interview me. Most men I meet — even the so-called newspaper ones — are not so polite. Which I understand, to a point. I mean, I'm a stripper. I know what people say about the girls in my profession and especially about me. But we all have feelings. We all get hurt.

But that nice young fellow was so polite and so sincerely interested in me. And I knew he was genuine 'cause I could see it in his clear eyes and hear it in his honest voice. To prove my point, he still wrote to me, even twenty years later, even after he'd got married and had a daughter. I liked when he wrote to me about her. I cried buckets when I read about her accident but it seems she turned out just fine: strong and opinionated and with a heart of gold. I like that she wants to be a journalist, just like her dad and momma. My husband and me had no children, though I wanted at least one, a girl, but I can see why that blessing was denied me.

James Andersen

We prepared for most every contingency (food, medicine, first aid, replacement gear, backup technology) and planned never to be more than a couple of kilometers from each other's group, just in case we needed to sound the alarm, which would mean our immediate extraction to a place of safety — and the end of our combined assignment.

Feeling oddly fatalistic (in a way that had nothing overtly to do with the mission's inherent dangers), I wrote to Busty, as if she were somehow involved or responsible for my mood. When two weeks passed and I had no reply, I called her home (which, in recent years, I normally did on only on

Christmas Eve and her birthday). For the first time, a gruff male voice answered. Rather than hang up (which I considered), I said, "Hello, may I speak with Sondra Lou Churcher?" I'd listed her phone number under her real name, so I had it at hand.

"Who wants to know?"

I explained who I was and he explained that he was her husband. We'd never spoken before.

"Of course, that nice writer fellow. How are you?"

Relieved by his friendly tone, I said I was well and that I was going on a long business trip that could last a month or more. "I thought I'd call up, say hi and wish her a happy holiday season."

"That's very nice of you but you missed her by a few days. Crazy thing, she's on the first major business trip of her life. Even took her first airplane."

"Really? May I ask where?"

"Guam."

"Guam? The Pacific island where we have that naval base?"

"Well, you are as smart as Sandy says."

"Thank you. But why Guam?"

"The commander there — I forget his name — anyway, like you, he's a devoted fan. He invited her — and a couple of her showgirl friends — to stay in Guam for a few weeks to put on some soft shows for the boys."

"That sounds wonderful. I'm sorry to have missed her. When do you expect her back?"

"Well, here's the thing, the commander told his friend about the upcoming shows and this other commander — an admiral stationed somewhere in Kenya, I forget exactly — well, he invited Sandy and her friends (all successful showgirl strippers, though not quite as well-known, or as old, I might add) to do several shows for his troops."

"Wow, that's amazing. Do you know when the ladies arrive there and how long they expect to stay?"

"I don't think Sandy and the girls will arrive there for several weeks ... and I expect them to stay a couple of weeks. As she said to me — and I think she's right — if you travel some place really far, it makes sense to stay a while, if you have the time."

"I guess she has the time."

"Indeedy, we're both slidin' into retirement. Sandy considers these trips the last two of her professional career — and a chance to go out in style. Me? I have a bad back, so the last thing I want is to fly around the world in a cramped space, fit for a poodle."

We spoke a few minutes more and then said a pair of warm goodbyes. He invited me to come see them someday. I said that sounded real nice and thanked him for the invite. I did not mention that I was also headed for Africa, as it sounded too strangely coincidental.

Gloria Applebaum

Having kept up with the news in Rwanda for many years, I'd never felt the need to engage anything more than my passive sympathies — until the day I read of the plight of the women and their maiming. At that moment, recalling images of the Holocaust and the degrading of Jewish women (and remembering that Francine and I were both Jewish, as was her daughter Molly, born of a Jewish mother), it suddenly seemed imperative that we should all help the injured Rwandan women in a big and newsworthy way.

Alongside the moral issues, I confess that I immediately began imagining how our stories of genital mutilation and rape would incite our flagging audience, putting our magazine back on top and maybe earning us a Pulitzer or two. In fact, recalling how we had already declared ourselves feistier feminists than our good sisters at *Ms.*, it seemed our great fortune (and moral obligation) to act quickly on this rare opportunity.

Perhaps not surprising, there also was my personal motivation: I needed some time away from Francine. Having lived alone for so many years, I found it difficult to share my home — and my heart — with only her. Part of me hoped she'd never come back.

Francine Rose

Of course, it wasn't only about helping Rwandan women. I'm not that selfless. But who is? Mother Teresa? Joan of Arc? Maybe. Certainly not me.

Don't get me wrong. I'm not making excuses or selling myself short. I'm just being real. Modern life is complicated. And political. You scratch my back, I scratch yours. Sure, I was passionate about wanting to help maimed Rwandan women but I also had personal motives: like enjoying time and space away from Gloria ... a unique bonding experience with Molly ... the opportunity to save *Virago* ... and the chance to show the world that I was the number-one journalist in my family — *not* my soon-to-be ex-husband.

Lawrence Schielding

Some newspapers rely on wire services for most of their news coverage. But the best newspapers do original research and writing, discovering news in hidden accounts, shallow graves, secretive hearts.

Into the fray I sent two great writers, two brave ethical souls: James to report on the Rwandan men and boys who'd been emasculated; Francine to report on the women and girls who'd been raped and mutilated. My plan was to have them work separately, using different sources, generating independent stories.

Despite our safeguards, I began to worry (with increasing nervousness) that one or the other of my two dearest friends — and possibly both — might be killed in action. I reveled in the imagined horror while wiping away real tears.

By the way, had I foreseen that Mark would join James's group and that Molly (my goddaughter) would join Francine's, I might have shaped my entire proposal very differently — or canceled it altogether. I have a special soft spot in my heart for beautiful youth.

FLIGHT LISTS AND FOREBODINGS

Lawrence Schielding

In my mind I still heard the voice of Bill Carter, our former executive editor, exhorting me to focus less on the new bells and whistles and more on giving the world more hardcore reportage, à la Watergate.

Like all business managers I had to balance our paper's high standards with the proposed project's bottom line. To do so, I made dozens of decisions that considered both the scope of the work and the safety of our two teams. Failure to bring them all home safely (while itself a newsworthy story) might blemish my reputation and even cost me my job (always depending on the circumstances).

I spent a lot of time weighing the pros and cons of sending our team of journalists to Rwanda, focusing especially on what we might get out of a particularly promising news-gathering location: Cyanika, right up in the North on the border with Uganda. In favor of such a decision was my honest belief that war-reporting was a time-honored profession. Rwanda was a still-simmering zone of conflict, and any journalist willing to accept the inherent dangers—regardless of personal motivations—has a God-given right to follow his (or her) own conscience.

Mitigating my concerns was my understanding that the worst of the violence had now declined, having peaked back in late spring. Still, my sources described Cyanika as a busy, militarized border-crossing, the site of an endless flow of refugees in both directions, and violent flare-ups with both countries' border guards. It's not where I would have wanted to spend time.

But by December 1, 1994, I was getting reports suggesting that things were calming down a little. The government —intent on brokering a reconciliation between the main warring parties—was working to establish basic administrative functions. Even so, I remained on the fence.

And then one of our assets came up with a first-rate idea. Rather than set up our journalists on the edge of Cyanika, he proposed that we locate them about nine miles southeast to a small village named Umuhanda, near some lakes. The plan wasn't foolproof. Umuhanda had seen its own small share of horrors, but it had been relatively quiet for several months.

Finally, it seemed that Rwanda had two rainy seasons — one in the spring, one in the fall — and when I found out that the one in the fall would be about done by the end of November, I greenlighted the plan to house the two teams in a pair of medical outposts by the second week of December.

Having approved the insertion of untrained, non-military personnel into a war zone, I knew I'd have a lot to answer for if things went south, despite my folder of signed waivers and consents.

James Andersen

I'm not sure why I was filled with such dark forebodings. I'd taken an active role in the planning, enlisting the advice of other journalists who'd traveled to Rwanda in recent years, reviewing their procedures for communication, transportation, health and so on.

Because we were expecting to interview natives who'd been emasculated, raped or mutilated, we'd hired a local doctor and nurse for each group to serve as healers and extra translators. As safeguards for our personal protection, we carried special papers from the Rwandan consulate in New

York, signed by both Hutu and Tutsi officials. But we carried no weapons. Not even edged tools, other than the scalpels and scissors employed by our medical personnel.

I shared all the details of my preparation with Francine — except for my knowledge that Busty would soon arrive at the American base in Mombasa (nearly 1,000 miles away) and that I had a great desire to see her again, believing, in my heart of hearts, that it would be for the last time.

Francine Rose

I hadn't seen James for the better part of a year and Molly only a half-dozen times during that same period. She'd been angry with me for leaving. I'd been angry with her for being angry with me. Eventually, I recognized that the greater fault was mine. After all, I was the responsible adult who'd left her for Gloria and *Virago*, shutting her out during those early days of separation, pretending it was for her own good, telling myself she needed to develop fortitude and resiliency to become a strong woman. Eventually, I saw that I'd been selfish — and wrong. Molly was already strong. And independent. And wise beyond her years. The parts of her that had been messed up were my fault — and Jim's. Ironically, it wasn't her accident that had messed her up but our rehabilitative parenting. Strict one day, lax another, our mixed signals drove her to the park to hang with the riffraff, like some streetwise druggie.

But all this is beside the point: deflection on my part. Here's the thing: I was proud of my daughter's recent maturation. She was altruistic, progressive, intellectually curious, dependable and unequivocally kind. She was also sexually equivocal, claiming (aloud and publicly) to like boys and girls.

I wanted to support her in this but wasn't sure how — other than being emotionally supportive, which I was. Still, it didn't seem quite enough. I mean, it would have been enough for anyone else I knew but she was my only child — my daughter — and still growing into her womanhood. As to her orientation, I wouldn't say that I wanted her to be gay but I certainly wouldn't have minded. After all, I had a lifetime of insights I could share with her. She could learn from my mistakes.

This had been my thinking when Larry and I first discussed the Rwanda project and he'd floated the idea of separate teams, male and female. Immediately I saw the opportunity to choose Molly for my team in order to make amends for having left her. I hoped we'd grow together, not only as mother and daughter but as women.

As a result of this thinking, I decided not to fly to Paris on the same jet out of New York that would carry Jim and Mark, Felix and Dativa. Instead and on my own dime, I decided to fly with Molly to Paris five days earlier, for five days of personal girly time ... and then on to Kigali.

James Andersen

I should have been angry with Frankie for taking Molly to Paris on an earlier flight and then transferring to Kigali. That wasn't the plan. We'd all agreed to fly together, have a nice meal together when we arrived and then split into our separate teams.

I hadn't seen Frankie in about a year, since she'd left me to live with Gloria. Past enmities aside, I'd been looking forward to seeing her. We still had Molly in common (along with Larry and a lot of other history) and I wanted to know what her intentions were regarding the apartment we'd shared for twenty years.

I was even more disappointed about not seeing Molly before I left. At the time, I didn't read too much into it, figuring she needed to reconnect with her mother before their Rwandan adventure. Still, I'd wanted to spend my own prep time with her, discussing the rigors and responsibilities of journalism, safety precautions, cultural insights and taboos concerning the Hutu and Tutsi — and her relationship with Mark. Though young and in many practical ways immature, I was hoping she would marry him. Having noted their many shared interests and complementary personalities, I thought they'd make a good couple.

I had another equally compelling reason for wanting them to marry: I no longer trusted myself living alone with Mark. I'd become too sexually attracted to him and worried that I might do or say something that betrayed my passion, like pretending I didn't know he was home and coming out of a room naked, hoping to arouse him into doing something impulsive.

Of course, I didn't actually want any of that to happen (for it would certainly ruin my relationship with Molly and possibly Mark too) and yet I couldn't seem to rid myself of my compulsion.

Despite the tension, I relished my time alone with Mark. The real-time fantasy provided by his cohabitation stimulated my creativity. For months before his arrival, I'd done little to advance my novel, *Ecce Homo / The Beholding*. Despite Larry's florid praise, I knew the book needed more depth and development. But I was stunted. My real-life, brief and furtive sexual encounters had failed to inspire fully developed characters, much less a riveting and satisfying plot. But Mark's wit and youthful exuberance were a stimulating boon and I thought that with another six months I might complete my crowning achievement and with its publication announce (at long last!) the kind of man I am. But it would have to wait: Rwanda called.

Francine Rose

Having learned that some of the western world's most famous Classical nudes were collected in the Louvre and Musée d'Orsay, I planned to spend one day at each museum with Molly, followed by a day of park strolling and café conversation. I hoped our shared viewings would steer our conversations to sexuality — personal and political.

Everything went according to plan. At the museums we were one pair of eyes, one hungry heart, intuiting together where to go, what to see. Floor by floor, room by room, our eyes devoured dozens of the world's most delicious nudes. On approaching *The Sleep* (Courbet; two young women entwined on satiny bed covers; a peek of ginger crotch), my hand flew to my mouth but Molly only giggled — her way of coping, I thought.

During all those hours of savoring artistic nudes, we never questioned the limitations of the two-dimensional canvas. We never considered turning over a painting to see what delights might be hidden on the other side. And so, when we came upon a room of nude statuary (our senses already heightened and sexualized), we were jolted by the sculptures' three-dimensional charms.

With unrestrained prurience we examined every aspect of the nude torsos, exploring every neck and limb, every nook and cranny.

Despite the physical idealizations (perfect derrieres; uniformly rounded, small-nippled breasts; hairless vulvas, bronze burnished or shined to a perfect marble gloss), the statues suggested a variety of complex feminine expressions. Our two favorites were *The Three Graces* (a sisterly sorority) and *Diana of Versailles* (the huntress goddess reaching for an arrow from her quiver), which we both agreed could be used in *Virago*'s future marketing.

We occasionally separated to follow our own paths but mostly we walked together, arm-in-arm.

Molly X

I mostly enjoyed those five days alone with my mother, although our focused discussions became repetitive and tiresome. Though I thanked her (repeatedly) for clarifying my (personal) opinions, my greatest takeaway was that I was in fact heterosexual, with a deep and abiding affection for Mark Goldstone. I just didn't know how to tell her.

Mark Goldstone

Molly was in Paris and I missed her terribly. My feelings were complicated but I knew Jim had a lot to do with it. He was, after all, my mentor ... my friend ... a father figure who'd invited me into his home to share his rent but also to befriend his wayward daughter, to be a positive influence on her life. I betrayed that trust, I think.

In my defense, Molly and I had got off on an unplanned, intimate footing: me, tripping on the floor vines and falling into her arms; her, disentangling (with all the guile of Salome) and then sashaying into the kitchen, the switch of her hips focusing at least part of my attention on her slim, boyish ass.

I liked her immediately. Her sarcasm, her gender-bending Joan of Arc defiance and, yes, her lame gait. Something about it drew me but it certainly wasn't pity. Molly was no three-legged dog. She was unselfconsciously bold and self-determining. She was an original. She was Molly X! And yet, from that first day onward (despite her attractiveness and forward ways) I maintained a degree of separation. Even after we'd become intimate, I withheld some part of my heart, as if safeguarding some secret or insecurity.

Looking ahead, knowing we'd likely experience some real danger in Rwanda, I decided to share with her some part of my most honest feelings (as best I could), as soon as we had a private moment.

Felix Kwizera

My sweet Dativa did not take the news of our impending separation well.

"Why two teams? Men and women? Why we not stay together?"

She was shy and did not make friends easily. I was open and my drug business had developed my people skills.

Also, I was already familiar — even friendly — with my teammates, while Dativa knew only Molly and not very well. While I did not know Jim well, he seemed very interested in getting to know me personally. In addition, I had a history of sorts with Mark, who'd already explained to me the situation between Molly's parents (the two team leaders), which I then shared with Dativa.

Her face grew dark at the news. She did not approve of husband and wife separating. She was dismayed by their lack of commitment and resolve.

Dativa Natukunda

Many times I made Felix look at the ring on my hand, the beautiful circlet of bone and shell that had been his mother's.

"Your parents were in love?" I knew the answer but liked hearing his words.

"They were. Very much," he said.

"What separated them?"

"My father's death."

"Are they together now?"

"I don't know. It is the main reason why I return to Rwanda. If my mother lives, she needs me. If she is dead, she is with my father. But I need to know."

BIRD'S-EYE VIEW

Mark Goldstone

Because of the troubles in Rwanda in 1994, direct flights from New York were not available, so we all had to change our plans. Our group — me, James, Felix and Dativa — took a Boeing 747 to Brussels, where we connected with a Sabena World Airlines flight (leveraging Belgium's historical ties to Rwanda). Francine and Molly, having finished their trip to Paris, flew Kenya Airways to Nairobi and then flew on a connecting flight to Kigali.

Our flight to Brussels was special. It was my first time on a wide-body, jumbo jet and I felt extremely privileged. Somehow, Jim's boss at the *Times* had got us all business-class tickets in the jet's upper deck (which was reached by carpeted, winding staircases). Not only were our seats wide and comfortable but there was a snacks and drinks bar with café-style seating. Jim took it all in his stride (though it was his first time too) but Felix and I were like gleeful kids. Dativa was quiet. Interior. Technically, she wasn't part of our team — but I didn't think that was the reason for her reticence, her separateness.

After about an hour, Jim led Felix and me to a space that was like a mini-conference area. (Dativa remained in her seat, staring out the window.) The three of us sat in hassock-like chairs around a circular white table. From his old, leather briefcase (whose scars I admired as marks of hard-won experience) Jim removed two, string-tied packets and handed one to each of us. Inside were various documents but we focused only on the procedural checklists and maps, which were three: a large map of Rwanda; another that showed only the northern area where we would be housed; and a more detailed map that showed the positions of the two campsites, along with the surrounding roads, paths, trails and points of interest for a radius of about ten kilometers. "That's a little more than six miles," Jim reminded us. "One point six kilometers to the mile. Don't forget that."

Felix Kwizera

I felt like maybe Imana the Creator was on my side — or, at least, taking an interest in me. I had no illusions as to my worthiness but I did not stop to ask questions.

As I understood it, James's boss at *The New York Times* had been informed of a couple of dozen possibilities where a pair of camps might be settled: valleys, lakesides, mountain foothills, etc. With no suggestion being especially persuasive, Mark suggested to James (who suggested to his boss) that my hometown, the small village of Umuhanda, southeast of Cyanika, would be a good choice. Mark did not mention that such a location would facilitate an investigation into my mother's fate. (He kept that plan close to his vest.) Instead, he offered the impressively plausible notion that my village in northern Rwanda, close to the borders of Uganda and Zaire, would see some of the two-way traffic of beleaguered Hutu and Tutsi, either fleeing Rwanda or looking to return. In such a village, there would be no shortage of damaged souls wanting and medical attention and willing to be interviewed.

Dativa Natukunda

I was no journalist. I was no nurse. I felt no connection to the women and girls who'd been raped and maimed. It was all very terrible, of course, but I didn't want to know their pain. I didn't want to see their stumps and scars. That would upset me and I was already upset. In short, I didn't want to be there. I was there because Felix needed to be there and I needed to be with him.

I was no longer Rwandan in my heart. Rwanda was the place of my birth, a fact on my passport. In my heart I was American. I belonged in New York, strolling through the park with my lovely white baby ... though I had strong hope (given the ring on my finger) that I would someday soon be a married woman with my own baby to stroll.

Still, Felix's mission was very important to me, for Felix's mother (whether dead or alive) would determine when I might marry and get on with my life, as Americans say.

Mark Goldstone

All my journalism professors emphasized the importance of absorbing as much about the subject as reasonably possible. In this case, as my team leader's right hand (who happened to love his daughter and who'd pledged to help our native assistant find his mother), I was especially thorough in my preparation, pursuing a self-directed crash course in Rwandan geography, culture, history and politics.

James Andersen

On our connecting flight to Kigali, the captain announced that a delay in clearing the runway would delay our arrival by thirty minutes. Before we could process our regret, he added that he would use the time to circle widely, affording us excellent views of this "land of a thousand hills".

Because Rwanda is so relatively small, our circling runs gave us a good sense of the mountainous, landlocked nation. We saw silver rivers and impressive lakes but it was the large national parks, best known for their mountain gorillas and volcanoes, that fired our excitement.

We all groaned when the captain eventually announced the beginning of our descent.

Mark Goldstone

As the jet approached Kigali the views grew less impressive. The Nyabarongo River looked like a muddy, indolent snake. The capital was a scrabbled oasis of short buildings, scant trees, humble awnings, old cars and trucks. The boulevards were wide but mostly empty. In the near distance, shanty-towns crowded the hillsides.

We approached the airport: a small squat control tower; a half-dozen illuminating pylons; two large windsocks; two runways.

After our passports were checked and stamped, we were met by a thickset African with a peppery beard. Behind him was a tall young man with a clean-shaven, narrow face and out-going disposition. Both were dressed in white-buttoned shirts and black trousers.

"How do you do?" said the older man with an outstretched hand. "I am Dr. Auguste Karekezi and this is my assistant, Albert Bizimana. We will be part of your team."

After we'd all introduced ourselves, including Dativa, the doctor continued, "I've borrowed a van from our district hospital to convey us to our camp. The road north is not perfectly smooth and the light will soon wane. So, please, let us now gather the luggage and proceed."

James asked, "How long a trip, doctor?"

The doctor shared his easy, bedside smile. "As the gold crested crane flies, about 75 kilometers. Driving, about 120. Should take at least three hours. So, shall we begin?"

"Three hours?" Jim asked. "Why so long, if you don't mind my asking?"

Dr. Karekezi spoke with practiced indulgence. "The road is mostly paved all the way to Cyanika but the village is more than fourteen kilometers to the southeast, and there is no paved road leading to it. There is a dirt track that's the main route south to the lakes, and it gets foot traffic, but it's not made up. It will get us there but it is narrow and rutted and requires slow and careful driving."

"I have a plan for that," called out Albert.

Dr. Karekezi smiled proudly. "My none-too-bashful student is Rwanda's future."

With a sarcastic smile, Albert explained: "One day, I'm

going to use my modest savings to rent a thousand bulldozers to smooth out the roads and pave them properly for the rainy season. It will boon the economy and help us reach outlying patients."

"One day!" laughed Dr. Karekezi. "Albert thinks large. That's why I chose him."

Normally, Jim and I would have jumped at the opportunity to chat more but, at that moment, we were both exhausted from our travels and wanted nothing more than to reach our destination and settle in.

"Have they finished putting up the camp and equipping it?" asked James.

"Almost," said the doctor. "But there's been a change in plan, which was my decision. I did not think you would be comfortable in a tent for six weeks. After a while, the rigors of life under canvas would detract from your business of interviewing physically and emotionally traumatized males. To keep you in better condition for your important work, I have acquired a simple, two-room house on the outskirts of Umuhanda, a kilometer or so from the camp. It can accommodate the five of us. You, Dativa, will be placed in a similar situation with the other four members of your team, which, by the way, includes my wife and daughter." The doctor looked to Albert but Albert looked away.

While James and the doctor continued to talk off to the side, I worked with Felix and Albert to gather and load our belongings and equipment, which included a pair of portable typewriters, three 35mm cameras (one for Felix) and a pair of camcorders (then new to the market). It was our plan and expectation that Dr. Karekezi would have overseen the acquisition of everything else we would need.

Felix Kwizera

Entering the van, I made sure to sit beside Dativa, leaving Mark and Albert together. I looked forward to knowing the new fellow (whom I assumed was Tutsi) but at that moment, the emotional challenge of returning to my homeland was overwhelming and took precedence over everything else.

Staring through the van's open windows, I felt as though I had been returned to my childhood, so suddenly and intensely did I recall the humid climate, the landscape of mostly high grasses ... the fields of tree tomatoes and yellow passion fruit ... the occasional sweep of sparrows ... the cawing of blue-winged ducks. I was home.

Dativa Natukunda

Felix took my hand, something he had never done before in public (not in the rear pews of our church, nor in the green shadows of the park). I let his hand lie on my lap, finger-laced with mine. I suppose it was a declaration of sorts, though I don't think anyone noticed.

While holding my hand, he kept his eyes on the passing scenery. He looked sad. I assumed he was thinking of his parents. When we first met, he'd asked about my parents and I'd told him that I did not remember them, which was the truth and he let the matter drop. But in all the days that followed, he never asked how I felt about not remembering them. That was disappointing. I don't think I would have had anything to say ... still, I think he should have been more curious about my feelings.

As to my parents, I was happy I did not remember them. Had I remembered their smiles or how it felt to be held by them, I think it would have saddened me terribly. So, not remembering them was a kind of dark blessing, which made me think of all the injured females we would soon be interviewing. For me, it was better not to know.

Albert Bizimana

Though Felix and I were both in our early twenties, he seemed more mature to me. He lived and worked in New

York City. He knew French. He had a fiancée. Yes, I was studying to be a doctor, a great practical goal, but his acquirements seemed more worldly.

I asked him if it would be okay if we spoke mostly in English and he said, "Yes, of course. Whatever you like."

"Thank you," I said. "My English needs practice. I hope not to embarrass myself."

"Please," he said, "we are now friends and teammates. No reason for embarrassment."

What a wonderful beginning! We would be friends! And he could be my contact in America. In New York, no less!

Felix Kwizera

I was glad to get along so well with Albert. He had been born in a neighboring village to a Tutsi family (as I had guessed) and been selected from each school he had attended to move ahead, as he had always been the star pupil. He seemed very smart but also quite humble. He was around twenty years old, same as me. But, unlike me, he had never left Rwanda. He'd remained in the general area (where'd I'd also been raised) and knew it well. Some years before, he'd got to know Dr. Karekezi, a doctor and surgeon in residence at the nearby Butaro District Hospital, who'd made him his personal project, pledging to guide him through the remaining stages in his quest to become a licensed medical physician. In a whisper, Albert confided that he'd known for some years that Dr. Karekezi was grooming him to marry his daughter, Augusta, who was planning to be a nurse. I did not ask Albert about his relationship with Augusta. I was mildly curious, of course, but I wasn't ready to reciprocate by answering questions about my relationship with Dativa.

"How do you assist him?" I asked, keeping the conversation professional.

"I keep stock of his medicines, help organize his files, type up his notes."

"You assist when he visits patients?"

"Oh, yes. I enjoy that very much. But then I am usually part of a group of other young medical students. I like it best when we visit patients outside the hospital, just us two."

"He makes house calls?"

"House calls?"

"In America, that's what they say when a doctor visits a patient at home."

"*House calls.* I like the sound of that. Thank you for that help! And, yes, I've gone many times with the doctor to make house calls. And sometimes not to a house!"

"What do you mean?"

"I mean, sometimes a person requires help outside of a house, like in a forest or on a mountain and we go to assist."

"Could be dangerous, yes?"

"Very. Say, a person was hurt by a boar or panther and the animal is still nearby, lurking."

"Of course."

"And then, you know ... there are the terrible attacks between Tutsi and Hutu. We are both Tutsi and carry identity papers to show we are medical professionals. For protection, the doctor keeps two guns in his jeep — a rifle and a pistol."

"Protection from ... ?"

"Whatever. Whomever. These are dangerous times."

I nodded. "I know too well. My father was killed right in front of me. Not ten feet away. I watched from a window. I wanted to go to him but my mother held me so tight, I felt her nails in my skin."

Albert patted my shoulder.

"I am very sorry for your loss. We treat many people who have been injured by violence. Sometimes they need surgery."

"Dr. Karekezi does such procedures?"

"Mostly he addresses bone and flesh wounds. Bad wounds to ... certain organs ... are not his specialty."

"But he tries?"

"If the situation is an emergency and no other doctor is available, he will try. But often, there is only so much he can do. Especially if there's been an attack and many people are injured and brought to the hospital at once. We only have twenty beds and that's not enough. Staff and resources are limited."

"What happens then? Some wounded patients die?"

"Sadly, that happens too often."

I nodded. And then he nodded too.

I thought to mention the situation regarding my mother but the timing didn't seem right.

Francine Rose

Molly and I were met at the Kigali airport by two angels, Debora and Augusta Karekezi, mother and daughter, both nurses. I introduced ourselves as Francine and Molly Rose, mother and daughter, both journalists.

I hadn't planned on using my family name to introduce Molly. In fact, I hadn't given it a second's thought. But at that moment, in the heart of Africa, shaking hands warmly with those two beautiful African women, I couldn't bring myself to say *Andersen* (my ex-husband's name, or so I already thought of him) and I sure as hell wasn't going to say Molly *X*. Though I didn't regret my words, I endured several long seconds awaiting Molly's response. But Molly said nothing, other than a polite greeting about how excited and honored she was to work in Africa to assist African women.

Molly X

Of course I noticed. I'd never in my life used the name Molly *Rose*. I was born Molly Jean *Andersen* and for the past year had insisted on being referred to as Molly *X*. Ironically, during the week Mark and I had been separated, I'd practiced writing my hoped-for future name: Ms. Molly

Goldstone. But I never told anyone that. Not even Mark. Certainly not my mother.

Francine Rose

Our time in Paris had not been emotionally satisfying. I'd hoped to make up for the past year that Molly had spent mostly alone with her father. I knew it was unreasonable to expect her to jump ship, so to speak, but I thought that her avowed bisexuality, along with the opportunity to throw her hat in the professional feminists' ring, would draw her closer to me. It didn't happen but I wasn't terribly disappointed. I knew we'd be living together in close quarters for the next six weeks, part of a five-woman team ministering to wounded native women in the heart of Africa. I loved challenges.

Molly X

I really liked the two women, especially the mother, Debora. She was tall and beautiful, graceful and confident. She wore a nurse's uniform: a white, knee-length smock-dress, collared, front-buttoned and cinched at the waist; and white nurse's shoes that were impressively clean, considering. Her only colored clothing was a headscarf of swirled stripes: red, yellow, green — the colors of the Rwandan flag. Her daughter was shorter and a bit darker, and had more meat on her bones. Her bright eyes flashed like a pair of searchlights. She was dressed like her mother (without the headscarf) but named for her father. "I'm Augusta," she said. "Nice to meet you."

I liked them both right away but I think Frankie was put off a bit by the mother's beauty. She'd never have admitted it but I think she was competitive that way — and somewhat insecure. Despite having celebrated her fortieth birthday loudly and proudly, I'd heard her recently in the bathroom, groaning at every newly discovered gray hair, cursing facial creases that were no longer the mark of passing emotions, like smiles or frowns but were now just her: the forty-something version. Apparently, even Gloria had remarked that she was looking a little older. That must have stung.

Debora and Augusta, both very efficient and friendly, made us feel welcomed and safe. They helped us load our belongings onto a luggage trolley and then into the van, which was parked right outside the terminal. Within forty minutes of arriving, we were on the road. During our long, three-hour journey north, I did not see another female driver. I saw cars, trucks, old buses and some cattle-drawn carts but no other female driver.

Augusta Karekezi

I'd half-hoped Molly would arrive in a fancy skirt and boots so I could feel justified in my jealousy. I mean, she was from the United States … New York … Manhattan … and I was a village girl from Northern Rwanda who owned two skirts, two plain dresses and never had a boyfriend. (Albert was *not* my boyfriend, no matter what my father said.) Anyway, since we were going to live together, I needed to feel superior in order to even the playing field.

My first impression of her was spot on. As she approached, she had an exaggerated bounce to her step, like a runway model flaunting her stuff. *Oh Lord*, I thought. But then all my expectations went poof!

To begin with, she wasn't tall. If anything, she was a little on the short side and, though slim, rather angular in ungraceful ways. And her boyishly short hair wasn't pretty. And what I'd thought was a bounce in her step was actually a side-to-side side lurch, as if she were spastic or broken. She wore a blue T-shirt with white lettering that said THE NEW SCHOOL and ripped jeans, which surprised me, as I'd assumed she could afford a nice new pair.

Debora Karekezi

Joining this team thing was my husband's idea, not mine. Frankly, I resented it. We had plenty work to do in the hospital without looking for more. But Auguste thought differently. Nothing new there. And his will triumphed, as usual. Oh, his arguments made sense, I suppose. Publicity in *The New York Times* might lead him to a top position in the Ministry of Health, perhaps even Surgeon General someday. And I don't say he didn't deserve it. He was a wonderful doctor and a wonderful leader and free to plot his own path to success. What I resented, with every cell of my furious heart, was the way he'd long schemed to have our daughter become a nurse, just so she would one day make the perfect wife and helpmate for a future son-in-law.

I never gave Auguste a son (not through any fault of mine) but, in Augusta, I gave him a wonderful daughter whom he loved. Sadly, I knew that his sense of fatherhood would not be complete until Augusta had snared a man to follow in his footsteps. And so, a half-dozen years ago, when he told me about a particularly bright young boy he'd met in a district school, I sensed he had targeted a strong candidate to join our family. Of course, he never actually explained as much to me. And he never said anything overtly to Augusta. But it was obvious in the way he guided our lives — and Albert's — which had all the subtlety of a cattle prod.

Lawrence Schielding

Ironically, although I'd essentially banished Jim and Frankie to the other side of the world, I couldn't get them out of my mind. Sitting in my glass perch above the ever-busy newsroom, I couldn't stop imagining how they were getting on in that tiny, land-locked war zone. Sometimes I imagined them battling each other to a draw. Sometimes I imagined one or the other emerging victorious and crawling back to me, wounded and needy — or would it be the loser crawling back to me, begging me to lick his or her wounds? Either way, I liked to imagine one or the other ringing my doorbell, pleading for my help, begging my forgiveness.

The two groups were under no illusions that they themselves could influence the violence between the antagonistic Hutus and Tutsis. But they did believe that their mission might alert the wider Western world of the situation, which might (through third-party mediation) lower tribal tensions and eventually, perhaps, lead to binding peace accords.

Publicly, James and Francine were in Rwanda to record the stories of people who had survived physical traumas, especially of a sexual nature. Privately, they were there to boost their respective careers and to find out who they really were, as man and woman.

Gloria Applebaum

I gave her my blessing. "Go to Africa," I said. "Help as many women as you can. Write their stories. Save our magazine!" And I meant every word.

But *Virago's* sales continued to dip while Francine was away and I'd had to reduce the size of our office space and do more of the work myself from home. To make sure we'd stay afloat, Francine agreed to go on half pay while she was away and I let go all but three of our staff.

I was lonely in my big house but not at all sorry that Francine was away. We'd been fighting for some time, mostly catty shit, like sisters — except, we weren't sisters. Sisters have an insoluble bond and I no longer felt anything like that for Francine. But I did need her to succeed, as much for my personal credibility (especially with my brothers, who'd never expected me to succeed) as for the magazine itself and its dedicated readers and sponsors.

I made another cost-savings decision while Francine was away. I changed our production cycle from monthly to seasonal. Producing four issues, rather than twelve, would save us a bundle. Also, we'd only to need to develop enough top-notch content for four yearly issues — a huge relief, given the pressure to come up with great material every month. My accountant, aka my masseuse, aka my therapist, all applauded my decision.

Following the splashy announcement that *Virago* was going quarterly, I killed the next three issues and set ourselves to relaunch sometime in June, with our first-ever summer issue. With more time on my hands, I fell back into old habits, seeking out my favorite Village cafés and book-stores, especially Djuna Books, where I'd first met Francine and remained a minority partner.

On my third visit back to Djuna Books, romantic lightning struck again — a trite conceit, I know, but that's how it felt. I was sitting on a barstool near the cashier when I was approached by a youngish woman, dashingly outfitted like Zorro's twin sister: black blouse with ballooning sleeves; black gaucho pants, gathered with a silver-linked belt; thigh-high, black leather boots; and, as God is my witness, a chain-trimmed black fedora. Before she came to a halt, she asked me, in richly accented Castilian Spanish, "*Excúsame, por favor,* do you have any books by Teresa Claramunt or Teresa Mañé or any of the other great Spanish feminists?"

Estrella Delgado

When I was nineteen, I lived unhappily with my parents in our old home in the lonely outskirts of Seville. I knew I had to leave or watch my young heart wither on the vine. But go where? I dreamed of Hollywood, where sexy actresses drove red convertibles and sunbathed by pools overlooking valleys of fertile vineyards. I had money from my abuela, who'd passed the year before.

I left for America but never made it to Hollywood. I got as far as Greenwood, which is Brooklyn, which is New York City, which is three thousand miles from Hollywood. But that's where I landed in 1981, intending to stay a couple of months before heading to L.A.

I was lucky (I suppose), because I quickly found an apartment to share with a man and two women. Very soon I got involved with the man … and then with one of the women … and then with the man and the other woman … and then, just the two women.

I stayed in Brooklyn, Hollywood fading from my mind. So much for the best laid plans.

I wasn't unhappy but I wasn't satisfied either. I wasn't sure what I wanted. Maybe write. Maybe paint. Maybe act. Maybe marry. Maybe not. I didn't know what I wanted.

To help me understand, I decided to study what other modern women were thinking, so I enrolled in Brooklyn College, where I met a history professor by the name of Renate Bertenthal, who was very interested in expanding women's understanding of how they'd been systematically restricted by male-dominated social norms and politics. Her revolutionary ideas whet my appetite.

One day she asked me to help her stuff fliers into the mailboxes of female faculty, to spread the word of a meeting that would lead to the formation of the Brooklyn College Women's Organization (which would lead to the formation of the Women's Studies Program, which would eventually win academic legitimacy for the field of interdisciplinary feminist inquiry).

Though it didn't take long before I was a committed feminist, I saw myself as something of a fraud because I knew next to nothing about feminism in Spain, not to mention my woeful lack of knowledge of modern Spanish women's literature.

So, after graduating from Brooklyn College, I returned to my roots in Seville, enrolling in the School of Inter-disciplinary Studies, where I was able to fashion a doctoral program that integrated advanced courses in Modern

Spanish Women's Literature, Gender Studies and Feminism. I returned to New York City in 1981 with my reinvigorated Spanish accent, my framed doctoral certificate and my feminist passion.

With these cutting-edge qualifications, I was able to get a job teaching at New York University's campus in Greenwich Village. It was my first teaching assignment but as the course was only two days a week, my main recompense was prestige and free time, which I largely spent visiting Village cafés, bars and bookstores and preparing a few articles I'd written for magazine publication.

As to the bars, I liked them all: straight, gay, anything goes. Lucky for me, I was sexy and fetching and many people seemed eager to meet me, including a middle-aged man who said (behind my back but not out of my hearing), "*Ella es un zorro!*" Now, I'd been called a fox many times but I'd always laughed it off or ignored it. But this time was different. For some reason, the same comment in Spanish inspired me. I decided to own it, to make it my mark.

Busty Evans

I received a letter today, delivered to my quarters (a small hotel, not far from the harbor, where I lodged with three other girls from my show) by a nice young man (an ensign, I think), who said, so politely, "For you, Ma'am."

The letter was from my sweet Bobby (my husband of many years), who'd recently retired his bakery truck business and now had a lot of time on his hands, especially when I was on the road, working. A couple of months back, to help with some grief I'd had, he'd brought home a pair of sibling kittens (a female with sparkling eyes and a male with snaky stripes) and named them Sequin and Boa, which gave of us both a good laugh.

I missed all three of them; Bobby the most, of course, and cried when he said how much he and the kittens missed me. He ended the brief letter with a reminder not to get our boys in uniform too riled up because they had important work to do. Then he added, like it was a passing thought, that James Andersen, that nice writer fellow from New York, had called to wish me a happy holiday season and had asked for my address. I thought that was just the sweetest thing. All these years that nice man had kept in touch, never asking anything of me, except to know my thoughts, like they were something special.

James Andersen

Having learned from Sondra's husband that she would be leaving Guam and arriving in Africa before I got there, I worked hard to learn all I could about her next stop.

I learned plenty. For one thing, I learned that while Guam is a major American naval installation in the Pacific, the United States did not have a single permanent military base in all of Africa.

But that didn't mean we were powerless. Even before the seizure of the U.S. Embassy in Tehran in 1979, President Carter had announced the formation of the Rapid Deployment Force, a potent mobile strike force enjoining elements of the Army, Navy, Marine and Air Force that could operate independently without the use of established forward bases. Thus it was that Eastern Africa — within striking distance of the Middle East — became a major focus of the RDF.

Before long, in exchange for military and economic aid, the United States forces had access to several African air force and naval facilities, such as the one in Mombasa, Kenya (where Sondra would be staying for nearly a month), and which was within hailing distance of Rwanda, if one yelled loudly enough.

James Andersen

Before we could begin our work efficiently, we needed to acclimatize ourselves to our new home and so Felix, Mark and I followed Auguste and Albert up and down the rolling hills of the nearby village. All around we saw small, grass-thatched huts (called *Nayakatsi*) set in the shade of banana trees. Most of these huts were unstable and drafty but we saw others (covered with dried animal dung, sand and straw) that were reasonably stable, and even relatively upscale homes made of cob, that added cement to the dung. A few of these larger homes had windows and doors and roofs of iron sheets, though most sheets had been scavenged. The owners of the largest homes also owned banana plantations of several acres, surrounded by barns, a well house, out-buildings and animal pens. In two cases, the owners also owned a flock of goats, a few cows and some chickens and rabbits. Albert pointed out (very matter-of-factly) that by living next to their fields, these farmers were able to protect their crops from thieves and famished refugees.

Albert Bizimana

For much of the past year, Rwandans — Tutsi and Hutu alike — had been turned into refugees. Some were badly maimed, with an incomplete set of limbs, castrated or ruined genitals, missing an eye or an ear. Hobbled, bleeding, they fled to different towns and villages. Depending on their means and location, they might seek safety by crossing borders to neighboring nations. In our part of the country, that meant Uganda to the north or Zaire to the northwest. Sometimes, a lull in the local bloodlust would beckon them home; or they got evicted by their new country.

Understandably, many were poor and angry. They all wanted to survive; many also wanted revenge. Though some had injuries that had healed (leaving permanent scars or disabilities), others still required medical attention of the kind that we were able to provide. All who visited us were interviewed by the medical staff and by the journalists.

Francine Rose

Though Molly and I were anxious to begin our real work, Debora suggested that we first establish a regimen of daily chores and a familiarity with our immediate environs. She said this would make our actual work more efficient — and help keep us safe. She didn't elaborate but there was something in her tone, and her emphasis on safety, that gave me a jolt of anxiety, and led me to recall the day I lost Molly.

The two of us had been picnicking on the fringe of one of Prospect Park's great meadows when I momentarily screwed up my eyes against the summer glare. When I opened them again, four-year-old Molly was nowhere to be seen. Maybe she had wandered away to chase a squirrel or a butterfly. The vast meadow was empty; the woods behind us, dark and unnervingly quiet. I panicked. Heeding my cries, a dozen good-hearted Samaritans joined in my frantic search. It all worked out in the end and, remembering this, I readily agreed to follow each of Deborah's practical suggestions to keep us safe. After all, we were on the outskirts of a rural village — smack dab in the heart of Central Africa — during a reciprocal genocide.

Molly X

For every question I asked Augusta about her life, she asked me three about my life in America, especially New York. And by New York she did not mean the homey streets of Queens and Brooklyn, the gangsta Bronx or extra-galactic Staten Island: she meant Manhattan as pictured in the movies.

I answered all her questions carelessly because I didn't like the way she stared at me, like I was some odd, feral

- 105 -

thing. I wouldn't have minded if she'd answered my own probing questions but getting her to share personal info was like yanking healthy molars.

Finally, I decided to be the bigger woman (figuratively speaking; Augusta was way bigger and beefier than me) and began by telling her about my name: "I don't use *Rose*, my mother's name, and I no longer use my father's name, *Andersen*. I've baptized myself *Molly X.*" She was still processing that information when I added, "My boyfriend Mark is on the other team, the male team that includes your father and mine." Yeah, I said *boyfriend*. I wanted to be very clear on that point, though I wasn't opposed (then or now) to the idea of having a *girlfriend*.

Augusta Karekezi

I couldn't help staring at her, especially at her misaligned hips; one leg shorter than the other. She never referred to it but she did seem oddly shy, never undressing in front me, which only made me more curious.

Anyway, she must have thought I'd stop staring if she shared her story. Boy was she wrong! I mean, I loved her story about leaving her apartment one winter's day to pick up her father's prescription at a local pharmacy and how, having been distracted by a local bad-boy sitting astride his motorcycle, she forgot about the prescription and climbed aboard the bike (her twelve-year-old arms locked around the boy's black leather jacket), which kickstarted a wild, winter joyride, which resulted in her waking up in a hospital, with doctors examining her leg, which had now been repaired, and staring at her partially exposed nakedness, while her essence floated up to the ceiling, beyond their reach.

My shocked eyes must have indicated that I wanted to hear more (which I did) and so she continued confiding, relating how her injury led to terrible arguments between her parents, who eventually separated to lead lives of gender activism, which eventually led her father to invite his favorite grad student to share his home to help pay the rent — but also as a check against his wayward daughter's involvement with local park druggies.

Molly was the most fascinating person I'd ever met. After learning so much about her, it was impossible for me not to stare at her just a little.

Molly X

After I did my part to break down the barriers between us, Augusta unlocked her heart, telling me all about her father, wonderful in many ways but regimented and authoritarian in many others, especially when it came to directing the lives of his wife and daughter. Teary-eyed, she confessed that she no longer loved nursing and had never loved Albert, her father's professional protégé and her unofficial (and unacknowledged) fiancée. I was so moved, I embraced her like a new best friend — and she kissed me.

Augusta Karekezi

Unlike my mother, I never wanted to be a doctor. But for a long while I dreamed of being a nurse, as she was. I liked that she was a respected professional; that she wore a pretty uniform and worked in the hospital. I liked that she befriended patients who were sick or broken. I liked that she knew a lot about science and medicine but did not have to make life-or-death decisions.

But when I realized my father was pushing me towards becoming a nurse, my dream began to sour. And when I realized he was grooming me also to be the wife-partner of his hand-picked son-in-law, I began planning my revolt. But I never thought my first salvo would be a kiss — with another woman.

Molly X

Whoa, baby!

Flattered, but also shocked, I looked about to see if there'd been witnesses. But we were alone. No parents. No Mark. No Albert. Which begged the question: *What next?*

Debora Karekezi

I may have looked like the most docile and compliant wife but deep inside I seethed. Having fallen in line behind yet another of my husband's self-serving mandates, I recalled our shared childhood, and especially our school days when I'd been the better student but not the better prospect — all because I wasn't a boy. Ask him. He won't lie. Not on this matter. He will tell you bluntly that I was prevented by an age-old patriarchal system from attending medical school, despite being more academically gifted and deserving.

Despite my long-seated rancor and the fact that I'd been against joining this program from the start, I was determined to make the best of it. Having already explored the village and the area surrounding our office campsite, I announced my readiness to share my knowledge about health and safety.

"Don't worry about me," said Molly. "I'm New York tough."

Her innocence shocked me.

"Molly, compared with Rwanda, New York is a playground. Please listen carefully."

Dativa Natukunda

Debora was smart, beautiful and caring. While she spoke to us about safety, I watched for those moments when she made eye contact with her daughter. She loved her so completely, so obviously, I wished she were my mother.

My mother gave me up for adoption, though I don't know why. Maybe she was dying or already dead. I don't know. I have no memory of her. Not a single picture, not one fact. Not even a name. I know even less about my father, if that's possible.

The not knowing made it easier for me to imagine Debora as my own mother and Augusta as my sister. This made me feel better about being in Rwanda and helped me even the score with Molly. You see, I knew she didn't like me very much. I felt like she'd always been more interested in Felix than me. I was just someone she'd been forced to deal with. So when she hit it off with Augusta, I felt sad and lonely, like I was left outside a locked door. Still, I took pride in knowing that Molly could never be Augusta's sister, the way I imagined myself. I mean, she wasn't Rwandan. She wasn't even black. Besides, she had her own mother, who was white and no kind of motherly, just as Molly was unfriendly and no kind of sisterly, at least to me.

Albert Bizimana

I had mixed feelings about Augusta. Having known her — and her parents — for so many years, I saw her as more sisterly than sexy. Perhaps it's hard to believe but we never discussed her father's hope that we'd someday reprise the doctor-nurse partnership he'd modeled so successfully with his wife. Though I did not love Augusta, in any romantic sense, I still thought we might enjoy a successful cooperation, according to vague rules I hadn't yet entirely worked out.

Felix Kwizera

Ironically, despite all the violence of my African childhood, I did not remember many of the things that could kill me.

"Please listen very carefully," said Auguste.

We were gathered inside our large work tent for the first time. There were three cots, a writing desk, cheap metal shelving filled with antiseptics, pain-relief medicine, bandages, splints, etc. I was told the women's tent was identical.

I wondered how Dativa was doing. By nature, she was not brave. When we went back to our respective camps, she cried.

"My wife," said Auguste, "a most competent and caring nurse, has compiled a list of deadly and dangerous things to recognize and avoid. Let us review."

Mark Goldstone

I must have blanched during the recitation of all the things that could poison, bite or rip us asunder, because I did not immediately notice Jim's hand on my lower back. Perhaps it was meant to be comforting but just then I wished it was Molly's hand, not Jim's.

James Andersen

I was crossing lines, left and right, threatening to violate every personal and professional code I espoused — and for what? Cheap thrills?

I pulled my hand away but not before tapping Mark's shoulder twice, as if to reassure him, the way a friend or father might. I needed to exercise more self-control.

Felix Kwizera

We'd just arrived and already I was sick with worry, figuring I'd be the one blamed if anyone got stabbed or poisoned or eaten alive. In my mind, I was the main reason we were gathered there.

I mean, I was the one who'd been saved by Jesuits and sent to New York. I was the one who'd decided against going to college, the one who'd taken a job in Washington Square Park. I was the one who'd envied Moby3 and taken his place after he got pinched. I was the one who became Philippe du Jour, the one who sold weed to Molly, who then introduced me to Mark and her father.... I was the one who fell in love with Dativa, who reminded me that I'd always be Rwandan. I was the one who gave her my mother's ring of bone and shell, who convinced her to return to this dangerous place. I was the one responsible for all this — and all because my father had been murdered and my mother had gone missing. It was all on me, because I had big holes in my heart.

REFUGEES 2

Lawrence Schielding

As managing editor, it had been my responsibility to conceptualize the project, curate its staff and continually assess its live schedule and content.

While waiting with lurid curiosity to see how my writers would reveal themselves through their stories, I spent many hours imagining how they might relate personally in close quarters, surrounded by jungle threats. Twice a day I got off, imagining their sweaty couplings against the backgrounds of twittering birds, growling beasts and the buzzy drone of innumerable insects.

More soberly, I entertained what I might say to any of them who actually faltered and required my special supportive attentions. But never — not in my wildest fantasies — did I consider the possibility of traveling to Rwanda to assess the situations on the ground. Not my job.

James Andersen

It was not uncommon for thousands of Rwandan refugees who had fled to Zaire and Uganda to be pushed back across the border months later. In response, some Rwandan officials found it convenient to declare that their country was too overpopulated for the refugees to be allowed to return. When the migrants affirmed their right to return home (by force, if necessary), there was talk in Rwandan government circles of creating a commission to deal with the problem. At the time, though, we did not think such a policy would ever affect us directly, other than to increase our paperwork.

To cover ourselves, Auguste and Albert carefully vetted the biographical and medical history of each refugee who found their way to us. After they had been given whatever medical attention was needed, Mark and I conducted our own interviews, using a questionnaire that focused on the circumstances that had led to their injuries and then on to the emotional, psychological and social effects that resulted.

Though always sympathetic, we made it clear (through our translators) that we were journalists, not psychologists or social workers, and that we requested their permission to tell their stories, truthfully and forcefully, explaining also that they were perfectly at liberty to withhold agreement.

That was of course the very opposite of what we wanted them to do, so we emphasized how important it was for the world to know about the atrocities they had suffered. In spite of that, some of the refugees did refuse to work with us, claiming their injuries were too terrible to discuss publicly. Others balked, fearing our published stories might bring them further reprisals. In those cases, we encouraged them to change their minds by providing written assurances that we would protect their identity. Other cases led us to be more calculating. We never exactly bribed anyone but we sometimes tempted them with decent meals or clothing in exchange for their testimony, especially when what they had to tell us was dramatic. Only if a disfigured or partially dismembered refugee with a great story insisted on money did we offer coins. The gray ethics of these exchanges disturbed me but I forced myself to see the greater good.

Dr. Auguste Karekezi

As a humanitarian and a doctor, I make no distinctions about the Rwandan peoples on the basis of their skin, or ancient tribal affiliations, or paper-thin colonial definitions meant to sow hierarchical enmities. True, some groups still appear more generally stocky and flat-nosed and the Batwa are still discernibly smaller, but over generations, inter-tribal sex, rape and the occasional marriage have resulted in notable genetic diffusion. One cannot always tell, is all I'm saying. For example, though Felix and Dativa are Twa, he is of average height and could pass for either Tutsi or Hutu, if it were not for his two-tone Twa accent.

I never try to guess a patient's ethnicity. I block it from my mind. I treat all my patients equally, my Hippocratic Oath looming imperiously high, like Blind Justice.

Francine Rose

As a young mother I'd convinced myself that Molly could take care of herself, leaving me alone to write and muse. But in the aftermath of the accident, my better judgement kicked in and I had to deal with my burgeoning guilt. Though I still mostly blamed Jim's irresponsible laziness for what had happened, I came to see that I hadn't been a great mother: that my laissez-faire approach to child-rearing had played a big part in shaping Molly's impetuous character. As epiphanies go, I thought mine might be too little, too late. Watching her hobble through her teens was my daily penance.

It was during that decade that I began to self-identify as a revolutionary feminist. I wanted positive changes in my life, in my marriage and for women everywhere. Though I was increasingly intense and aggressive in my writing and teaching, I was always gentle with Molly. If something else were to go south in her life, I didn't want to bear more responsibility.

The prospect of a mother-daughter trip to Paris had seemed like the perfect remedy for our imperfect relationship. I saw Paris as a launch pad to make adult amends. What better way to quick-fix our mother-daughter relations than to bathe ourselves in the loving City of Light?

Unfortunately, despite our arm-in-arm visits to galleries of female nudes, I sensed her emotional retreat. That made me sad and even more furious with Jim, as I suspected he'd poisoned Molly against me. That's why I skipped out on our agreed-upon meeting at the Kigali airport, though I knew Molly would be disappointed not to see her father. But it couldn't be helped. It'd been the right thing for me to do.

You see, in some ways Molly was still young and naïve. She didn't fully appreciate her father's penchant for passive-aggressive relations — how he'd claimed, for example, to cherish our once-fine record collection but had let it die a slow death in his indifferent conservancy, discs and covers cruelly disassociated and left on the floor so the cats might scratch and crap on them until they were no more fit for music than a cow patty. She didn't know of her father's unmitigated gall in deriding my dedication to the Women's Movement, and his claiming that it stemmed from emotional, womanly impulses (which is damnable bullshit, as my fervor was dispassionately articulated in my many published writings, and applauded by both sexes). She didn't know that her father refused to believe that I supported the Women's Movement because I thought it addressed the biggest human travesty on the planet. She didn't see how he was headstrong in protecting the trammeled rights of gay men but questioned my dedication to protect the planet's nearly three billion females (as we were then) — the world's largest human group in crisis!

When I learned that women in Rwanda were being raped and mutilated by the thousands, and that my magazine was faltering and needed to be revived with some kickass female journalism, and that my daughter needed to be reclaimed from the poisonous influence of my husband, I realized that my world was a gold mine of political, profitable and personal opportunities.

Albert Bizimana

The Rwandan community in exile was in the hundreds of thousands, most of whom had taken up residence in the countries surrounding Rwanda. Except in Tanzania, where the government had encouraged their integration into the local population, the refugees existed precariously, with few rights or guarantees.

I wasn't much of a nationalist. I just wanted the problems to go away, so I stayed on the political sidelines and kept quiet, with my medical credentials blatantly pinned to my chest, which seemed my best hope of warding off partisan violence. (Proportionately speaking, the Tutsi suffered most and I was Tutsi, as were Auguste, Debora and Augusta.)

Bottom line: I just wanted to be revered as a successful doctor who worked in a politically stable and economically progressive nation. To that end, I dreamed of finishing my training in the United States and then (with the ink still fresh on my framed sheepskin) returning to Rwanda like a medaled hero.

James Andersen

As I had hoped, hearing the raw stories of men coming to grips with their ruined manhood reinvigorated my belief that my work-in-progress, *Ecce Homo / The Beholding*, would be my masterwork. Back home, I'd been reluctant to talk openly about my book. When asked to describe it, I would respond vaguely: "It's a kind of fictional memoir." If asked what it was about, I would offer the well-rehearsed line that it was about what it means to be a man among other men, in a world half filled with women, and left it at that. If pressed for more detail, I would smile slyly and say, "I'll let you know when it comes out."

Since its inception, I'd spent a thousand hours imagining the shape of my narrative and twice as many imagining how I would crow my success to the world, beginning with Larry and Francine. I also spent hours imagining how I would tell Sondra. In these musings I was a fully grown man who still felt guilty for spying on her enormous breasts through a partially shaded window as young boy.

Mark Goldstone

I was thinking of Felix's history (and how it had brought us all together), trying to imagine his mother's state of mind after seeing her husband murdered in broad daylight, right outside their home. I imagined her grief, her worry for her own safety and her anxiety to protect her young son. But why did she leave Felix? Did she think he would be safer without her? Did she think she could travel faster without him? What other reasons might she have had?

These questions haunted me. They seemed a thousand times more compelling than the testimony of nameless refugees. Any good journalist could write those stories. But Felix's story, despite its unknown details, felt personal to me. I felt connected to him. He was the reason I was in Rwanda. In fact it's no stretch to say that I felt fated to write the story of his search for his mother.

There was another reason that compelled me to pursue Felix's story. Professor Andersen was becoming uncomfortably intrusive. Even back in New York, in that crazy apartment with its entangling floor plants, sexually suggestive wall art and murky light from the never-washed windows, I'd sensed his subtle preying whenever Molly was away from home.

Please understand: I have extraordinary admiration for the man. He's a brilliant teacher and a ground-breaking journalist. His essays on media ethics were widely published and his crusade to protect the rights of homosexuals was brave and laudable.

More personally, he was an ideal mentor for my doctoral thesis, driving me to ever-higher degrees of objective thinking and passionate reasoning. I'd been honored when he'd asked for my help about his wayward daughter and then (some weeks later) further pleased when he'd suggested that I share their apartment (recently vacated by his wife) — a win-win-win for the three of us, so it seemed at the time.

The thing is, not long after my arrival, he began twisting the expected rules of privacy and decorum. Initially, I wasn't suspicious but his indiscretions became more frequent and obvious. Worse (I think), I found myself unexpectedly attracted to him ... just when I was falling in love with Molly.

There is no telling what might have happened if Larry Schielding (Jim's friend and the Managing Editor of *The New York Times*) had not offered him and his wife Francine the opportunity to lead two independent teams of journalists to cover the civil war atrocities in Rwanda. As far as I know, this pair of potentially life-changing opportunities was welcomed by all. For me, the promise of adventure and professional bylines in *The New York Times* was a huge inducement. But the idea of leaving the unsettling situation in Jim's strange apartment was also a big plus.

What I didn't know was that Jim's predatory advances would intensify in the relative seclusion of our new home in Africa. Without Molly to turn to, and wanting to avoid long periods alone with Jim, I found relief by focusing on the story of Felix's mother. I knew that helping Felix would be a good thing and writing a great story would be a big win for everyone — especially me. I felt some shame keeping all this from Jim but the complicating ethics seemed to absolve me.

ALLIANCES

Felix Kwizera
I would never enter the tent while the doctors or journalists were working with the maimed. The space was too confining

and I was too cowardly. Instead, I remained outside, where I could hear every word, even those contorted by screams. Always, I stood very still, my eyes closed, my teeth clenched, blood pounding in my brain like war drums. This was my penance for having watched my father's bloody murder — and done nothing about it.

James Andersen

Despite the basic sameness of the wounds (dismembered limbs, ears, noses, genitalia), I never got used to the physical horrors. Each day I wondered anew about man's inhumanity to man. I prayed that scientists would one day identify the metabolic imbalance or faulty synapse responsible for such incomprehensible savagery.

Alfred Bizimana

Early on, I wanted to be friends with Mark and Felix. And why not? We had a lot in common. We were all in our early twenties. We were all ambitious. We were all working with wounded refugees. We all had a girlfriend of sorts in the female camp. But early on they showed it wouldn't be easy. For example, we had never discussed sleeping arrangements before moving in. Our group was five in number and I think it was assumed by all that three of us would occupy the larger of the two rooms. But which three? The three Rwandans? The three from America? The three youngest? I was in all three groups and my choice was to be with the youngest, but that's not what happened. As soon as we arrived, Mark rushed into the smaller room, gleefully claiming it for himself and Felix. I don't think Auguste minded but I sensed that James was as disappointed as I was.

James Andersen

I was outraged. What possessed Mark to do such a thing? Had I been too obvious in my overtures? Was this his response? An escape from my clutches? I panicked: Did Auguste and the others know? Would the women soon find out? Would it all get back to Larry?

A master of the seething smile, I gathered my belongings to move into the larger of the two rooms. And then it hit me: Wait a second. Mark never rushed ahead ... never spoke without consideration ... never even wrote a paragraph without first organizing his thoughts. Why start now? Answer: He wouldn't. That meant he had his own good reasons for doing what he did, which might have little to do with me. I blew a deep sigh of relief, promising myself to exert greater self-control.

Dativa Natukunda

Bad enough that I couldn't be in the same house as Felix, where I could have cooked and comforted, but I was far away, where we couldn't even speak. Then things got worse. Much worse. When we moved into our small house (not too far from our work campsite), I assumed I would room with Augusta and Molly and that we would eventually become a friendly circle. But no. The most horrible thing happened. *Both mothers insisted on rooming with their daughters.* I was shocked. *No one wanted me.* I was orphaned — again.

While the girls happily settled into their new rooms, their mothers sectioned off the far corner of the kitchen with enough rope and rough blankets to make it pretend-private. With a straight face, Molly's mother said to me, "How lucky you are to have your own space!"

That night, alone and abandoned, I wept for my own mother, whose face I couldn't see.

Molly X

I had trouble sleeping that first night. It wasn't the heat. Our village was set among high hills and our house, with its mud-brick walls and thatched roof, was naturally well insulated. No, it was the voices in my head, all talking at the same time, as if vying for my attention. It was Mark in the Pink PussyCat, faking an easy laugh when I could tell he felt frightened and out of place among all the dildoes and whips. It was my dad, talking to me while standing on a stepladder, pushing a shoebox full of homo porn into the top closet shadows. It was my mom in her old room, talking to me while she gazed longingly at the prints of female nudes tacked to her walls. It was that local boy, Billy, daring me to climb aboard his motorcycle and wrap my arms around his black leather jacket. It was Augusta explaining why she'd just kissed me. It was Dativa's wordless wail (like a kitten's hungry mewling) coming from the kitchen, from behind a screen of woolen blankets.

Debora Karekezi

I had many good reasons for wanting Augusta to share my room. For one thing, I wanted to separate her from Molly. Though I'd sensed a clash of cultures the first time they'd met, they'd soon become thick as thieves. But I did not trust Molly. She was too worldly. Too advanced, like other privileged American girls I'd met. Girls should be proud and strong — but also humble and eager to learn from their mothers. I did not think Molly was humble. And she did not seem eager to learn from her mother.

Also, Molly's arrival seemed to excite Augusta's westward fixations — her delight in all things American. To rein this in, I gave Augusta a beautiful headscarf (the bold colors of the Rwandan flag) to match my own, reminding her that while she was free to live as she pleased, she should never forget the debt she owed the country of her birth. Yes, I agreed, it was good to grow with the times but she should also honor the memory and customs of her Tutsi ancestors. Remember, I said, Rwanda is your home!

Augusta was young and short-sighted; she saw Molly and

her mother as fashionably exotic. My head said maturity would clear her vision. My heart said she should emulate Dativa, who wore a traditional engagement ring of bone and shell. But first, I thought, she should find a man she loved, someone not Albert.

Dativa Natukunda

I have no family that I can remember. When I was young, before coming to America, I saw other families — whole families with parents and children — and would magically insert myself into their circle, where I would be safe and happy. But dreams aren't meant to last. All too soon I'd awaken to the reality of my lonely life in the orphanage.

I was getting older and something had to be done with me. I was a mouth to feed, a body to clothe. The Jesuits wanted to marry me off to the first good offer but I begged them. I said, "Please, send me to America. I will work hard. I will make my own life there."

Sending me to America was a big expense but the bishop, who visited every few months, had a cousin in New York who was about to have a baby. The cousin wanted to return to work and was already looking for a nanny. She had a successful husband — a businessman of some sort — and they both trusted the bishop, so papers were drawn up and signed and arrangements were made for my move to the US.

The husband and very pregnant wife met me at the airport. They had lovely smiles and were very nice to me. It was a good thing that the Jesuits had been so demanding with my English, for I was able to converse and understand.

They were — they are still — a lovely couple. Very generous and accommodating. I lived with them, in a nice apartment building on lower Fifth Avenue. They apologized for the small room, right next to the baby's nursery, but I joked that I am a small person, which is true, and I found the room beautiful and large, with fairytale clouds and rainbows.

Though I worked long hours, six days a week, it was lovely. Outside the building was a man in a fancy uniform, who opened the door for residents and visitors. Sometimes I did local shopping. The husband had given me a plastic card and explained how to use it to buy whatever was needed. America was crazy rich!

My greatest delight was discovering Washington Square Park. For one thing, many of the men were dark-skinned like me, though some had crazy braided hair, piled high or stuffed into colorful, knitted caps. These were Jamaican: they were very nice and had musical voices. Their talk was like song. Unfortunately (in my opinion), they seemed always to be holding homemade cigarettes, whose smoke hung in the air, sweet but bitter.

Still, I loved going to the park. I loved the music. And the sense of freedom. I loved that many dark-skinned women were there, pushing baby carriages, all the babies white, like mine. Most of the women were from the Caribbean. A few from Africa. But none spoke my language.

I went to the park every day that the weather was fine, entering through the monumental arch, then strolling round the central fountain, hoping to catch the eye of some handsome young man who would see what a good mother I would be.

One day I noticed a handsome young black man in a modest green uniform. He looked very impressive, even when he was only collecting trash or raking leaves. Sometimes I saw him standing in the far corner of the park, in a shady arbor. He seemed very popular, for many people stopped to talk with him. I decided I wanted to meet this popular young man. So, I studied his schedule and met him one day outside the building that housed the public bathrooms. Joy and amazement when I learned he was Rwandan, just like me!

Felix Kwizera

Something clicked when I met Dativa. She was so giving, so nurturing ... and besides being Rwandan (and mostly Twa, just like me!) she had also lost her parents and been cared for by the Jesuits. How were so many coincidences possible? Surely, God's hand was in our meeting.

Molly X

When I'd first learned of Larry's two-team approach, I conflated *Heart of Africa* and *Heart of Darkness* into dangerously exotic opportunities for romance. Subconsciously, I think I was giving Mark another chance — giving *us* another chance. Technically, we already were lovers but there had been nothing lovely in our love-making. It wasn't even fun.

I'd heard that some pussycat men were real tigers in bed but that hadn't been Mark. At least, not with me. In fact, he'd seemed so hesitant and low-key, I began to suspect he might not be a committed heterosexual. That led me to suspect that he might have accepted my father's offer to move into our home as much for the hoped-for pleasure of getting to know my father better as for the opportunity of knowing and influencing me. But then it occurred to me that I'd been just as guilty of deceiving him, having led him to believe that I was sexually experienced when, in fact, I'd never fully been with another male — or touched, or been touched by, another female — until Augusta kissed me.

So, I thought, we were both frauds — or naïfs. Thing is, because I liked Mark and respected him, I determined that our African adventure would be, at the very least, a fact-finding mission for us both.

Albert Bizimana

I'd grown up in a local village that was mostly Hutu. I was by far the best student and one of only four Tutsi boys, none of them studious like me. I had no close friends.

My father owned many cattle and was always busy, moving them from pasture to pasture before marching them to the slaughterhouse. He never expected me to join his business; he had bigger plans for his only son. Through a friend of a friend, he connected me with Dr. Karekezi, who immediately saw my potential and began grooming me by giving me private lessons that would prepare me for my rigorous medical training to come.

During holidays and vacations, Dr. Karekezi sometimes brought me to his home for dinner. That's how I got to know Augusta. We liked each other right away — not so much like boy and girl but as co-conspirators, laughing behind our hands when her father was too serious to be taken seriously.

Eventually, we both understood that her father wanted us to marry and carry on the roles of doctor and nurse that he and his wife had modeled. As it was unthinkable to argue with Dr. Karekezi, we went along with his program, trusting that all would work out favorably. In truth, we had no shared notion of what *favorably* meant, other than that we both dreamed of going to the United States for our final training and certifications — preferably to New York City. To say we hadn't thought out our plan would be a gross understatement.

Augusta Karekezi

Before leaving for our separate camps (where Albert and I would have no ability to communicate directly), I'd spoken to Manzi, who had worked at the district hospital all his long life as an orderly and driver. Albert and I were both very close to him and called him *Nyiarume*, meaning *Uncle*. Originally, we'd intended to speak to him together but I thought that might draw attention, so I quietly pulled him aside one day and quickly made him complicit in our plan to exchange written messages as part of his bi-weekly supply trips to both campsites.

Nyiarume had known me as a baby and used to love

bouncing me on his knees, and I knew he loved Albert too. Seeing himself as the conduit bringing young lovers together, Nyiarume was happy as a lark on these missions, and Albert and I were able to keep in touch. Initially, our plan was to endear ourselves to the Americans' children in case they might later be useful in helping us get to America but it did not take us long to realize that it was the American parents who held the real power. That did not change our calculus; it only meant we had to foster alliances with the young Americans in order to get to their elders.

Albert Bizimana

Mark and Felix often spoke in huddled confidences, as if protecting some special secret. I felt angry and shamed when they'd made such a romp of excluding me from their room, and was desperately jealous of their intimacy. Quite aside from my ulterior motives, I really did envy them. Although we'd grown a little closer by the end of our first couple of weeks together, I knew I needed a more efficient way to insinuate myself into their company.

TESTIMONIES

Mark Goldstone

Journalism is not like creative writing, at least not the way I'd been taught. One didn't look for bolts of inspiration. Drugs or drink only blurred the lines. Character motivation was a plus but not essential. I needed facts — and a sense of compelling importance — to make a strong article.

In Journalism 101, I'd learned that there are proven facts, probable facts and probable untruths, and how to tell one from the other. For example, it's a proven fact that more Tutsis than Hutus were killed in the Rwandan genocide: there were corroborated body counts and expert testimony to prove it. It is a probable fact, and possibly provable, that the Rwandan government bore much responsibility for the deaths. But it is a probably untrue that almost all the attacks and killings were of a sexual nature. Though there was great enmity between the groups, as a result of colonially constructed divisions and jealousies, it is all but certain that most of the killings were not sexually motivated. Though a great many were.

As to Felix's story of his mother, I had no proven facts. At the time of the killing of his father, Felix said he was nine years old, but even that could not be verified. Believe me, I tried. As to the killing itself, the act was committed in broad daylight — or at night, just before Felix went to bed. The story kept changing. He was not a reliable witness. Did more reliable witnesses exist? That's what I needed to discover.

It seemed my best bet would be to find out the name and location of the village that Felix's mother had fled to, and seek help from her, if I could find her, or her family. Felix said he had forgotten the name of the place. Perhaps he'd never known it. Perhaps it had been knocked from his mind by the twin traumas of his father's murder and his mother's disappearance. All he could recall were unconnected details ... a live volcano ... a tiny village ... strange, rocky terrain ... dark forests ... a place of mountain gorillas ... and Cyanika somewhere nearby.

Felix Kwizera

It was shocking to me how much I'd forgotten. Was I stupid? Was I damaged? Why couldn't I remember more of what my mother had told me of the journey from her home village to my father's? As I recalled, she'd been the talker in our family, not my father. Then why did I remember only fragments: mountain gorillas ... impenetrable forests ... a volcano ... a tiny village hidden by fog?

Then it occurred to me that the fragments I recalled

must be of special significance. That made me wonder what they might mean. Perhaps each might stand as a kind of landmark. Which led me to think: Could these landmarks be ordered into some kind of map or even a route?

It was an exciting thought but I had no idea where or how to start. The only routes I knew were Manhattan subway lines. I was useless in the wilds of Northwestern Rwanda. Then I remembered that Albert had been born and raised in the area. And that his father had raised cattle. And that Albert had worked summers for his father, helping to drive the beasts from distant pasture to distant pasture, following common trails ... going off-trail looking for strays ... cutting new trails where old ones had become impassable. I joked: "Even on a moonlit night, I wouldn't trust myself to walk alone from our village to our tented campsite." Albert laughed hard and bragged, "Not me! Impossible for me to get lost. I know unmapped trails that go every which way for forty kilometers. And I have a great sense of direction."

Albert Bizimana

After weeks of ministering to victims' wounds and taking their testimony, the flow of mutilated refugees had slowed considerably. Dr. Karekezi said this was completely normal, even expected. He explained that the migration of refugees was largely a response to weather, politics, crop yield, sanctions, new violence, retaliations, etc. The stream of refugees was almost predictable, he said — except that it wasn't. The stream had unexpectedly dried up, which meant that we had free time on our hands.

Dr. Auguste Karekezi

The temporary halt in the flow of maimed refugees did not mean long rest. I had a backlog of paperwork awaiting me at the hospital, not to mention a number of minor surgeries and specialized treatments that required my personal attention. Inasmuch as Albert was by then fully capable of dealing with the campsite's paperwork and basic medical treatments, I instructed him to remain while I returned to my usual hospital rounds, and instructed my wife to accompany me, leaving Augusta, Francine, Molly and Dativa at the women's camp, holding down the fort, as the Americans say.

James Andersen

Most of the refugees responded to our interpreter's questions as if filling out routine work applications. I could not understand what passed between them and barely listened. But my interest piqued whenever a refugee began to ramble excitably. The interpreter would then turn on the tape cassette and the refugee would vent his pent-up rage. Sometimes this exhausted itself quickly but in the most dramatic cases the refugee would scream and cry until they'd reduced themselves to a howling mass.

At that point, the interpreter would tell me what had been said and I'd tell the interpreter to ask follow-up questions: *Who did this to you? ... Why? ... What kind of weapon was used? ... Did you fight back? ... How do your wounds make you feel about yourself? ... Do you have a place to live? ... Do you have a place to work? ... Do you still have family? ... Are you still with your wife or girlfriend — or with someone else? ... Are you able to have sex? ... Are you looking for vengeance? How would you want to carry it out?*

Sometimes a refugee became suddenly quiet, unable or unwilling to continue. But we always did continue. I insisted on it. There was no point in stopping, even if the subject had to be calmed or fed or mildly sedated. We had a job to do.

At the end of each week, I reviewed the collected testimonies. Invariably they fell into three categories: those that did not serve my further interests; those I might consider for a *New York Times*-destined article; those I might reference in my book in progress, *Ecce Homo / The Beholding*.

After several weeks, the stream of refugees temporarily dried and I decided I needed rest and a break in routine. I considered traveling to the other campsite to visit my wife Francine — but then thought better of it.

Francine Rose

The interviews were wrenchingly personal. Every female I saw was a mother and a daughter, and each had been victimized by a male, which meant that every assault had been a hate crime — a rape or a variation on a rape.

I was consumed with rage. My every dream was bent on violent redress: Like a sword-wielding ninja, I smote every man I met, gangs of them falling like sheaves before the blade.

My bloody vengeance made me think of El Zorro (as my sources called her), the woman costumed in black and silver who'd taken my place in Gloria's bed and who (purportedly) was looking to cut me out of the magazine. Hah! Let her try! My cutting-edge journalism would save *Virago* from financial ruin. Gloria's choice would be easy: I'd be the last woman standing!

READINESS

James Andersen

I was right not to visit Francine. Our respective work had further polarized our gender allegiances and we simply were not ready to reconnect, even as friends. But I desperately needed soothing ... and knew only one suitable person on the continent.

Busty Evans

"Fifty-something" is how I describe my age and the size of my enormous breasts: my pride and joy ... my ticket outta Hagerstown and away from my Mennonite grandparents, who never taught me a lick about what Mennonite meant — other than all the things I wasn't supposed to do or even think. Think *Mennonite* and you probably think German Bible thumpers but I don't remember reading Scripture or having it read to me when I was young. Growing up, I knew very little about religion. It wasn't until years later, while watching the TV miniseries *Jesus of Nazareth*, that I began to understand what it was all about. But then I figured I was too old and too far gone to get into it.

As for godly, the closest I ever got was falling in love with Robert Gray. And the best day of my life was marrying him and moving into his home outside Syracuse, where no one knew me — a major plus.

Bobby's a good man and made me a better woman. Thank God he was with me when my little Tico died, right after my good friend Rose LaRose from Detroit passed. For weeks I was so sad, I couldn't bother to put on my slippers to walk about the house. Bobby said I was bereft. I knew what he meant, but I'd never before heard the word spoke.

One day Bobby came home with a pair of sibling kittens to help with my grief. He's the one who named them Boa and Sequin, which shows how much sympathy and humor the man has. With his love and support, I passed that sad summer by training the kittens, reading the Bible, gardening and playing church bingo.

We had ourselves a good quiet life. Nowadays, my oversized breasts — once regarded as the Ninth Wonder of the World — don't seem so special, not with all those silicone jobs out there.

Crazy thing, now I'm windin' down my career, I'm doing some real travelin'. Having never been further west than Dayton or north of Toronto, I wound up last month in Guam (somewhere in the middle of the Pacific) and now I'm in Mombasa, the capital of Kenya, so I'm told. Weatherwise, I was crazy to visit Guam and Central Africa. They're both hot and I never liked the heat much. I got me a pair of super special glands that can overheat like you wouldn't believe, which is why I never worked summers.

Couple of weeks back I heard from my sweet writer friend, James Andersen. He wanted to know how I was doin' and was kind enough to say that he'd spoken to Bobby and regarded it as a privilege to finally make his acquaintance. He said he was going to Rwanda for a writing job and would be there while I was in Kenya and how wonderful it would be if we could meet up again.

James is just the sweetest man. I'd do most anything for him, though I expect I'll go to my grave without understanding why he kept in touch with the likes of me all these years.

James Andersen

I'm not naturally introspective. It certainly wasn't a requirement for journalism. Journalism is mostly an outward exercise. But when I started writing my fictionalized memoir, *Ecce Homo / The Beholding,* I had to ask myself hard questions, like: *Who am I really? What do I believe in? What is most important to me?*

Eventually, I got down and dirty: *How close a friend is Larry? Why did I marry Francine? Why did we grow apart? How do I really feel about Mark? What about Busty?*

Mark Goldstone

James seemed preoccupied, which made it easier for me to quiz Felix more about our unfocused mission.

He had said that he did not remember the name of his mother's village but he thought it lay somewhere to the southwest. When I pressed him, he admitted that it wasn't that he'd never known the name but that the village was so insignificant that it didn't have a name. He was embarrassed by this, as if it reflected poorly on himself and his mother.

Having reviewed all the challenges, Felix and I concluded

that we would not be able to find his mother's village by ourselves and that our only hope was to enlist Albert's help.

Albert Bizimana

To their credit, they didn't beat around the bush.

"We need your help," said Mark.

"We can't do it without you," said Felix.

Before I could say what I wanted in return, Mark added, "I'd owe you, big time."

That's all it took to for me to enter their precious circle.

Mark Goldstone

The prospect of a jungle adventure was incredibly exciting. I mean *me* (a nebbishy Jewish guy from the Bronx) was about to play Allan Quartermain, handsome adventurer, seeking King Solomon's mines in the heart of darkest Africa. Sure, our goal was only a small, nameless village but Albert insisted that the trackless forest, the live volcanos and the mountain gorillas were all very real.

Still, we needed a plan. Actually, two plans — or a two-part plan. First, we needed some reason (or excuse or subterfuge) to explain to James and Auguste why we'd left our medical tent untended for an uncertain number of days. Second, we needed a map (or marked route of some kind) to avoid wandering aimlessly through dangerous territory.

Albert Bizimana

Two days after Mark and Felix had asked for my help, I told Mark I needed time alone with Felix.

"I need to talk to him in our mother tongue. I need to talk with him naturally, simply, like his mother might have done. I need him to relax, to close his eyes … to concentrate and remember … to answer my questions calmly, specifically and without reservation. I mean no disrespect, but I think you'd be a distraction."

Felix Kwizera

I said to Albert, "My mother wasn't unhappy but I knew she missed her home village a great deal. It made her feel better to tell me stories. She told me many, especially about the journey from her village to my father's, where I was born and raised."

"You've seen it all through what your mother told you," Albert said. He asked me to close my eyes and imagine my mother talking to me, as she had done, and walking me through her village. He asked me to describe the streets, the trees, the clouds, the direction of the sunset. He asked, "Are the houses grass-thatched or corrugated iron? Are there goats or cattle in the pens? Do you see banana plantations? What fruit trees do you see? What birds are flying about? From what direction does the fog arrive?" He said, "Describe the nearest hills and those far away. Recall your mother's voice. Tell me her stories."

We talked for ages. He said my memories were very helpful.

Albert Bizimana

Felix's patchwork of memories were helpful and insightful but insufficient; they helped confirm the sequence of landmarks on our itinerary but weren't extensive or specific enough to connect one landmark to another. My own experiences leading my father's cattle were more helpful in this regard. Still, if not for our work interviewing the fleeing and return-ing refugees and all we'd learned about their many desperate routes, I never would have been able to create a nearly uninterrupted foot trail from our village to where we surmised that Felix's mother had been born and raised.

Mark Goldstone

We made a good team as we all had skin in the game. Felix wanted to learn his mother's fate but couldn't do it alone. I wanted to accompany him in order to acquire experience for a first-rate article — and to put additional breathing room between myself and Jim. Albert wanted to demonstrate his impressive package of life skills so Felix and I would feel in his debt and to prove to Dr. Karekezi that they each could function well, independently of each other. Because we all had skin in the game, we had each other's back.

PREPARATIONS

Mark Goldstone

Albert dubbed our destination *Umudugudu wa Mama* ("Mother's Village") and estimated its distance at about twenty-five miles, but this figure, he admitted, was based on Euclidean efficiency: i.e., the sum total of dozens of relatively straight-line jaunts. Of course, in our case, traveling through rough unknown territory, distracted by real and perceived threats, it would be a rare thing to walk even fifty yards in a straight line.

So we really had no idea — distance-wise or time-wise — how long the trip would be. This made planning, especially in terms of provisioning, very difficult. As we were unlikely to pass a grocery (or even a roadside food vendor) and even more unlikely to fish, hunt or harvest a meal for ourselves, we had to carry an excess of foods and potables to guarantee our survival. Of course we also had to carry clothing, tents, sleeping bags, the portable stove, dry fuel, tools, utensils, medicines, bandages and so on and so forth. After assembling it all, we projected that each of us would need to carry nearly fifty pounds of rucksack weight — just below the standard for members of a Marine Expeditionary force.

Albert Bizimana

Felix contributed little to the planning, leaving most of the work to Mark and me. We did not complain as we knew he already bore a heavy emotional burden and would, in any case, have to carry his share of the supplies. As to that, it did not take us long to realize that each of us, being slightly built, would be unable to hoist our loads over any considerable distance. It was Felix who suggested, "I think we need our women. We cannot do this on our own."

Felix Kwizera

In addition to sharing our physical burdens, we expected our women to provide emotional support. Personally, I was counting on the facts of Dativa's Twa background, orphan history and brave hopes for a better future to help me face the truth of my mother's fate.

Mark Goldstone

Through our forced separation I came to appreciate how essentially alike Molly and I were. We both self-described as *basically* heterosexual, were both sexually tentative with each other, both harbored vague feelings of same-sex attraction. Moreover, we both were uncomfortable in our naked bodies: she, for her slightness and deformity; me, for my under-whelming physicality. But it was our shared outlook on politics and ethics, our egalitarian hopes for a better future and some special *something* that drew us together and made us feel like a romantic couple, however uniquely defined.

Albert Bizimana

My relations with Augusta were beautifully complex. What does that mean? It means that while most every aspect of our personal relationship seemed ill-paired, we privately cele-brated our oppositions for the greater good of our individual freedoms. Despite the long-term planning of her father (my boss and mentor), we knew we weren't meant to be together. We also knew that if we became formally engaged, her father might sanction and assist our travel to America to complete our studies — with the understanding that we would return to Rwanda to live and practice. Of course (from our point of view), once we were beyond her father's influence, there was no telling what decisions each of us might make.

Augusta Karekezi

I hadn't been completely honest with Albert. I'd let him glimpse my dissatisfaction at being a nurse trainee and my infatuation with America but I never gave him solid reasons to think I wanted to continue my studies in New York. Truth is, through my mother's cajoling, I'd begun to see Rwanda through her more mature eyes and while I still desperately wanted to visit America, I no longer dreamed of transplanting myself there.

In essence, I hadn't made any decisions. Not even close. I'd agreed to join Albert in the search for Felix's mother because it promised to be exciting and because I relished the chance to spend time with Molly. Also, I was curious to see how she behaved with Mark, another interesting American. For the record, I hadn't told Albert (or anyone else) that I'd kissed Molly. I'm not even sure why I did it. I liked her but not in a romantic way, I don't think. It was almost like I'd dared myself to do it. The next day I regretted it and wished I could take it back. But then I was okay with it. I liked to think of myself as spontaneous.

Molly X

Living in the heart of Africa, I had the time and perspective to review the responses of my parents to my name change, since they were now separated in gender-defined camps.

My father's disappointment had shocked the shit out of me. I mean, he's the one who'd always joked about our presumed cousin Hans Christian Andersen. And he's the one who'd stopped communicating with our branch of the American Andersens. And he's the one who (according to Frankie) had wanted a boy to validate the surname "son of Anders". And yet, he's the one who was surprised and disappointed when I ditched *Andersen* and replaced it with *X*!

Unsurprisingly, my name change pleased my mother, who saw it as a revolutionary feminist expression: the ripping off of a male-assigned label. At that point she'd already begun plotting the end of her marriage and likely saw my name-change as the announcement of my alliance with her cause (as if I couldn't simultaneously support both the men's Gay Movement and the women's Feminist Movement). Neither of my parents fully appreciated that *Molly X* was a personal rather than a tribal battle cry for independence and freedom.

Francine Rose

When the stream of female refugees dried, I used the extra time to review my interview notes, assigning each case to a category (mutilation, unwanted pregnancy, profound psychological trauma, etc.) and then assessing which ones might be right for a *New York Times* article and which might be better for *Virago*. I expected the work to take maybe five days. If the dry spell threatened to last longer than that, I promised Molly I'd take her to Kigali for some R&R, if it was safe.

Mark Goldstone

I liked to think of myself as part of a venerable line of young journalists — Bret Harte, Ambrose Bierce, Samuel Clemens — who'd blazed westward trails through their reporting. Their successes helped me believe that I might also succeed. But it was Jim and Molly who were more directly responsible for my uncharacteristically adventurous leap. To Jim, I felt the need to prove I could find my own story, pursue it and write it marvelously well. To Molly (and myself), I needed to prove I had the balls to pursue adventure, even in places that were dark and harrowing.

Felix Kwizera

Mark's approach and mine were very different. He was all about adventure, proving his manhood, writing a story. Mine was uncertain, reflecting my ever-changing feelings about my past, my true home and my future with Dativa.

Albert Bizimana

Jim left a note explaining that he was going to use our downtime (the temporary halt of refugees to our campsite) to visit a friend at the United States military base in Mombasa, Kenya. He did not mention the name of the friend, or how he would travel there or how long he would be gone.

Jim's departure left us with a big problem, for we had counted on him remaining alone at the camp ("manning the fort", as Mark put it) while the rest of us ventured into the wilderness. With Jim gone, we'd need to explain our disappearance to Dr. Karekezi, who had already left our campsite to return to the district hospital.

Surprisingly, it was Felix, who'd been quiet during our preparations, who offered the best plan: "Just say a little native boy came to us, saying there had been an accident. That his parents and others were hurt — and that he needed us to follow him, though it was more than a day's travel."

We liked it. It was simple and believable. And, inasmuch as we had no other refugees to attend, the lie would alleviate most of our professional guilt. Still, how would we get Augusta, Molly and Dativa to join us?

I worked out a plan with our dear Manzi before he arrived with his weekly supplies.

"Uncle, it is most important that you give Augusta this sealed letter and wait for her response." The letter described our mission in much the same way as the letter we'd left for James or Auguste (whoever returned first).

I also gave him a second sealed envelope, instructing him to open it (and share it) if he hadn't heard from me in a week's time. This second letter was a copy of my map, with all the landmarks and possible routes noted. Just in case.

Augusta Karekezi

While Manzi waited, I unsealed the envelope and read its note, which described how a little native boy had come to the other camp, crying, saying there'd been an accident and that his parents and others needed help — and that the little boy needed them all to follow him, though it was more than a day's travel. The note, written in Albert's hand, asked that I come as soon as possible, bringing Molly and Dativa with me, along with some supplies.

The letter was brief and understated (so unlike Albert) so I assumed it was code for something else that was also urgent. I showed the note to Molly and Dativa, explaining my feelings and, as we had no other commitments, we all agreed to go. With Manzi's help, we packed the van with enough clothing for a week and all the requested supplies (including some additional items of our choosing) and drove to the other campsite, which none of us had visited before.

Molly X

The day before Augusta received her letter, Frankie left for Kigali by herself, clearly disappointed, as she'd been counting on my company. But I had no interest in reprising our weird Paris experience, where all things feminine had been laid out front and center, like an all-you-can-eat, twenty-four-hour buffet. It was too much. Also, I'd been thinking a lot about Mark, mostly what I liked about him, and then — voilà! — I had plans to see him, which made me so unexpectedly happy that I slipped the thought of Augusta's barely remembered kiss into my back pocket.

Dativa Natukunda

Augusta read the letter aloud to me and Molly. Though she

said the letter was from Albert and written in his hand, I heard Felix's voice between the lines, calling for me: *The time has come to search for my mother. Come with me. Be with me when we find her!*

Just thinking back, girls and boys did not mix very much at the Jesuit Urumuri Centre, where I'd been brought by a stranger who'd found me (following some violent calamity in my village), a naked and hungry toddler, wandering alone.

For many years I lived in the Centre, waiting to be adopted. Other children were adopted but not me. I don't know why. A thousand nights I cried into my pillow, thinking I was too puny and ugly for anyone to want. And so the years passed. If I'd been in the care of some other order, maybe Benedictine or Franciscan, I might have been tracked to become a nun but the Jesuits do not have sisters and nuns and, eventually, I aged beyond the possibility of adoption.

But I was a good girl, a helpful girl, and I think the Jesuits liked me, which is why they eventually made special arrangements for me to join the young American couple in their fancy building on lower Fifth Avenue to serve as their nanny.

Had I stayed in Rwanda, I suppose I would be married by now, walking down a village road, holding my own child's hand, with another child wrapped snugly to my back. Instead, there I was in New York City, caring for a beautiful little baby named Stewart James. In fact, I'd been with the family on the day of his christening, holding the child when his mother was tired, or busily greeting guests, adoring his warmth on my chest and cheek. For me, the experience confirmed what I'd always known: that I needed to be a married mother to be fulfilled.

And then, astonishingly, I had met the handsome young man in the park and discovered that he was also Rwandan. And now I was going to be meeting him again!

After Augusta read the letter to Molly and me, we set off to join him and the others. Manzi was driving. Augusta sat beside him in the passenger seat. I sat in the back, behind Augusta and beside Molly. The front windows were open, the forest-scented wind rushing in. Up front, Manzi and Augusta must have thought they were talking privately, for they never addressed us and used only their native tongue to speak to each other. They must have forgotten that I spoke and understood Kinyarwanda — or just didn't care.

I was leaning forward, concentrating on what Manzi and Augusta were saying, unaware that Molly was concentrating on me. At a pause in the conversation, I must have sat back in my seat, for it was only then that I noticed Molly staring at me, as if I'd suddenly become an object of exquisite interest.

Molly X

For a long while I'd been dismissive of Dativa. I'd thought of her as somehow inauthentic because she'd left needy Rwanda to move to New York to work for a wealthy businessman and hunt for a husband, and had snared our good friend Felix, whom I regarded as very authentic for having survived Rwanda and reinvented himself as a New York City park employee and black-market businessman and who was now risking it all to learn the truth about his mother.

But just then, sitting beside Dativa in the back seat of the van, a million miles from Manhattan, I saw her in a new light: despite her own personal history of death and abandonment and her culture-shock move to New York, she had eschewed her beautiful new life to accompany Felix back to the bloody terror that was Rwanda and for no good reason that I could see, other than love.

James Andersen

Reckoning it was too far to travel by road to Mombasa (southeast, about 750 miles, mostly across Tanzania), I decided it would be more practical, though more expensive, to go first to Kigali and then fly to Mombasa from there.

At the time I was doing a lot of reckoning, mostly about my closest human relationships. To my mind, Frankie and Mark were my problem relationships. Basically, I think my life with Frankie might have turned out better if Molly hadn't been injured. That tragedy snatched our marriage in its jaws and turned it into a death spiral of regret and blame. Maybe I'm fooling myself but I think our relationship became cruel and retaliatory only after the accident.

As to Mark, this was a quirky thing because nothing demonstrably illicit had occurred between us. But I'm not obtuse. I realize now (and I think I realized then) that Mark had guessed at my ulterior motives. But I'm not sure. I'm not even sure I had ulterior motives. At least, not at the start.

Here's how it started: For a long while I'd been really worried about Molly. In her last year of high school she'd been arrested for smoking dope, buying dope and consorting with felons who smoked dope and bought dope. Several times I'd had to use my position in the community to get police charges thrown out or reduced to misdemeanors. If I hadn't interceded, Molly might have gone to jail.

I worried that Molly would soon age out of our protective abilities, by which I mean *my* protective abilities, as Frankie already seemed more invested in her career than in the well-being of our daughter. She behaved as if Molly's "acting out" was much ado about nothing, which infuriated me.

Anyway, because Molly and I both feared that her blemished public record might scotch her applications to some colleges, she wisely chose to accept the full-ride scholarship The New School had offered her.

At heart, we all were happy with the outcome ... until recidivist Molly started acting out again. That was when I thought that Mark Goldstone (my prize grad student and protégé) might become a regular visitor to our home, ostensibly to meet me to review his doctoral thesis but also to act as a mature and responsible influence on Molly's reignited rebelliousness. At first, my idea appeared to be succeeding, as Molly seemed more focused on school, politics and social issues. In fact, Mark and Molly seemed to get on so well that I invited Mark to move in with us — at a fair rent. Molly aside, I thought his presence would also make up for Frankie's sorely missed contribution to my costs.

I suppose I'd been aware, in a shadowy way, of my burgeoning attraction to Mark but self-awareness has never been my strong suit.

Francine Rose

Right before I left for Kigali, alone, I received a note from Jim, asking if he could visit so we could "talk it out". *Talk it out?* Really? If he came offering an olive branch, I would have shoved it up his unlubed ass. That's how angry I was. I blamed him for Molly's rejection of my offer of a girls' vacay in Kigali, assuming he'd poisoned her ear against me. Just like the buggering bastard to hit out at me through backdoor channels, rather than face me head on.

Furious, I flashed back to our many heated arguments, blotting out his idiotic avowals, remembering only my own high-minded, honest assertions:

How could you minimize the importance of my work? Of course, you don't in public. In public you say the right words, the perfect phrases, so everyone will think your heart and head are in the right place. But I know better. I know what's really going on. And I've known for a long time. It's not just that I left you. I left you to live with a woman. And when people ask me why, I've been saying simply, "It's more satisfying."

I know that galls you. You've said as much. But I also know it's not at the heart of your anger. What galls the fuck out of you is the fact that I had the courage to finally live my authentic life as a woman-loving woman, while you are still a cowardly dog, unwilling and unable to admit that the sharpest impulse behind your estimable journalism and teaching is not a fight for

Gays' equality before the law but avoiding admitting publicly that you are gay yourself — an indisputable, died-in-the-wool homosexual who hides in a lightless closet.

How pathetic that two of your friends, out-and-out gay men, had the balls to co-found the edgy Gay Alliance chapter, the Flaming Faggots, while you only cheered from the sidelines like a proud but scared little boy. This hypocrisy is infinitely worse than conveniently forgetting to wash the dishes or do the laundry. This is a form of suicide. The murder of your truest self. Because you lack the courage to fight for yourself, you have fought instead against me as I have ventured — slowly, tepidly, but ever closer — towards fulfilling the promise of my most authentic self: a proud and loving gay woman.

James Andersen

Technically, I suppose, I had violated the age-old proscription against making sexual advances towards a student. But that worthy law had been written for the protection of adolescents, not consenting adults. It was a superannuated law. A law that desperately needed updating. Same with adultery and homosexuality. Sexuality outside marriage — with a man or a woman — is the most normal thing in the world. Legislating against it is pure madness.

Still, theory is one thing, lived life quite another. My personally relevant facts were these: My student Mark and my daughter Molly had developed a deep friendship (and possibly something more) and yet I still considered pursuing Mark myself in the name of advancing my most authentic self (and possibly his too), despite all the countervailing professional strictures, social mores and feelings of my daughter. Damned if I did, damned if I didn't.

As for Frankie, she never answered my invitation to meet, which is why I went ahead with my plans to go to Mombasa. I wasn't sure of all my motives for seeing Busty; but, at the very least, my visit was a way of postponing any further reckoning of my complicated personal relationships.

SOUTHWESTWARD HO!

Albert Bizimana

When Uncle arrived with the women (his van stuffed with their belongings and additional supplies), he handed me an unsealed envelope, saying, "I took the liberty of making photocopies of the map, thinking everyone should have a copy and know how to read it."

At first, I was not pleased. Seeing myself as the group's unquestioned authority, I did not welcome the idea of anyone seconding-guessing my decisions. But I soon recognized the value of Manzi's action. The fact that everyone had a map would attenuate my responsibility should the expedition fail. Especially if it failed tragically.

Having prepared for all the most reasonable contingencies, we were ready to embark. To find our destined village, we would have to locate several major landmarks, if Felix remembered right: stretches of strange rocky land, deep forests of bamboo and birds, a mountain or mountains populated by gorillas, more dark forests, and a volcano. I was thinking we should head to Mgshinga Gorilla National Park and then make our way to Mount Nyamuragira, since the route between them and the village of Umuhanda (where Felix's father had brought his mother and settled) made basically a straight line. If we were able to follow this route, we just might discover the truth about Felix's mother.

Although we intended to enter Uganda where the border wasn't monitored, rather than at the Cyanika crossing, the trip was not without peril. Rwanda is so small and densely populated, and tensions were still so high, that our discovery could easily put our lives at risk. In the past year, long-standing enmity between our peoples had given rise to an unfathomable bloodlust, with neighbors, villagers, even former friends, murdering and violating each other in the most unspeakable ways. Bodies were still being counted. The worst seemed to be over, but we still had to be very careful.

Mark Goldstone

We all had faith in Albert's navigational skills. It was his idea to travel westward in order to pass into Uganda unobserved. And it was his realization that Felix's gorilla reference likely referred to the Mgahinga Gorilla National Park. It was also his idea that we should continue traveling due west, crossing into Zaire, where we would pass through more forests and a strange volcanic landscape before approaching the foothills of Mt. Nyamuragira—where we hoped to find Felix's mother. All this was Albert's plan.

Molly X

I used to make fun of Mark for being mature and responsible. But when we took our first break, only three miles from the campsite, he drew a fresh, thick notebook from his rucksack and started writing. I was mortified. Though I thought of myself as a journalist, I hadn't even thought to bring pen and paper. I was such a fraud!

I was sitting quietly beside him, my eyes welling with tears when, without even looking at me, he drew an identical notebook and pen from his rucksack and passed them to me without comment ... and I thought: what a deep and complicated thing love is.

Dativa Natukunda

Walking behind Felix through the forests and fields of Northern Rwanda, I imagined ourselves being followed by a low cloud filled with the rumbling voices of our ancestors, blessing our happy union, praying we'd produce a beautiful baby, hopefully a boy.

Augusta Karekezi

As soon as my father returned to the hospital, Albert took charge of most everything. For sure, it was Mark and Felix who'd put forward the idea to find Felix's mother but the actual planning, logistics and leadership came from Albert. Once embarked, I followed his lead through the Impenetrable Forest, matching his every trailblazing footstep.

Without my father hovering nearby, I had time to reassess my opinion of Albert. To me, he now seemed taller, altogether more substantial. Without the depersonalizing rules and regulations of our district hospital, without the standard hospital uniform that made him appear a mini version of my father, he showed better. To me, Albert now seemed a more mature version of the nice boy I'd met years before, the one I'd mentally dismissed once he appeared to be just another part of my father's plan for my future success and happiness.

Molly X

When Mark took my hand, I recalled the day in the Pink PussyCat Boutique when I'd taken his hand to reassure him. On that occasion, the surroundings had made him nervous. But on this day, he seemed a new man: an indefatigable, truth-seeking explorer. Color me impressed!

Mark Goldstone

Uganda is a place of fog and shifting winds, and in no place is the fog more mysteriously foggy than in the Impenetrable Forest. Because of the region's high altitude, the fog is a more or less perpetual thing, an expected presence in the low sky, attenuating the sun's glare. This is one reason why the primeval region is called *Bwindi,* which means "place full of darkness".

The other reason for the darkness is the leafy forest hardwoods and extensive stands of giant bamboo that block the sunlight with their dense canopies. Sunlight that does fall between the trees and bamboo is absorbed and muted by the thick ground cover of ferns, vines and other entangling tendrils that severely hinder foot traffic.

Felix Kwizera

We didn't walk so much as grapple our way through the forest. Although we weren't required to do any jungle-like slashing, we each carried a machete. Sadly, such weapons were common and easy to acquire throughout Rwanda.

I had my machete with me (hanging off my belt, like an improvised holster) when I went off a little ways to relieve myself. While watching my stream of pee shower some tiny buttercup-like flowers, I heard a nearby snuffling. Immediately, I stopped peeing and zipped up.

Only then did I turn my head in the direction of the snuffling, in time to see an animal that looked like a short-eared, spindly-legged, pregnant deer. As soon as we made eye contact, it bolted.

Albert Bizimana

I might have seen the same animal later that same day. The one I saw was a yellow-backed duiker, fairly common in Uganda. Hunters and poachers shoot the adults and catch the young ones by snare, then slitting their throats. To be fair, farmers sometimes hunt duiker in reprisal for raiding their crops. Personally, I would not kill an innocent creature like a duiker. But I knew, even then, that I could kill any creature, man or beast, that threatened me or someone I loved.

I had two guns (a rifle and a pistol), which I had taken from Dr. Karekezi's van. (They'd been kept in a long tool box, beside the spare tire, and he probably did not know they were gone.) When we went on very rural visits, we were always aware of the guns as a last resort of self-protection.

The doctor had trained me in their proper use, just as he had mentored me in all my pursuits.

When preparing for our expedition, I knew I should train someone else in our group on the use of the guns. That meant Felix or Mark. Call me sexist but I did not think of training any of the three women, though I'm sure any of them might have proved proficient. In any case, they were all self-protected. Each carried a machete, as well as a walking stick, which could serve as an excellent bludgeon.

Molly X

I loved that Mark (and some others) saw me as a daring firebrand but I wasn't really daring at all. Back home, I avoided rough neighborhoods at night, didn't have casual sex, didn't do hard drugs — just smoked some weed without even enjoying it. What I did enjoy was the high I got from being associated with the faintest fringe of the local black market: the dope users and sellers in our sunny neighborhood park. It was the *idea* of being a renegade that excited me.

One day Moby3 had offered me something new. "Girl, swallow this and you be flyin' like Lucy in de Sky. First one on me." I took the tablet (wrapped in tissue and sealed in a tiny plastic packet) and sold it to some kid on a red bike, who'd been looking to score. But after I sold it, I was nervous: almost sick to my stomach. *What if it was poison? What if he had a bad reaction and flipped out? What if he permanently lost his mind?* Three weeks later I saw the same kid on the same red bike and wanted to give him a hug. But I held back, real cool like, and he came to me. "That was unbelievable. You have any more?" I asked him what his experience had been like and he told me all about his kaleidoscopic world of butterflies.

I recalled the incident on our third day in the forest. We'd been walking on a cool dewy path below an immensely high canopy of trees, slowly approaching an open, low-rolling field of wild orchids (most shaped like purple-pink starfish or leopard-spotted elephant ears) when, suddenly, we were enveloped by a million darting butterflies, their patterns and colors fast-shifting. We were all stunned into silence, as if sharing a collective dream ... and I was taken back to the boy on the red bike and his drug-induced, kaleidoscopic world of butterflies.

Dativa Natukunda

In my early days walking from lower Fifth Avenue towards the park, I said to another black nanny pushing a baby carriage, "Where are all the birds?" Other than the gray pigeons, whose oily opalescence disgusted me, and the tiny brown sparrows that were common as dirt, I saw no birds. Certainly not beautiful ones, which made me sad, as I'd seen so many during my years in the orphanage: green broadbills, the Red-throated Alethe, the Blue-cheeked Turaco. While crossing the Impenetrable Forest I saw another of my favorite birds and pointed to it while whispering in Felix's ear, "look, my handsome francolin."

Augusta Karekezi

When I first began working at the district hospital as a nurse trainee, I was surprised at how noisy the place was: alarms and beeps, rattling trolleys, ringing phones, conversations rising and falling; altogether, a very different kind of setting from what I was used to. As my father was a relatively eminent doctor, we had a relatively eminent home with a shady porch and a small back veranda facing the forest. I often sat alone on the veranda, and what I enjoyed was the relative quiet.

I'm thinking back to our crossing of the Impenetrable Forest. I'd walked single-file, behind my male partner, just as Dativa and Molly had. I'd been second in line, following

Albert's footsteps, careful not to disturb his focus. On our third day in the forest, Albert had seemed particularly preoccupied and while I didn't want to distract him, it seemed like a good opportunity to get to know him better.

"What are you thinking?" I ventured, in a low whisper.

He paused several seconds.

"Not thinking at all. Just listening to the trees."

"The trees?"

He gave me a quick smile over his shoulder.

"Every tree sings its own song."

"That's a new one," I said. "Singing trees."

He smiled again. "Think of it as a duet: trees and wind together."

I looked at him coyly. "Unlikely partners. How do they make it work?"

After another pause, Albert answered: "We don't see the wind, only what it moves. We don't hear the wind unless it flows past something and makes it vibrate — like branches and leaves. Tree and wind are codependent, like a couple."

I liked this new Albert. Beyond the reach of my father's shadow, he seemed entirely different. And now I wanted him to like me.

"It's like light," I added. "We can't hear it or see it — unless something reflects it."

"Exactly!" he said, turning at last to look me full in the face.

Encouraged, I added, "We cannot see wind but we see how it rustles tree leaves. We cannot see love but we see how it flutters lovers' eyes."

He thought the words were mine but they weren't. They were song lyrics from one of my teen magazines. Still, my feelings were legit: straight from my suddenly stirred heart.

Albert Bizimana

She'd been a silly girl when we'd first met, idolizing every-thing American, especially its acting and singing stars. Silly brainwashed girl, she'd talk about Broadway and Hollywood and Miami Beach as if she had some idea where they were or what they were like. But she didn't, trust me. There'd been no newspapers for her to read, no television or movies either. So, how did she come by her knowledge, such as it was? Two words: Uncle Manzi. He'd felt sorry for the girl whose father was the main doctor in the district and who over-protected his daughter to the point where the other girls in the village resented her. Not surprising, Augusta was afraid of them, with their simpler lives and cruder habits.

Manzi wished there was a way he might allay her loneliness, even if it were only with some trifling amusement. As it happened, Kigali Airport had recently begun hosting more direct flights from Europe and the United States and Manzi, who worked at the hospital as a janitor and driver, was often asked to go to the small airport to pick up or deliver passengers or packages.

Now, Manzi had a wife named Clarisse who worked at the airport as a cleaning woman. One day Clarisse told Manzi her idea for a little side business: When removing passenger refuse from the landed planes, she often came across full-color, glossy magazines that had been left behind (mostly American but sometimes from France and Germany and Italy). Many of these magazines looked unread and in mint condition. With Manzi's help (and the use of the hospital van and jeep) they could sell the magazines at the villages or use them for barter. Manzi kissed his smart wife and put the plan into action.

Because the plan was immediately profitable, Manzi could afford to choose a couple of magazines from every new batch, twine them with pretty ribbon that he found in patient waste baskets and then present them to Augusta.

When Augusta was a young teen, *Tiger Beat* had been her favorite magazine. Under her bed she'd kept secret scrapbooks of her heartthrob singers and actors. When she grew older, her favorite magazines were *Life* and *Look,* for these (she believed) were the ones that provided the most realistic sense of America's greatness.

Dativa Natukunda

After moving to America, where I was generally happy, especially after having met Felix, I was better able to weigh up the strengths and weaknesses of Rwanda.

For example, poor Rwandans live with the country's wildlife but do not waste much time thinking about pets. In New York City, there is no wildlife (so to speak) — nothing big — but many people have pets, although the city has odd pet laws. For example: you can't own a capybara but you can raise a fennec fox. You can have a pet snake (even a large one) but not a constrictor, though you can own almost any breed of dog, even potentially aggressive ones like Pit Bulls, Dobermans and Rottweilers.

I know a woman named Giselle who's from Haiti and knows a lot about rare and exotic dogs. It is her hobby, although she is a poor nanny like myself. Sometimes we'd walk our baby strollers around the park together. Sometimes we'd walk to other neighborhoods, even as far as Soho, and she'd point out all the rare dogs we saw along the way, spelling their breed names whenever I asked. One crazy week we saw an Icelandic Sheepdog, a Pharaoh Hound, a Portuguese Podengo Pequeno and a Dandie Dinmont Terrier. Though these Manhattan dogs had all been collared and leashed, their exotic breeds and strange looks reminded me of the incredible variety of Rwandan wildlife. Strange how my lives mixed together.

Molly X

Walking the forest in Mark's company, I had an incredible, animating revelation. While he always kept his pen and journal within easy reach, I was suddenly inspired to let go all my professional hopes and goals; to surrender myself to my immediate surroundings, absorbing all I could using only my unanalytical senses.

Expectations, deadlines, responsibilities instantly evaporated. I might be a journalist; I might not. I might like girls; I might not. In this new mindset, feelings and freedom rose to the fore: perception and immediacy became my main filters.

In that moment I put journalism aside and decided to focus on poetry. I knew nothing about meter. I knew rhyme was no longer cool. I knew I needed strong literary images and line breaks and deep thoughts and emotions and good sounds. Because my newly inspired brain felt like a shaken snow globe, I ran with that idea. The forest canopy would be the globe; the birds and monkeys, the colorful confetti:

> Through the thicket of giant hardwoods, blue turaco and
>   red-faced barbets glided like winged streaks of color.
> Sunlight broke through gaps in the trees like insect-buzzy
>   spotlights.
> Huge trees were festooned with creepers and parasitic
>   plants that poisoned and strangled.
> Monkeys leaped and lunged from branch to branch like
>   screeching gymnasts.

These details (and dozens more) pushed from my mind the stories of Rwanda's raped and mutilated women. With this new focus, I felt less like a journalist but more like myself. No longer in competition with Mark and my parents, I felt closer to me.

Anyway, when we went through the Impenetrable Forest, I carried my machete, like a swashbuckling Anne Bonny. But I never went very far. Just far enough where I couldn't be seen by the others, beyond the carry of their conversational voices, but not beyond the estimated range of my blood-curdling scream, should it come to that.

Look: I'm no hero; I'm not brave. I'd already learned that

when I first met Mark. I might pose like Joan of Arc but I was nothing like her. While she ventured out alone to face her enemies (and even God Himself), I needed a dependable partner. For a while I fooled myself into believing that this partner could just as easily be a woman as a man. But no. My feelings on the subject began to clarify as I got to know Mark: not the manliest man but someone who paired well with me. If I looked calm in the Pink PussyCat, it was only because he was with me, more scared than I was.

Buying a nickel bag from friendly dealers was about as daring as I got. In truth, I had attempted only one daring escapade in my life — and it had left me crippled and chastened. I was like my father. He talked a good game but rarely broke a sweat. He liked being known as daring, without actually putting skin on the line. Still, I think I was closer to him than to my mother, because we were more alike.

Ironically, my admiration for him grew after I found the pictures of Busty Evans in a clasped folder in the dark recesses of his closet. I admired the fact of his secret life. I knew the strength it took to hide such secrets. I'd been looking at his Busty collection (personal photos, news clippings, magazine stories, letters) when I heard him enter the apartment unexpectedly. I quickly went up the ladder to re-hide the folder but in hurrying down again I turned my right ankle and fell with a yelp. My dad came quickly to my aid, carrying me to my room and then leaving me alone while he prepared an ice pack. We never spoke about why I'd been in his room but I figured he knew that I'd learned his secret.

Neither of us ever mentioned the event until the day when Manzi arrived at our campsite with the letter from Albert that would change our lives. While we were all busy packing the van for our big adventure, Manzi privately handed me a sealed envelope with a handwritten note from my father:

I reached out to your mother but she wouldn't speak with me. I tried. Anyway, with our work temporarily slowed, I am going to the American base in Mombasa to see my special friend who is there performing for the troops. I think you know who I mean. I met her, in a manner of speaking, when I was a boy and got to know her through the years as a fan and journalist. She's a good woman with a good story to tell. I don't think you'll ever meet her but I'll tell you her story — and how it relates to me — next time we are together.

—Love, Dad

IN THE WINGS

Busty Evans

I'd done a show for almost every squadron and team on the base and, just like in Guam, the boys were pretty well behaved. Even their hoots and shouts were mostly respectful. I think the uniforms — and the presence of officers — kept the rowdies in check. Whatever, it was certainly better than the disgusting XXX theaters where I'd mostly performed in recent years. I had only one or two more shows to go but already I was feeling nostalgic.

When I got the offer to go to Guam, I figured it would be a nice change of pace and a nice way to say goodbye to my career as a dancer. That's still how I saw myself. I'd learned dancing when I was little and that's all I'd ever wanted to do — and so that's what I did — and made a good living of it.

Now, some people try to tarnish what I've done by calling me an *exotic* dancer or a *burlesk* dancer. But when people say such things, I say to them, "I'm a *working* dancer." And that's God's simple truth. For years I earned my daily bread by taking whatever dancing jobs were available to me. Lucky me, I was blessed with a pair of obvious recommendations that were better than most resumes.

It was nice work in the early years. Burlesk shows were

still popular. Along with the dancing, there was comedy and singing. The paying crowd was polite, even well dressed — the ladies too. But that was the tail end of the good times. Society was getting harsher and meaner and the glamor of burlesk was fading fast. One day I looked around and realized the whole damn business had gone seedy and disreputable. And it's only gotten worse. Now, it's one worn-out place after another. And once a place loses its self-respect, the people who work there go to hell too. In the past few years, I've been groped and pinched and damn-near raped a dozen times, usually by theater managers who figured I owed them something extra for all those crazy requests I made, like a working lightbulb in my dressing room.

I was just about done in, ready to retire my boas and pasties, when I got the invite to go to Guam. Rear Admiral Jack Shemnar, the commander of the naval base there, was an old friend and fan and I knew he would provide a respectful audience for a relatively tame show. So I went with a couple of my dancing gals and we had ourselves a lovely time. So lovely, I decided it would be my swan song: a good way to cap my career. I figured I'd return to Syracuse after my last show and live out my days like a good quiet wife. But when my commander friend asked me, with a touch of honest pleading in his voice, to go to Africa as well for a friend of his, I felt like I couldn't say no. I figured that would be my last dance, for sure.

Rear Admiral Colston Thomas, the Commanding Officer in Mombasa, had a lovely residence in Kilindini Harbor, not far from the small hotel where I was housed, along with the other dancers. He was just the nicest man. He and Jack were cut from the same braided cloth. He was very respectful to me and the other girls and we enjoyed the few weeks we were there. Each week he took me out to dinner and asked me dozens of polite questions about my life and career. During my last week, I told him that my special friend

James Andersen was coming to visit me. When I added that James was a *New York Times* reporter, sent to Rwanda to cover the terrible bloodshed, he seemed very impressed. And when I suggested that maybe James could interview him for an article about the Rapid Deployment Force under his command, he seemed genuinely enthused.

James Andersen

I hadn't seen Busty in quite a few years. When I called to tell her I'd arrived in Mombasa, she seemed thrilled and invited me to meet her on the main seaside boulevard where my hotel was located.

When I'd interviewed her in the past, it had always been after a show and she'd been in the theater dressing room, covered up with some worn, frilly robe. Now, seeing her at a distance, it appeared the years had been kind to her. Walking towards me, she looked lovely and understated in a simple frock, despite the high-stepping advance guard of her bosom. As she drew near, I saw her hair was thinner, and restrained behind her neck with a pink plastic clam. Two strides closer, I saw she wore shoes that looked like beaded Indian slippers; her quirky attempt to go native, I supposed. In all, she looked like somebody's lovably eccentric grandma.

She gave me a big hug, like I was a favored nephew.

"You look the same," she said, which I took as a compliment.

"You look beautifully relaxed," I said, which was the honest truth.

We began firing questions at the same time, which made us both laugh.

"Please," I said. "Ladies first."

She smiled demurely and almost immediately told me how happy she was, stepping into retirement on her own terms.

"I'm one of the lucky ones. I have my health, my pride,

my savings … and a husband waiting for me in a lovely house, just the two of us. And our cats. I have my gardening, my church bingo … and my nephews and nieces, too young to know my past. Not that I'm ashamed. I'm not. But it does makes life easier."

"You've always been an important part of my life," I said, my voice suddenly cracking.

"How long has it been? No, don't tell me!" she said, her well-timed laugh covering my emotion.

We talked a bit about how we both came to be there. But then she suddenly broke ranks and asked me pointedly why I'd continued to seek her out over the many years.

It wasn't the first time she'd asked that question. I knew she was asking again because I'd never satisfied her with anything close to the truth: how, thirty years earlier, I stood nervously outside the far end of a Catskill casino, trying desperately to peer through a partially opened curtain to see my first ever naked woman … and how my best friend Larry, also fourteen, crouched beside me, our flanks touching … and how the excitement I felt watching Busty was redoubled by his breathy nearness and the fact that his own parents (who knew my parents) were inside, less than thirty feet away, enjoying Busty's naughty show. Everything was so close and complexly compounded. Everything threatened to reveal everything else.

Stumbling and bumbling, I was unable (once again) to articulate for Busty a clear explanation of why she'd remained in my head all those years.

"Oh, sweetie, it's okay," she said. "I don't have to know everything. It's enough for me to know that you grew up thinking of me … and that you traveled miles in that old jalopy of yours to see my shows … and that you always wrote such nice things about me in your articles … and that you were always such a gentleman."

I was glad I didn't have to explain myself more fully and

personally, for after all those many years, the truth remained jumbled in my mind. Though I'd become a well-respected journalist, known mainly for espousing the rights of the ethically disenfranchised, I'd never been able to think through my feelings about Busty. I'd never been able to put words to my feelings, even though words were my stock and trade. So, instead of trying and failing again, I pivoted, "So, tell me about your husband," I said.

When Busty finished telling me about Robert, she asked about my wife and daughter and was surprised as heck to learn that they were also in Africa. Excitedly, she asked questions about them both but never said a word about meeting them. In her way, Busty was as polite and thoughtful and as intuitively respectful as anyone I'd ever known.

We talked for hours. When evening approached, she led me to the Castle Hotel on Kilindini Road. We had a lovely dinner there on the rear portico, facing the harbor and the Indian Ocean beyond. The sunset felt oddly romantic.

After dinner she said goodbye. She said she had another show to do. Before she parted, she told me that Colston wanted to meet me for breakfast the following morning.

"Colston?"

"Rear Admiral Colston Thomas. He's very interested in you doing a story about the base here and his Rapid Deployment Force. He's facing funding issues and could use some good press."

Busty amazed me. She'd come a long way. But before I could muse more about our just-concluded meeting, I had to email Larry to see if he'd be interested in the story, and that would mean telling him what I was doing in Mombasa and why the hell I'd left Rwanda. Thing is, I knew he'd understand. He'd been with me that steamy night in the Catskills (when we both watched Busty Evans bare it all) and some years later during that Christmas Eve organ recital when we'd both fallen for Frankie.

Lawrence Schielding

I received Larry's email and called him back immediately, without any concern for time zones. He answered the phone after the first ring.

"Listen to me," I said, skipping all pleasantries: "Your story is a go. After all the U.S. casualties at Mogadishu, there's been a shift in foreign policy, and we've been withdrawing forces from Africa. That means that next time American forces in Africa are surprise-attacked, everything's going to depend on the RDF. I know you need to get back to Rwanda, and your first drafts from there were great, but let's hold off on them while you run with this one. And be careful."

As soon as we disconnected, I had a dark presentiment that I'd never see Jim again. As so many times before, I flash-imagined his sudden and violent death, and felt very mixed emotions. Then my thoughts turned to Frankie, who'd contacted me just the day before from Kigali. Her early drafts had also been brilliant: brazenly dramatic; filled with graphic outrages perpetrated against Rwandan females. Then I flash-imagined *Frankie's* sudden and violent death.

In theory, I figured I could wind up with one or the other. Unsure which of them I preferred, I let the pair of violent images commingle in my fevered brain.

Francine Rose

I felt unmoored. Not just untethered but drowning too. That last letter to James, in which I'd blasted him for his cowardice, had taken its toll on me too. While it had felt great to kick him to the curb, I'd assumed my female relationships would immediately fill the void and that my work with injured Rwandan women would bring me some good sisterly karma. It didn't. Debora and Augusta seemed not to like me — and Molly hurt me. It never occurred to me that she wouldn't want to go to Kigali with me. I mean, what's better than mother-daughter love, when the mother is me?

And yet, she'd turned me down. So I arrived in Kigali all by my lonesome. Purposeful and self-directed, I planned to see Kandt House, Rwanda's Museum of Natural History; the Al-Fatah Mosque, built in 1913; and the quarter where Swahili traders congregated. But mostly I wanted to seek out Rwandan women who spoke English, to understand how they saw a world that was daily bloodied by Rwandan men.

Even without Molly, I might have enjoyed my visit to Kigali, had I been able to clear my mind of the backstabbing bitch, Estrella Delgado. But I couldn't. I had too much at stake and the bitch was stealing it from me ... while my back was turned ... while I was trying to save Rwandan women! How selfish and heartless was that!

But the facts were clear: When I sent the draft of my first article to Gloria, she didn't immediately reply, and when I followed up, she admitted she hadn't yet reviewed it because Star (her nickname for Estrella) had scored interviews with a half-dozen notable, Latina feminists including Alicia Escalante (Chicana warrior) and Sylvia del Villard (Puerto Rican activist), which were sure to steal thunder from *Ms.* and put the spotlight back on *Virago*. Gloria said she was sure my draft was terrific and promised to read it ASAP.

Gloria Applebaum

I'm a very lucky woman. Though born to parents who over-favored their sons, I'd been sent to college and grad school, where I learned what I needed to know to provide for myself. Eventually I could buy my own home (a beautiful townhouse on Minetta Street in Greenwich Village) and help launch Djuna Books, which led to my relationship with Francine Rose and later to my relationship with Estrella Delgado. I'm publisher and president of *Virago* and a person to be reckoned with.

Estrella Delgado

I admit it. It was a calculated stunt, strutting into Djuna Books, dressed like Zorro's twin sister, knowing that Gloria Appelbaum, *Virago* publisher, would be there.

And it worked, grandly! I'd hoped to simply catch her attention, make conversation, introduce myself as a feminist writer. I did not imagine that I'd rise so quickly to become her star writer, much less her lover and house companion. As for Francine Rose, I respected her then and I respect her now, no matter how low her star has fallen.

THE SNARE

Mark Goldstone

According to Albert's estimates, we had reached Mgahinga Gorilla Park, though we didn't see a single sign or any other people. To stay out of sight, we climbed into the foothills, which offered good cover. We hacked through thick shrubbery, then found ourselves in a grassy clearing. Far off, we saw three men on the edge of the forest. Albert signaled *Stop!* and whispered down the line that we should all drop low to the ground and remain still.

Molly X

I held my breath until I heard an otherworldly screech — and then gasped. Animal? Human? I wasn't sure. Then I heard a gunshot. And another ... and another. I swore an oath before God: Just let me be brave. I didn't want to die a coward. Especially in front of Mark. Let me be brave — and live — and I will write brave poetry for the rest of my days.

Dativa Natukunda

Why did we ever come back? To die in the dirt? Oh God, dear Jesus, let us live and I promise to marry in Church.

Felix Kwizera

This whole country is a place of darkness. First my father. Perhaps my mother. Now Dativa and my friends. Oh God!

Augusta Karekezi

Albert put an impassioned finger to his lips to beg my silence, touched my own lips with that same finger, then turned and crawled away through the high grasses toward the source of the screech. I lifted my head just enough to watch. It was the bravest, most beautiful thing I'd ever seen. Just like in the movies.

Albert Bizimana

I crawled away slowly to draw attention from the others. If they saw me, I wanted them to think I was alone: a solitary hunter. My guns proved that; and if I had to, I'd use them.

Mark Goldstone

Albert crawled off: I'm not sure why. But there appeared to be something brave and purposeful about his snaking movements. Then I heard a gunshot.

I was too frightened to lift up my head to look about. But I finally did. I had to. After all, it was my story that was playing out. Inquiring minds would want to know *Who? What? Where? When?* and *Why?* and I was the only reporter on the scene. I also didn't want to disappoint James, and certainly not Molly, whose head was buried in my side.

Then I heard a second shot. And a third.

GORILLA MISTS

Albert Bizimana

She went by four names: Professor Dee, Professor, Dee and Nyirmachabelli, meaning "woman who lives alone in the forest", although, as far as I could see, she wasn't alone. She wasn't even the only woman. But she certainly was the only white woman around, except for Molly.

But I'm getting ahead of myself. I should be describing what happened out there in that field within the forest, where we heard what sounded like gunshots.

Augusta Karekezi

With each shot I buried my head deeper into the grass. I don't know how much time passed before the sound faded.

And then I heard yelling, and running. Or maybe the running came first. Either way, when I opened my eyes and lifted my head, and there was brave Albert crossing the open field, his rifle braced across his chest like a trained infantryman. (He looked very brave. I used to think of him as my father's pet weasel, but in the past week or so, Albert's face had assumed a more handsome, manly cast.)

From a distance I saw him addressing a white woman and three African men, each of whom carried a rifle. She was the tallest of them and seemed to be in charge. After a minute or two, Albert turned to face where we all lay in the high grass, and beckoned us to join him.

Mark Goldstone

All of us — Professor Dee, her three native helpers, me and my friends — stood in a rough semicircle facing the sprung snare and its sliced noose, dangling high and empty. I was so nervously excited, I dashed notes into a barely readable scrawl while Dee comforted the still-screeching infant ape.

Facing what I thought might be the makings of a good feature story, I imagined how its success would bring me fame and respect. I wanted Jim to be proud of me but I also hoped that a big, successful article would make me more independent of him: place me beyond certain aspects of his reach — which, admittedly, I both feared and desired.

Molly X

Dee's three men had fired three shots to scare off poachers. Though they hadn't actually spotted any poachers, they'd been drawn to the site by the unmistakable wails of Guseka, an infant gorilla, one of Pinky's brood. Pinky was a favorite of Dee's. Dee said she'd learned more about mothering and parenting from Pinky than from her own mother — or from any other human female, for that matter.

Dativa Natukunda

Thank you, God, for sparing Guseka's life. The "laughing imp" really is a little darling. I will have my baby baptized, in gratitude.

Watching the white woman cradle him in her loving arms, I wondered what had it been like for Guseka to be separated from his mother. These thoughts reminded me of Felix and of myself, since neither of us knew our mother's fate. But while I had long ago given up hope of ever meeting my mother, Felix had made it his life's mission to find his.

I didn't know my true mind on this subject. I wasn't sure how I really felt about it. Did I want Felix to find his mother? What if she didn't like me? What if she wanted Felix to stay in Rwanda, in her childhood village? What would I do? What would become of me?

Felix Kwizera

I didn't know my mother's fate but I knew a lot about poaching. Even in my village (where my father was killed like a dog), we knew bush-meat hunters set thousands of rope-and-branch snares in the forests where the mountain gorillas live. I'd seen such traps: a noose tied to a springy branch or bamboo stalk; a stick or rock to hold the noose to the ground, keeping the branch tense. The traps are meant for large game like antelope but sometimes catch apes. The adults are strong enough to free themselves but the little ones — so light — are hoisted high into the air, where they screech for help.

Molly X

The trail to Professor Dee's camp was steeply inclined, jagged and twisting. Vines like tripwires lay across the barely trodden path and small lizards leaped at our every step. I hate to admit it but I don't think I would have made it if the professor (tall, wiry and resolutely strong) hadn't ordered her three native associates to carry our rucksacks.

Except for Mark, we all remained quiet, focused on the trail. Somehow Mark had found the strength to ask Professor Dee a dozen questions about her mission in Uganda. I sensed he was already on to yet another journalistic scoop. Ironically, the more enthused he was to explore this new lead, the happier I was to be an introspective poet — no longer in competitive mode.

Mark Goldstone

Having studied journalism at Columbia University and The New School, I'd already met dozens of impressive scholars and newsworthy people but I'd never met anyone quite like Dee. She was amazing: expansive and exuberant about her research; completely unassuming about herself and her stunning accomplishments. I mean, all great people stand on the shoulders of giants but Dee was working with Dr. Louis Lazar, one of the world's most famous scientists and all he did was rearrange anthropological history by proving that mankind had begun in Africa. In fact, Dee was so grateful to her mentor, she told us that it was Dr. Lazar's connections and fundraising efforts that had led to the establishment of Dee's camp in the southwest corner of Uganda, in the northern part of the Virunga mountain range, where she was studying the gorilla.

The campsite was surprisingly — almost shockingly — comfortable. In addition to a latrine with a wooden seat and a generator for electricity, the professor had installed glass windows, curtains and charcoal stoves in three cabins, meant to accommodate herself, staff and guests.

So it was that we stayed with her for two restful and instructive days. We allowed ourselves that luxury because she had already promised us great assistance. Having heard our story and seen the map that I had drawn, she said she had a good idea where Felix's mother's village might be and promised that one of her men (who knew the region well) would use "Lily", her old, canvas-topped Land Rover, to take us as close as the regional roads and tracks would allow.

Lucky for us, driving in this part of Uganda was reasonably safe. Also, Moses, Professor Dee's driver, carried with him a copy of the permits that sanctioned Professor Dee's research. But we had to wait a day, because he was on a trip to the local village to restock the tinned produce that sustained Dee's group, and would not return until the next morning.

I remember that during our time in her camp, Professor Dee shared with us her personal history and professional highlights. We learned that after what she called some "false starts", she eventually received a PhD in zoology from Cambridge University and lectured for several years at Cornell, where her research on gorilla societies brought new data to our understanding of one of our closest evolutionary relatives.

On Day Two she started right in on the subject of poaching. "Poaching is a vile snake and I'm the mongoose to bite its neck and kill it." That got our attention. With all eyes on her, she began her speech. (I say *speech* because her words had the flair and formality of a public address.)

"Hunting for survival is good," she began. "It's part of the natural process. Almost all vertebrates prey on other living things for sustenance. But poaching — which is killing for profit — is a crime against nature and a tragedy for the whole environment."

She then described how gorilla-poaching had become popular and profitable — how park rangers were known to accept bribes, allowing poachers to set traps and kill the animals routinely in the national park where she worked. With tears in her eyes she described how poachers had killed Digit, her favorite gorilla and ten-year companion, hacking him to death while he tried to protect his children. She slowly described how she'd personally dug his grave and helped bury him, less than a mile from her present campsite.

She went on to explain how, spurred on by this act of barbarity on her doorstep, she had launched a public and perhaps obsessive crusade to protect gorillas and punish poachers, describing in detail how she destroyed traps and attacked those who had set them, sometimes beating them with a stick or even with her bare hands. Fleeing poachers always cursed her, she said, and many swore vengeance.

A MOTHER'S VILLAGE

Mark Goldstone

Moses, Professor Dee's driver, must have returned during the night or in the very early morning, for he alone awakened us and suggested we be ready to leave within thirty minutes. I asked if we might first say goodbye to Professor Dee, to thank her for her hospitality and sharing, but Moses said no, it was Sunday morning; she'd already left for her weekly visit to Digit's grave and could not be disturbed there. "She said to tell you how much she enjoyed your company and hopes you will visit again on your return journey."

It occurred to me that because the Rover was green, with

a khaki-colored canvas roof, it looked like an army vehicle. This was somehow fitting, as we were, I suppose, an expeditionary force — of lovers and friends, sons and daughters, each with different hopes of the village that loomed momentous, like a fabled destination.

Felix Kwizera

Before we left, Moses reviewed a copy of the map that Albert had created, based largely on details I'd recalled from what my mother had told me about her journey from her village.

Regarding my mother's village, I reiterated to Moses all I remembered about the huts and animal pens; the tomatoes that grew on trees and the bananas that grew close to the ground; the direction of the sunset, the fog that came from the southeast, and, of course, the mountains and volcano.

"What about the smell?" Moses asked me.

"What smell?"

"The smell from the fiery lake."

"I don't remember a fiery lake. I mean, I don't remember her mentioning a lake. There's a lake?"

"If I am thinking of the right village, then yes, there is a fiery lake. Though she might never have seen it."

"How is that possible? If there's a fiery lake, she would have known. No?"

"It is the fiery lake of the volcano, which you mentioned. Your mother seems to have known about the volcano but not about the lake, and therefore did not have it as a memory to pass on to you. You said her people are Twa. If my guess is right, they live on the fringes of the village but mostly in the forest. Mostly Hutu live in the village and they control access to the fiery lake. The volcano has erupted many times over the years. On one occasion, when I was working with Professor Dee in the Gorilla Forest, we felt a thunderous rumbling in the earth below our feet. Not long after, we saw a faint glow in the western sky and smelled a terrible stink, which the professor said was sulphur. Later we learned that the mountain had erupted and that lava had poured from its lake and through fissures in its flanks. Some of the villagers were killed. If you haven't heard from your mother for a while, maybe —"

Moses paused, ominously.

"No, no!" I yelled, guessing at his meaning. "My mother left many years before."

"But this particular volcano erupts frequently. In fact, it's one of the most active volcanoes in Africa, and its lava flows considerable distances. You said your mother returned to her home village, perhaps looking for help, after your father was killed."

I paused for a few seconds, then asked him directly, "Do you know for sure what you are saying?"

"Forgive me. I do not mean to alarm you. All I am saying is that if she was in the village at any time when the volcano erupted, she might not have survived. Of course, one cannot know."

This was an unwanted complication.

"It is possible," I said in a low voice, "but I don't think so. I don't think God would have taken her like that. It would not make sense. Anyway, we are going to her village and I expect to find her."

Moses nodded, then asked, "When did you last see her?"

"Please, I do not wish to discuss that."

Albert Bizimana

Weeks ago, Augusta had been an associate, a necessary political ally, someone to help me ingratiate myself into the circle of the Americans' influence so they might somehow assist my vague scheme of going to America to complete my medical studies before returning to Rwanda like a medaled hero, ready to assume an important position, perhaps right beside Dr. Karekezi — perhaps his eventual successor. At the time, I needed that scheme to thwart the doctor's plan to have me marry his silly daughter. All that now seemed moot.

My future now seemed so much simpler. I did not need the Americans; everything I needed was right in front of me. As I'd gotten to know Augusta — out from the shadow of her father and beyond the reach of her well-meaning mother — she seemed her own person: a lively, intelligent, soulful young woman, with humor and guile too. And now she seemed to like me — even admire me!

Mark Goldstone

It sometimes happens that a daring journalist discovers a potential story much greater (or, at least, more pressing) than the one he or she has been assigned. It happened to me.

Inspired by Professor Dee's experiences, I was suddenly inclined to put aside my writing about maimed Rwandan males, and the story of Felix's mother, to say nothing of the potential future deployment of the Rapid Deployment Force, to write a blockbuster exposé on the horrors of gorilla poaching. Excited by this new idea (which, like my other ideas, was sure to launch my nascent career), I'd shared it with Professor Dee, who said she'd be grateful for my "politically persuasive prose". With that, she gave me her local posting address, along with Dr. Lazar's home address, though she cautioned me to delay contacting him until she could send a letter of introduction on my behalf.

Before we parted, Professor Dee exhorted me to understand the inherent dangers of my proposed work. "Enraged gorillas are among the most terrifying of all animals but they are trusting friends compared to the soulless poachers who kill without a qualm."

TO THE VILLAGE

Albert Bizimana

Moses drove in a westerly direction on mostly narrow, pitted tracks. Whether from experience or intuition, he seemed to know which byways could accommodate the Land Rover and thereby lead us as close as possible to the great plain at foothills of Mount Nyamuragira. His ability to navigate to reminded me of Albert's.

I sat in the passenger's seat, feeling uncoupled at last from my daughter. I hoped she felt the same. With the windows down, Moses and I spoke freely, knowing our words would be snatched by the wind.

"What exactly did you tell Felix?" I asked.

Moses kept his eyes on the road. "I told him there are some farms in the area, with huts and pens, but not really any villages."

"Anything else?"

"I reminded him that the Twa sometimes live close to the Hutu in these far-flung places, staying in the forests nearby but coming out to trade when it suits them."

"According to Felix, his mother used the word *umudugudu* to describe her childhood home, so he expects a village."

"Yes, he told me that too. But from all he said and the map you provided, I think his mother described a small village-like gathering of small farms in the foothills of Nyamuragira."

"The one that erupts?"

"Yes."

"Are you sure it's the village Felix hopes to find?"

"No. But it adds up. I don't know any other notable settlement within ten kilometers."

Mark Goldstone

Eventually, an hour later, Moses rolled the Rover to a slow stop and cut the motor. No one said a word. Twisting to his right and speaking over his shoulder, he said, "This is what you might call the end of the line."

The landscape was a patchwork of striking contrasts. Close at hand were plains of hardened black rocks, stands of trees and pockets of savannah. In the distance, the terrain shifted into a green wall of tropical forest. The air was heavy with humidity, the scent of damp earth and the gritty tang of sulphur.

Molly X

Sensing a potential poem in the frisson between arrival and expectation, I took out my notebook and pen — Mark's notebook and pen — and prepared to make art. Already feeling like a poet of some experience, I surrendered myself to the sensory forces that surrounded me, named them, and then paired each with a poetic phrase that expressed my mood. I had found my métier.

Albert Bizimana

When I was a young teen, I heard about the mountain's eruptions. Years later, Dr. Karekezi told me how he and his wife, along with other medical professionals, had been brought to the area to perform whatever triage was possible.

Augusta Karekezi

Looking at Mount Nyamuragira far off, I remembered my mother saying how she went with my father many years before to join a makeshift medical team set up two kilometers from the outer reach of the lava flow, and how embarrassed she was when my father ordered her about as if she was a mere adjunct, forgetting that she was also his brilliant wife, who might have become an even more accomplished doctor than him, had she been allowed to pursue a full medical career.

My situation was very different. As part of a new generation, I had every opportunity to pursue a medical degree but chose not to. Instead, I imagined myself as an excellent nurse, married to Albert and loving his doctorly ambitions with unstinting admiration.

Felix Kwizera

I thought:

> My mother walked such fields. Such grasses brushed her legs. Such tree fruits were not beyond her reach. She was happy here.

I never asked why she married a man from another village. I assumed it had been arranged but I never sensed that she was unhappy about it. Only once (I remember it was a rainy day and we were indoors) did she speak of regret and then only to say that she wished she'd been able to give me a little brother or sister so I wouldn't be so lonely. I should have told her that I wasn't lonely at all but I didn't then have the words. I thought:

> When I see her, I will tell her, first thing, that she was a good mother and need not have worried about me.

Dativa Natukunda

Watching Felix stare at the distant mountain, I knew he was in that special place of his imagination: one foot in the past, one in the future; uncertain, astride the present, where I stood.

Albert Bizimana

As soon as we finished unloading our packed supplies, Moses left hurriedly. I assumed he wanted to get back before Professor Dee returned from her weekly vigil at Digit's gravesite.

We all stood together, staring at Mount Nyamuragira. In my right hand I held the handsome compass Dr. Karekezi had given me on my eighteenth birthday, saying, "I know you know your way around this region but the simple science of the compass can sometimes help when all else confounds."

On my left wrist I wore the handsome analog watch Dr. Karekezi had given me on my twenty-first birthday, saying to me, "Always wear an analog watch to use as a directional tool with your compass. Hold up the watch. Point the hour hand at the sun. The half-way point between the hour hand and the 12 o'clock mark gives you a true north-south line. And remember: the sun hangs out in the east before noon and in the west after noon."

Mark Goldstone

When we were all settled and ready to march (again, in single file) I mentally put my poaching exposé on hold so I could refocus on the story of Felix's search for his mother. This time, I positioned myself right behind Augusta, who followed Albert, so I could more easily pick his brain.

Molly X

Though I was walking behind Mark again, I wanted him to know that our order was coincidental and that I had no intention of always trailing in his shadow. None of this *Whither thou goest, I follow right behindest* crap for me. Hell, if Frankie thought I was doing that, she'd never forgive me. Hell, I'd never forgive myself. So I said something to Mark like, "I hope you have my back like I have yours," thinking he'd understand my meaning. I suppose he did because he responded over his shoulder, "Of course. Always." But his response was so quick, it sounded insincere, so I gave him the silent treatment. A minute later, Mark turned to me and said, "Do you want to go ahead of me?" Before I responded, I pictured him behind me, his sad eyes focused on my hopelessly crippled gait. "Nah," I said, real casual-like, "I'm good."

Felix Kwizera

We seemed to be making good time, which worried me. Were we going too fast? Should I be preparing myself? But how? And for what?

Then I thought: *If I slow down, I might delay bad news.* And then: *If I never arrive, I'll never be disappointed.*

Dativa Natukunda

As we approached Mount Nyamuragira, I felt a force guiding us. I thought it might be Fate or the spirit of Felix's mother. I wanted to share this feeling with Felix but I sensed that he was in no mood to talk. That disappointed me, because he seemed not to understand that this whole experience involved me as much as it did him.

A VILLAGE OF SECRETS

Mama

I saw a group of people coming up the path. They looked like campers or explorers. We get quite a few around here. More than you think, because of the fiery lava lake. But this time I saw no one in charge. No one in uniform, anyway, like the ones who usually take guided tours to the top of the mountain. Just one of two middle-aged men, out ahead, leading the others.

And then I saw him, a younger man, walking in a line with three younger women. I recognized him right away: my little Felix, all grown up. I hadn't expected to see him again, except in my nightmares. I didn't know what he remembered.

Felix Kwizera

In my earliest memories, I am in her lap, looking up at her smiling face while I suck from her nipple; first her right, then her left. This is my earliest happy memory.

Mama

He was a happy and beautiful child, and I took pride in him. It was an agony when we separated. Later, some years after I arrived here, I took comfort in learning that he'd been taken in by the Jesuits, who would educate him. I knew they might make a priest of him and send him away, in which case I'd never see him again. But there he was, right in front of me.

Dativa Natukunda

It was magical. It was everything I dreamed it would be: the group of us entering the village, Albert taking the lead, asking questions of every adult man and woman who might lead us to Felix's mother. And then, after passing a couple of small farms with simple huts and rickety animal pens, this woman, dressed in the simple bark cloth made by the Twa.

She and Felix locked eyes.

Immediately, I sensed that this was the woman we were meant to find, though the two looked nothing like each other.

While the rest of our group hung back to give Felix and the woman some private space, I stayed close, pressing my special status. But neither Felix nor the old woman seemed to notice me. Instead, they began an intimate conversation in the two-tone patter of our Twa Kinyarwanda....

All the while I stood there, mute and increasingly disappointed, and then angry that Felix had failed to introduce me. Finally, brazenly, I introduced myself, offering the woman my right hand, on which I wore my shell-and-bone engagement ring, which, I believed, she would surely recognize as her own.

Mama

Though I was surprised to see a wedding ring on her right hand, I made the connection and offered congratulations.

"Oh, you must be Felix's wife. I am pleased to meet you."

Dativa Natukunda

Felix did not clarify my status. He just stood there while she asked me several quick questions. Not once did she hug me or Felix or make any other emotional demonstration.

"Please follow me," she said suddenly, taking charge. "I am poor but I have my own hut and will make tea for you all."

Felix Kwizera

I was first in line following her. As we walked, quite a few of the local children and teens and even several young adults like myself, called out to her, happily, "Hello Mama!"

I was confused. I knew this woman: her eyes, her huge breasts, even her scent. But I did not remember her being friendly or social. And I did not recognize her voice.

Mama

When I was younger, I had no trouble getting pregnant. What I couldn't do was keep a child alive. To my great shame and disappointment, every child I had (I think there were fourteen) died in its first year. I was almost as unlucky with husbands: I lost four to violence or waywardness.

Over the years there were outbreaks of violence that resulted in farms being destroyed — burned and pillaged — so that food was sometimes scarce. Eruptions did damage too, raining down lava and ash. When new mothers don't eat, their breasts don't swell with milk, which means their babes go hungry — unless there are other means. I was well known for my fertility and my great breasts were like a pair of milk fountains. In fact, I had so much milk, I rented myself out as a wet nurse, which was a pale pride for losing all my own babes and husbands, but I was able to make enough money (or trade) to have my own hut and a few animals besides.

I don't know how many children I nursed in the past thirty years. Sometimes mothers got sick or killed and someone would bring me an unnamed baby to nurse, without offering payment. Didn't matter. Any babe laid in my lap was nursed like my own. I love the little ones ... had plenty milk ... and a terrible guilt.

Felix's mother was one who couldn't get her milk to flow, so she came to me. Felix was such a good boy, pretty and smart, so I didn't mind nursing him a year or two longer than was strictly necessary. But there's a drawback to such situations, as I'd get especially attached to such a child, especially a boy for some reason. Still, I did not foresee that Felix and me would one day have a special connection, so painful and tragic, I think it caused both our brains to go a little fuzzy over time.

Felix Kwizera

I was inside my home. My father was outside, talking to a group of boys. They looked rough. I thought I recognized one or two. The boys were asking my father for food. They said they were very hungry. He said he had no food to share. I don't remember other words. I remember only that the sun was white ... that my father's clothes were white ... that it was an immaculately hot, white day. Then, suddenly, sharp knives were drawn ... my father was screaming ... blood flying ... his white clothes spattered with blood. I remember looking away.

Mama

Her husband lay in the white sand but she did not go to him. Instead, she followed the retreating Hutu gang at an unsafe distance. I followed her at a safer distance, knowing young Felix was in his hut, possibly watching.

At some point, perhaps when Felix could no longer see his mother, I heard him scream, "Mama! Mama! come back!"

It was then that she fitfully picked up a handful of stones and threw them at the boys — with great ferocity but little accuracy; no more threatening than a light rain. When the boys laughed at her, she dropped to her knees in defeat; perhaps supplication, I could not tell. But the image so inflamed me, I picked up a larger stone, a jagged one and threw it with greater force and intent than all her errant throws. It found the skull of one of the retreating boys and cracked it loudly. He was dead before he fell. As I had already retreated, the others turned and leaped upon Felix's mama like hyenas, flashing their knives and bludgeons. All the while, I remained unseen behind the leaves and shadows of the curved roadside.

When the coast was clear, I removed her bloody body from the road and gave her a quick burial in a nearby copse, having already removed from her left hand her simple wedding ring of bone and shell. The work was exhausting and I was emotionally drained.

Somehow I fell asleep. When I awoke it was dark. Slowly, carefully, I made my way back to the village, listening out for dangers, but all was deathly quiet. The body of Felix's father was gone. The place where he'd fallen had been swept clean of blood.

Inside the hut, I found no trace of Felix. I slept in his hut that night. The next day I tried to find any of Felix's living relatives but failed. It was then I committed myself to going to Felix's mother's village, where I hoped to find someone who might come and help the young boy. Before I left, I set the simple wedding ring by Felix's bed.

I told the villagers where I was going. As I was leaving, they all called out to me, "Goodbye, Mama, Good luck!" None of them knew my name. They all knew me as *Mama* because I had mothered so many of their children. Only later did I realize that Felix, hearing the story of my departure, might think it was his mama who'd left to find help.

Because I'd been closer to Felix than most of my babes, I'd also been closer to his mother and we'd shared stories of our childhoods. Recalling details from her stories, I eventually found her village, a loose settlement in the foothills of Mount Nyamuragira and extending into the nearby forest.

When I arrived, I did not share my story with anyone. Strangers were careful of villagers; villagers were careful of strangers. Whenever a visitor or a refugee appeared, I was careful with my mouth. Though I always quietly and tactfully inquired, I never met anyone who knew Felix's mother or any of her relations.

With nowhere else to go, I decided to stay. Truthfully, I harbored some slight hope that Felix might someday find me, though that very thought made me shiver with shame.

Over time I made friends but no one ever asked my name. Eventually, I became the local wet nurse and once again everyone called me "Mama."

I am outgoing by nature. In my new home I talked whenever I could with travelers who came to see the mountain and its lava lake. Many of those travelers spoke English. From them I learned that English and Kinyarwanda share several words, including *mama*.

After serving tea in my hut, I walked outside alone with Felix. His questions were tentative. He remembered me but his memories were vague and confused.

I told him that his mother had trailed the murderous Hutu boys, taunting them and that they eventually turned on her. I told him that I'd watched from a safe distance and that when the Hutu boys were gone, I cleaned his mother and buried her and then went to find his living relatives in his mother's home village but without success.

Felix did not press me for more information. He seemed satisfied with what I told him. I sensed he was glad he'd made the journey — but was anxious to get away.

When it was time to part, we cried in each other's arms. For a moment I thought of telling him the whole truth and begging his forgiveness. But I am weak and kept it a secret.

"Goodbye my Felix."

"Goodbye," he said ... and then stalled.

"Say *Mama*," I said. "Say, 'Goodbye, Mama.'"

My poor bloody Rwanda. It wasn't only men with bloodstained hands. Women's bloodlust sullied their role as protectors and providers. The boy I killed with a rock had a mother and father. He likely would have married and had his own children. If not for my rash rage, Felix might have grown up with his mother.

For years I bore in silence the burden of my terrible crime. In my old age the shame became overwhelming. My cherished self-image as nourishing caregiver was framed with an ever-tightening black border. Embracing Felix, sharing each other's tears, was an incomplete absolution. But it was all I would get. It was all I deserved.

Dativa Natukunda

We'd all remained in the hut while Felix and Mama talked outside. When we no longer heard their voices, we left the hut but saw only Felix standing by a tree. He said Mama had been too emotional to say goodbye. He said she wanted us to know that she loved us all and that we should always help each other.

I wasn't sure what to say or how to act. I was furious that my special relationship to Felix had mattered so little; that he hadn't singled me out, hugged me, loved me or made me feel special in any way. If this was the climax of the trip, I should have stayed home — in New York!

I couldn't stand to be there a moment longer. Thank God

Albert decided that we should get going. Luckily, because we were all tired, Mama asked a man she knew well — someone visiting from another village and who had a blue Isuzu truck, now emptied of its cargo — if he would take us east as far as he could. The man happily agreed and we all scrambled into the open back of the truck, stuffing in all our gear and supplies.

While traveling back east, Mark piped up, insisting we drop in on Professor Dee. Albert agreed at once, probably thinking the professor might be useful to him someday. Augusta and Molly said they'd love to see the professor again; that she was a great role model. Felix said nothing. I didn't care one way or the other. I just wanted to leave.

The truck drove us for a couple hours, and left us near the Gorilla Mountain. After the driver departed with a friendly goodbye, we resumed our single-file march. As before, I brought up the rear. Dead last. I used to like that position, as I could see everyone else (especially Felix) without anyone seeing me. Now I was just glad to be out of sight. In fact, I half hoped some wild beast would carry me away and that my ravaged body wouldn't be found until the following morning. Maybe that would get Felix's attention!

Felix Kwizera

I had never felt so close to Dativa. I supposed she was matching her silence to mine, respecting my turmoil after my meeting with Mama. With no father or mother, and no hope of finding any other living relative, Dativa was all I had.

EMPTY CAMPSITE

Albert Bizimana

Though we were all in agreement that we should make the effort to see Professor Dee again, we were put off by the prospect of climbing that height, on barely traversable trails, many at slopes of forty degrees or more, and without the aid of Professor Dee's native assistants. Lucky for us, however, we had gone through much of our provisions, which had lightened our loads considerably. Mark, Felix and I offered to shoulder some of the weight from our partners' rucksacks. Augusta and Molly quickly agreed (divesting themselves of at least ten pounds each) but Dativa dramatically refused, which seemed to embarrass Felix. But he didn't argue. He didn't say much of anything. He'd been almost silent since leaving Mama's village and we'd tacitly agreed to let him be.

Mark Goldstone

I put aside my notes for a story about Felix's mother to refocus on the story of Professor Dee, the gorillas she was studying in that misty altitude, and the poachers that threatened to ruin it all. I then readied myself for the arduous journey to the professor's camp.

After hours of climbing nearly vertical mud tracks (fringed with stinging plants and hidden vines, small, long-tailed lizards leaping at our every step), we arrived at the camp, which sat in a grove of large mossy trees, beside a small stream. This time, more clearly prepared for the journalistic mission at hand, I methodically noted the three cabins, each made of corrugated metal painted green, lined with grass matting and separated from each other by more than thirty yards of wild shrubs and bushes.

Professor Dee's cabin was the middle one and the largest. Because the front door was ajar, we peeped in like a gaggle of schoolkids, fairly bellowing our arrival. When we heard no reply, we entered cautiously. Inside, I recalled the impressive stone mantelpiece and the large photo gallery of gorilla faces above it. We called out again but again there was no answer. Only the odd stillness found in an empty home in the great outdoors. Where was everyone?

It was then we heard an angry shout from outside. I nervously moved to the doorway and peeped out. Immediately I recognized Professor Dee's longtime cook and houseman, a middle-aged Rwandan named Kanyaragana, running toward us. But why did he have a rifle and where was everyone else?

Augusta Karekezi
I'd got to know Kanyaragana during the couple of days we'd spent at Professor Dee's camp, just days before. With my mother's strong encouragement, I'd become interested in Rwandan traditional dishes, so I'd approached him, introduced myself as a Rwandan and told him I'd be honored if he'd let me watch him work in the kitchen.

Molly X
Professor Dee's cook recognized us but didn't put down his rifle. Apparently, he didn't know who to trust. "Where is everyone?" I asked. Whatever English he owned just then failed him. All he could manage was a flex of his hand — the universal signal that indicated we should follow him.

Felix Kwizera
Nothing about it promised good. In fact, I sensed it was bad — very bad. It was death, I was sure and I was in no mood for more death. Hours before I'd relived the bloody murders of my parents (hacked to death by monsters not much older than me) and while the scenes continually replayed in my adult brain, I still did nothing to save them.

I looked to Dativa. As always, she stood alone at the back of our group, looking terribly nervous. I moved to her. I touched her arm and she looked at me with fright, which was what we were all feeling. I tugged her gently to move us away from the others, then whispered in her ear what Mama had told me.

She breathed heavily while I spoke, keeping her eyes away from mine.

"But that is my past," I said when I had finished. "You are my future. I love you and I will always keep you safe." She turned to look at me but her eyes had a startled vacancy and I could not read her expression.

Dativa Natukunda

How many shocks can a person withstand? How many times can a person be twirled round and round without falling down dizzy? At that moment, having just learned the true horrors of Felix's youth and then facing new terrors, I would have fallen to my knees in panic had Felix not held me in his strong arms.

SCENE OF THE CRIME

Mark Goldstone

Although we were expecting the worst, we were not prepared for the macabre scene that greeted us. In a small clearing, maybe a few hundred yards southeast of Professor Dee's campsite, Kanyaragana, the rifle-armed cook, led us to a gorilla graveyard: fourteen, red-lettered headstones of murdered gorillas, each noting the deceased's name and age. Apparently, some of the dead gorillas had been quite young; juveniles, even babies, with such names as Dot and Dash, Pokey and Sweetpea. The largest headstone by far belonged to Digit, Professor Dee's long-time companion. Beside his grave was a canvas-covered body, which (we assumed) was Professor Dee's.

The area was now an active crime scene. At least two dozen black police officers (embroidered epaulets; berets; holsters and boots) were taking notes, touching everything in sight with ungloved hands.

Because we had visited the professor just days before (we were her last known visitors), we were all considered persons of interest in the investigation.

One by one, we were pulled out of our group to be interviewed. While each of us was questioned, the rest of us were forced to sit twenty feet away and spaced apart. Talking was fiercely prohibited.

There was one main interviewer (a large, potbellied man in an ill-fitting uniform) who emphasized his captain-like authority by rapping his palm with a black-lacquered baton.

As no identity had yet been officially established, this captain continually referred to the inert body under the canvas tarp as "the victim."

He asked each of us the same questions, in the same order, following up every hesitant response with a series of rapid-fire questions in an increasingly louder voice.

After interviewing Dativa, the last of us, he spoke loudly and freely with his subordinates, which provided us some understanding of the gathered evidence and the direction of the early investigation:

Because of the blood trail in the grass, it was thought that the victim had been first assaulted about fifteen yards away.

The natural position of the body, as discovered, suggested that the victim had crawled with her last ounce of strength to die beside the grave marked *Digit*.

The attack was so swift, that, apart from a few bruises, there were almost no defensive wounds on the victim's body.

The victim's face was twice lacerated. The death blow appeared to be a single blow to the head, so hard it split the skull.

A bloodied panga knife (a thick machete with a slightly upward curve) was recovered at the scene. The handle was studded with small wooden insignia that mystified everyone.

The investigation was rigorous but not meticulous. No one took our fingerprints; no one examined our clothing or rucksacks. The bloodied panga knife was examined by each of the two-dozen officers, none of whom wore gloves.

No autopsy would be performed because there were no coroners in Rwanda to do the job. The one doctor who did appear on the scene, a young French physician from the hospital in Ruhengeri (who, coincidentally, had been a friend of Professor Dee's and had performed several autopsies on dead gorillas), examined the body but declined to perform an autopsy because he said the cause of death was obvious.

Rwandan police were not accustomed to investigating this kind of murder. Internecine tribal butchery was an everyday thing but a murder involving a westerner — especially a white woman — was extremely rare. Even if the victim hadn't been famous, the mere fact that she was white made her murder newsworthy.

We understood that the lead theory was that one or more poachers might have murdered the victim in retaliation for her zealous crusade against poaching. We learned from the free discussion of the captain and his subordinates that dozens if not hundreds of poachers had been hauled into the professor's camp for interrogation and punishment during the past decade. We heard rumors of torture. We heard that the professor had allegedly destroyed thousands of duiker snares, confiscated spears and pangas, set fire to a poacher's hut and even been charged with kidnaping a poacher's child. We overheard the police say that terrible threats had been made against the victim's life.

One of the police officers, not the captain, brought up the similar case of Joy Adamson in Kenya some years earlier. Adamson, a conservationist raised and educated in Vienna in the 1910s and 20s, had worked with big cats, and most notably lions. In 1980, at the age of sixty-nine, she was reported to have been mauled to death by a leopard at her camp. Months later it was determined that she had been stabbed repeatedly by an itinerant camp employee.

Hearing this, the police captain beamed as if he had just had a revelation. Despite the unlikelihood of our involvement, despite the fact that the six of us had marched willingly right into the middle of the investigation, the captain ordered fiercely, "Collect their passports. No one is leaving here until I'm satisfied they're innocent."

Felix Kwizera

When I was interrogated, I did my best to sound American. Same for Dativa. No one had yet asked to see our passports. The guards did not know we were Twa or even Rwandan. They did not know we spoke Kinyarwanda. They did not know we understood what they were saying to each other within our hearing. That's how we learned that their captain was thinking of making an example of us. Even if we were innocent (and he seemed to think we were), he thought we should still be officially accused and brought to trial. Even if we were acquitted — even if it were a forgone conclusion — the much-maligned police could say that they'd acted as minions of law and justice. Perhaps bring some respect back to Rwanda.

Mark Goldstone

The police captain continued discussing his plans aloud with his subordinates, which allowed us to understand his motives. In this way we learned the captain had decided it would be too complicated and potentially dangerous to bring all six of us down the precipitous trails in handcuffs, just to be installed in a municipal jail that was not equipped to accommodate six new prisoners, much less women and Americans. And so, until he could figure out how and where to move the prisoners, he commandeered all three of the nearby cabins, dismissing its occupants (Professor Dee's staff), whom, apparently, he had already interviewed and cleared. Next, he decided that two of us should be secured in each cabin. First, he decided not to allow any of the three males (Felix, Albert and myself) to stay together. Then he decided not to pair either of the white prisoners (Molly and myself) with one of the Blacks. As fate had it, he finally chose to pair Molly and me, Albert and Augusta, and Felix and Dativa.

Each cabin had a single front door. The front and back walls had one large window, divided into six small panes. Each long side wall had a pair of similar windows. The windows did not open. The cabins did not have a toilet but there was a nearby latrine.

There were two trails that led directly into and away from the camp. One led to the gorilla graveyard and ended there. The other led into the forest, aka gorilla country. The police captain assigned two officers to guard each cabin and two others to guard each of the two trails. His orders were fiercely announced and implemented; it was unthinkable that anyone would challenge them.

Before we were led into our respective cabins, the police finally checked our rucksacks. All our food and canteens were taken. All metals objects, including eating utensils, can openers, knives, etc., were also taken. Mercifully, we were allowed to keep our plastic pens and notebooks.

Molly X

I don't think any of us was particularly nervous. We expected Professor Dee's staff to vouch for us; our parents were important and influential. I'm not sure about Felix and Dativa but I think the rest us were vaguely thrilled by the sense of danger. Also, the guards were reasonably lenient. They allowed Mark and me (and presumably the two other couples) to mingle in our cabin during the day, though we were locked into separate rooms, promptly at nine each evening.

Oddly, the arrangement reminded me of my early days

with Mark: how my dad (his academic advisor) had invited him to our weird apartment on the edge of Greenwich Village to be a positive influence on my wayward ways; how we slowly became intimate after he moved in with us (taking over my mother's vacated old studio); how we began hanging out in Washington Square Park, which led us to meet Felix Kwizera (who I already knew as Philippe du Jour).

Cohabitating with Mark in my parents' apartment had been weirdly romantic but also confining. Eventually, it tested our compatibility. But it wasn't until we shared a locked cabin on a mountain famous for its gorillas, supervised by local police who suspected us of murder, that I seriously began to suspect that Mark and I were not meant to be permanently coupled.

Augusta Karekezi

What a stroke of luck to be locked up with Albert! How ironic that my father had spent years planning for such an eventuality. Looking back, I almost laughed at how I'd chafed at his plans. Of course I didn't know then what I believed now: that Albert would not be an imprisoning chain; that he'd be a loving partner and that we would grow happy together. I could not wait to tell my father this news. Since becoming a teenager I'd given him too little joy.

I also thought of my mother, full of Rwandan sayings and bits of wisdom. Occasionally she'd say, *Akebo kajya iwa mugarura*, which translates: *The basket goes where it will be returned*. I'm still not sure what that means but that's the saying I thought of when I found myself locked up together with Albert. His love was the basket and my heart was the place where it would return. Something like that.

Albert Bizimana

What a fool I was to abandon the medical tent when Dr. Karekezi returned to the hospital, effectively leaving me in charge. And for what? To help the Americans with their crazy ideas so they might return the favor in ways I hadn't even thought through?

Relinquishing my watch and compass to the police had been a crushing indignity; symbolic proof of my having failed to repay the great man who had wagered much on my growth and promise.

How could I ever face him again? He who had chosen me from among hundreds of school children; he who had rescued me from a hard life of farming and raising cattle; he who had tutored me so that I might unlock the gifts only his prescient eyes saw. How could I ever again face the man who had given me the warmth of his own home, the promise of an eminently successful career and the hope of a blessed life with his beautiful daughter?

Adding to my guilt, the breathing symbol of my shame was right beside me, apparently devoted to knowing me better and loving me more.

Molly X

This is maybe the biggest thing I've learned: everyone keeps secrets. The ones most fiercely protected are usually those we keep from ourselves and the people we love best.

My parents' home was so full of secrets, you could smell them coming up the stairs. Unable to admit they yearned for same-sex partners more than they cared for each other, they excreted a repressive stink that had been palpable — though not, apparently, to themselves.

Well, my new vocation helps me immensely with my own secrets. As a journalist, the sheer volume of any topic's relevant facts always unnerved me. But as a poet, I don't need to know everything. I don't need to tease the truth from conflicting sources and then have them corroborated. I just need to understand and express that which seems essentially true to me.

Thank God I had my notebooks and pens. And thank god Mark was more interested in his own writing than he was in me. Ironically, while our recent experiences had drawn us closer in some ways, they also revealed the many ways we were not a great fit. That was my take. I was certainly interested in Mark's point of view but I suspected he'd want to keep it a secret.

Mark Goldstone

Which story to write first: Rwandan hellscapes of maiming and mayhem? … Felix's soulful journey to find his mother? … Professor Dee's jungle murder?

So many writing possibilities left me paralyzed.

I looked to Molly for support but she was busy writing another poem. I respected her poetry, I suppose, but it didn't really speak to me.

Felix Kwizera

Even as a Twa, I grew up relatively happy … until the boys came to our village and savaged my parents while I watched helplessly … which led me to be taken in by the Jesuits, who hoped I'd be adopted (I wasn't) or that I'd become a priest (I had no interest) … and so shipped me to a church in New York City, hoping this would lead me to salvation (it didn't). Instead, it led me to Washington Square Park where I met Moby3, who introduced me to marijuana (which reminded me of sorghum), which connected me to Molly, who introduced me to Mark, all the while I was building a relationship with Dativa, with whom I eventually returned to Rwanda, along with Mark and Molly (what were the odds?). And now we four are imprisoned in a pair of cabins, which until very recently had belonged to one of the world's leading authorities on gorillas, before being massacred by a gang of bastards, perhaps related to the thugs that killed my parents. You can't make this shit up.

Dativa Natukunda

My anxiety lifted (somewhat) when he took me in his arms and told me he loved me and would protect me. But it wasn't enough. I needed to do my part. I needed him to know what I wanted and what I expected.

I wanted to marry soon … in New York … and I wanted to have a baby and a nice carriage, so I could stroll my own child about the city. But not in Washington Square Park. I was done with that terrible place, built on top of dead souls…. And I was done with that stupid cabin.

RAPID DEPLOYMENT

James Andersen

My breakfast meeting with Busty's admiral friend went very well. After discussing our shared appreciation of Busty's charms (which went on for at least twenty minutes), he asked about my career as a journalist and how I came to be in Rwanda. He seemed impressed by my somewhat inflated status at The New School and by my close association with Lawrence Schielding, managing editor of *The New York Times*, who was responsible for my assignment in Rwanda (and my wife's and my daughter's and my prized grad student's, all of which I explained).

I told him we each were covering different aspects of the ongoing violence without getting into how the Rwandan maimings tied into the sexual politics associated with the Men's Movement and the Women's Movement back home. The admiral told me he'd appreciate a heads-up when any member of my team published an article in *The Times*. (I did not correct his notion that we were a single team and that I was its sole leader.) He then asked (as if he'd just been hit by a thunderbolt) if I might be interested in writing an article about his personal charge: the region's still relatively new

Rapid Deployment Force. He said certain Democratic senators were squabbling about the Force's ever-increasing budget and he could use a prop from *The Times*. I told him I thought it would be a fascinating article and promised to run it by my managing editor. When we were about to separate, he mentioned (seemingly in passing) that he'd only visited New York twice — both times for business — and didn't really know the city at all. I told him (truthfully) that New York City history was a hobby of mine and it would be an honor to be his guide whenever he visited and had some spare time. He thanked me (somewhat profusely) and, in turn, mentioned that if I should ever need some special accommodation, Robert Edwin Spearman, Ambassador Extraordinary and Plenipotentiary to Rwanda, was a good friend of his. With that, we shook hands warmly and I left, headed back to my hotel.

Dr. Auguste Karekezi

It had been more than a week since I'd left our medical camp and returned to the hospital with my wife, who would have much preferred to remain behind with our daughter and the two other young women but would not have said so, at least, not to me directly. As my long-time professional and social adjunct, she well knew that her place was by my side. She also knew that it was important and instructive that our daughter see her mother in this role so that she (our daughter) would assume a similar role someday with Albert.

Because it had been more than a week and I'd had no communication from either of the camps, I decided to pay them a visit that very day. Remembering that it was Manzi's day off, I realized I'd have to drive alone, which I did not care to do. It then occurred to me that I could kill two birds with one stone (as the Americans liked to say) and so I invited my wife to come with me, knowing she would be pleased. I even let her drive.

We found the women's camp deserted. Not only was no one there, we had the distinct sense that no one had been there for quite some time. I was immediately awash with fear but my wife was giggling!

"Why are you laughing? What is wrong with you?"

"Really, Auguste, sometimes you are impossibly dim."

I suppose I gave her a stupid stare because she put her hands on her hips and shook her head impatiently.

"Do you even remember what it was like before we married?"

"You don't think — "

"What else? Three young women … separated from their three young men!"

Just to make sure, we visited the nearby bungalow, only a kilometer or so away, where the women housed. The place was empty. Again, it looked like it hadn't been used for days.

Despite my wife's positive outlook, we drove to the men's camp in an anxious mood. At least, that's how I felt.

Once more, we went first to the medical tent. No one was there. Everything was still and in place, except for two white, unaddressed envelopes on the writing desk. Because I hesitated, Debora picked up one and opened it (it wasn't sealed), removing a single page of folded paper. "It's addressed to you," she said, handing it to me. "Just read it," I said roughly, because I was nervous and wanted her to be complicit in what I expected would be terrible news. It was from James. She read it quickly because she too was nervous.

To Auguste and all else, I am using this downtime in our mission to make a trip to Mombasa, Kenya, to see an old friend, who's staying at a hotel near the military base. Do not worry, I am traveling very safely. I should be back in a week or so. If I am delayed, I will leave a message at the hospital. Warm regards to all! — James

Though we were happy to know that James was well, we still had many questions. Debora handed me the second letter. This one was longer, also handwritten (I recognized the handwriting as Albert's) and again addressed to me, though more formally. I read,

Dr. Karekezi, I respectfully inform you that we have left these premises to make a house call, so to speak. A young boy, poor, from a somewhat distant village, showed up at our tent nearly in tears. It seems there was a cart accident in a forest near his village involving four or five people, including his parents. Someone who knew of our medical camp directed the boy to come here. According to the boy, the injuries seemed serious and so we moved quickly. Luckily, Manzi happened to come by on his weekly supply run; so we had him go to the girls' camp, explain the situation to Augusta, Molly and Dativa, ask for their help, help them pack and then bring them here. They have now arrived and we are ready to proceed on foot, the young boy leading the way.

We really don't think it will take much more than a week, provided we can get to the accident site within two days or so. If there is a way to contact you to share more specifics, we will do all we can. Rest assured, we have packed wisely and taken every reasonable precaution.

Francine Rose

I was productive with my time in Kigali but terribly lonely. It seemed like all my closest support systems had shut down: Molly, Jim, Larry, Gloria ... no one had contacted me in almost two weeks. So damn aggravating! I mean, how much can a girl give? I'd given all I could as wife, mother, friend and professional and still I was essentially alone.

Well, at least I looked great, I thought to myself.

I needed my looks to boost my flagging confidence. I mean, I was no kid but *forty* was the new *thirty*, so I was in my prime ... so I thought ... but I may have miscalculated. Thing is, other than from Gloria, I hadn't received the kind of attention I'd expected as a newly single, good-looking woman. Perhaps I hadn't accounted for the increased competition: the zillion other recently liberated forty-year-old women looking to turn back Mother Time. I certainly hadn't counted on Gloria throwing me out of her bed for a younger woman. How could she! What a slap in the face! If women treat each other so carelessly, we're no better than men! Then it struck me that there were articles to be written on the subject. Immediately, I saw myself leading the way, bravely sharing my hard-won, personal experiences.

Albert Bizimana

During an opportune moment (right before we were locked in our cabins, when the guards were not watching us so closely) I approached the French doctor from Ruhengeri (the one who had known Professor Dee and who had performed the autopsies on her gorillas) and told him that I was a medical student, almost ready for my residency and that I worked under Dr. Auguste Karekezi, head of the Butaro District Hospital. I asked for his card, one professional to another and gave him mine. I then asked for a favor: If another week went by and he hadn't heard personally from me, could he please call Dr. Karekezi at the hospital and tell him that I was being held here, along with my five friends — one of whom was *his daughter*. I reminded him that Dr. Karekezi was one of Rwanda's most eminent physicians and would look upon his assistance as a great favor.

Molly X

Jim had left a note explaining that he was going to use our downtime (the temporary halt of refugees to our medical camps) to visit a friend at the United States military base in Mombasa, Kenya. He did not mention the name of the friend, how he would travel there or how long he would be gone but I had a vague sense (based on nothing in particular) that he'd gone to see one of his famously outed friends, perhaps one of the Flaming Faggots from his Village haunts. It also occurred to me that he might be visiting Busty Evans (based on nothing more than the fact that I'd discovered her file in the dark recesses of his closet, right below his cache of homo porn).

In any case, I had to get in touch with my dad soon, before we were all sent somewhere to be formally charged. But how to reach him ... or get a message to him? My mind was a blank but it finally occurred to me: *Think like a journalist.* And I came up with this: *If it's true that he's visiting a friend at the United States military base in Mombasa, what good hotels are closest to the base?*

Before the French doctor left us, the police captain asked him to examine all six of us detainees, to prove we were all in good health and being properly treated. When he examined me, he insisted the guards stand back and turn away their prurient eyes. This gave me the chance to ask the doctor to call whatever hotels were near the American base in Mombasa until he found my father and explained to him that he had to get us out of this mess as soon as possible. The doctor confided that he'd already had a request from Albert to contact a Dr. Karekezi at his hospital but would also call the hotels in Mombasa in the hope of contacting my father.

The French doctor was very handsome and I wondered how he felt about a younger woman with a limp.

Debora Karekezi

Albert's well-written letter would have alleviated some of our worry if we had believed a word of it but we didn't. Sorry, but it seemed too coincidental that their rescue mission arose just when all the adults had left the room, so to speak. Albert could have told Manzi to get word to us at the hospital, so we could decide how to address the rescue situation. Of course Albert knew all that. So he must have had some other reason for wanting to leave the camp — both camps — without our knowledge and oversight.

Dr. Auguste Karekezi

Hearing from the French doctor that my daughter, Albert and the four others were detained in some mountain cabins on suspicion of murder was so shocking I was unable to process the idea for a full minute. Meanwhile the French fellow (I forget his name) continued to speak. Thank goodness Debora, who had been listening in, kept a cooler head.

Debora Karekezi

The French doctor suggested we move quickly. He'd overheard the police captain say that he wanted to get all six detainees off the mountain and into a courtroom where they would be officially arraigned. Once they were arraigned, the long legal process could not be interrupted and he (the police captain) could bask in the limelight of what promised to be a highly publicized affair.

Dr. Auguste Karekezi

We knew where Augusta and Albert and all the rest were being held but I had no good idea how to proceed. I was a relatively eminent physician with some middling national connections but the current government was crazily fractured with infighting between Hutu and Tutsi representatives and I didn't know where to turn. I needed an outsider's voice and leverage. Of course, I thought of James. "You still have that letter from James?" I asked my wife. "Yes? Please, let me see it."

Having reread the letter quickly, I called the hospital's telephone operator and asked her for the phone numbers of the hotels nearest the American military base in Mombasa,

Kenya. Through some miracle of fortune, we soon found the hotel where James was registered and I left an urgent message. Less than an hour later I was speaking with him. His reaction surprised me. Rather than expressing outrage against the Rwandan police, he was furious with his daughter and prized student for their demonstrated lack of respect and professionalism.

I'd never heard him so angry. You would have thought Molly and Mark had committed high treason. I did what I could to redirect the force of his response into something positive: "We really must get them released from police custody. Anything can happen if they remain there a long time." We argued awhile. "But you don't want to take chances," I said. "Besides, you don't want them to have records; their passports could be flagged and restricted for years." Jim finally agreed, saying he'd do all he could to prevent the ruin of their young careers.

James Andersen

With so much at stake I stupidly wasted precious time screaming at invisible Molly: *Why didn't you go directly to the drug store? ... Why'd you get on the motorcycle with someone you didn't know? ... Why did you continue to buy drugs at the park?*

And Mark: *She wrapped you around her little finger! I trusted you!*

And even Frankie: *Could you have been more permissive? Did you ever say no to her?*

Finally, I got to work. Though I felt like a fool, pressing for such a big favor almost as soon as it had been offered, I didn't see that I had any choice.

Busty Evans

I loved to dance for the sake of dance and that's the truth. But I also liked the special power it gave me when I was on a big stage facing a hundred or more desperate men, all practically begging me to fulfil their desires. No other part of my life gave me any such power.

Now, I happened to be in my admiral friend's office when he got the phone call from my own dear friend, James Andersen. I was there because we were making plans for my departure home. Me and the other girls had stayed a full three weeks and it was time we were off.

I listened to the conversation, trying hard to piece together what special situation involving James and his family might require the admiral's assistance. When the admiral thought he had the whole story just right, he told James that I had just walked into his office for my own scheduled appointment and that he would make some phone calls to see what he could do for him. As soon as he ended the call with James, I heard my admiral friend dial a long number, wait awhile and then address another man as *ambassador*. They seemed to be brainstorming the solution to a dicey problem. I think the admiral was trying to butter him up, because he used flattering words like *extraordinary* and *plenty potential*. I felt honored to be listening. The admiral and ambassador talked in a way that suggested rare power — the power some men have to get things done on life's really big stages.

James Andersen

In retrospect, the situation took a lot of finesse. Diplomatic relations between Rwanda and the US had changed greatly from the sixties to the nineties, morphing from ideological influencing to market liberalization to neglect and strategic disengagement. In April, 1994, the United States had evacuated its embassy personnel and citizens, effectively abandoning direct diplomatic influence.

But while the American ambassador no longer had plenipotentiary powers, he was still able — within the broader diplomatic network — to rely on personal connections and prior relationships to call in the odd favor from regional actors, international organizations or even other ambassadors, such as the one then representing neighboring Uganda.

Mark Goldstone

As I would learn, it was not a simple mission. Rwandan government officials had no radio contact with their police forces at such a high altitude. There were no other nearby police that could be sent to the area in a timely fashion, much less ordered to scale those heights, lacking maps and familiarity.

Also Rwanda had no helicopters or special forces to extract the prisoners into swift safety. Kenya could not fly a helicopter under its own colors and insignia across Tanzanian airspace and expect to land safely in Rwanda. Same for American aircraft. However (and very luckily), two helicopters belonging to the International Red Cross (which had been operating in the Iran-Iraq theater since 1980, when open hostilities erupted between those two nations) had been damaged a month earlier, seriously curtailing their humanitarian efforts. Self-serving efforts on behalf of the United States resulted in both helicopters being transferred to an American carrier and taken to the American naval base in Mombasa for repairs.

Busty Evans

According to my admiral friend, after both helicopters had been repaired and were ready to be returned to the International Red Cross, he and his ambassador friend worked out a deal to test flight one of the two repaired helicopters by having it fly to a site in southwestern Uganda (near the Rwandan border), land on a smallish clearing in the Mgahinga Gorilla National Park, extract four Americans and two Rwandan nationals, then fly them all to Kigali Airport, before returning to the American base in Mombasa.

"What happens then?" I asked my admiral friend.

"The two Americans and the two nationalized Americans from Rwanda will meet with James and his wife Francine at the Kigali Airport, where they'll all board a plane to Nairobi. Later that day, they'll fly to Brussels and from there catch a flight to New York City."

I sat numbly silent and vaguely disappointed.

"I was thinking," said my admiral friend with a smile, "since we were planning your own trip home, would you like to join your friend James and his family?"

Until James told me (many years earlier), I'd had no idea that he'd been to so many of my shows, driving as far north as Toronto and as far west as Ohio, and arriving at the Folly Burlesk in Canton in a red tin can, which he'd bought with his summer camp salary and tips. He certainly did a lot of driving; I guess you could say he was a driven young man.

I remember our first interview in my dressing room. He was adorably shy ... really, just a kid, trying so hard to be professional in his new slacks, button-down shirt — the pocket full of pens — and with a fresh notebook on his lap, open to a blank first page.

I remember being impressed with his questions because he took himself so seriously and because they were all so very proper — nothing naughty at all. In fact, he seemed particularly taken with the fact that I'd been born and raised into the Mennonite tradition. He asked if I still went to church. I said I made a point of going three times a year: Christmas, Easter and on my birthday. I asked if he went.

"Never been to a service," he said.

"Never been inside a church?"

"Oh, I've visited many," he said. "But just to look. I love the statues, candles, stained glass ... in fact, I went to college in New York near the Cathedral of St. John the Divine.

Magnificent. I used to go there just to think or read … and for the great organ recitals."

"Interesting."

Just then I thought of those dying burlesk theaters on Manhattan's West Forty-Second Street, which brought to mind the summer bungalow colonies and hotels in the Catskills. "You Jewish?" I didn't mean to be blunt. It just came out that way.

He said no, but his best friend was. He didn't elaborate, so I changed the subject.

"You have a girlfriend?" I asked.

Again he said no, but a little too quickly.

"No one you like especially?"

"I sort of like my friend Larry."

For the time being, I let that go. While I thought of what to say next, he asked me if I was married … or had a boyfriend … or girlfriend.

I said, "Someday I'd like to marry a special man who could accept my unusual life."

James and I simply clicked. In our long acquaintance, I shared with him more secrets than with anyone else, 'cept my husband Bobby and Rose LaRose, God rest her sweet soul.

Lawrence Schielding

At exactly 6:00 a.m. I was awakened by the ringing of my bedside phone. Startled, I reached for it frantically, like a drowning man.

"Hello?"

"Larry? It's me, Jim."

My mind cleared quickly. I thought (darkly hopeful): *Frankie's dead, killed by a crazed Hutu … mauled by a lion … swallowed by a croc.*

"You okay?" I asked.

"I'm fine. We're all fine."

"Francine?"

"All okay."

My hope deflated. "Then why call me so goddamn early?"

"I need your help."

Good. I liked helping him. Always have. (When I was a puny kid, he was my brawny protector. Without calling attention to himself, he always had my back. I think my parents understood this about our relationship, which is why they invited James to spend summers with us in the Jewish Catskills.)

Jim explained, "I need immediate authorization and payment for six adults flying from Kigali to Nairobi, Nairobi to Brussels, and Brussels to New York."

"What the hell?"

"Trust me. For now, just know that we're all okay."

"What about the work?"

"All covered. We have a ton of great copy for a series of articles about bloody Rwanda ... and — "

"And?"

"And a major scoop for the *Times*. You know that famous lady scientist living with the gorillas in Uganda?"

"Jane Goodall?"

"No. That's the chimp lady. The other one. The gorilla one. I just forgot her name."

"I know who you mean."

"Well, she's dead. Murdered, they say. Not officially announced yet. Molly and Mark were arrested as suspects."

"What!"

"They didn't do it — but they were there. And they were arrested, along with Felix and Dativa. But we got them out."

"Who's *we*?"

"The American Navy and the International Red Cross."

Silence.

"We had to sneak them out. A covert kind of thing, using Rapid Deployment assets and a helicopter."

Silence.

"It's okay. The Ambassador is smoothing it all out."

Silence.

"Just get your office to buy the tickets and have them ready for us at the airport. Also, please have your contacts make sure that all our visas are cleared."

Silence.

"As soon as I get to New York, I'll grab some sleep and then come by the office to see you. Have to run. Thanks!"

Pause, then: "Okay. Speak soon."

It took me a while to compose myself. I thought: *I guess they're both still alive.*

After all those years, I still harbored the secret hope of someday living with one or the other.

Francine Rose

When I returned to the hotel after another day of sightseeing and research, the concierge handed me a written message.

> We're all okay. But we have to leave immediately. All of us. Go straight to Kigali Airport. I'll be there with Mark and Molly, Felix and Dativa.
> —Jim

He couldn't take ten more seconds to tell me what's going on? Just like him to keep me in the dark. What a controlling bastard!

TERMINAL

Sondra Lou Churcher

I'd already said goodbye to the other dancers. I'd tried hard to be strong but we cried lots. My career was over and everyone knew it. We swore to keep in touch but we mostly knew we'd never see each other again. I was okay with that. It was time to move on. My mind and body were fifty-something, just like my famous breasts.

I was sad but not unhappy. I knew I'd look back on my career with mostly love and gratitude. For sure, it had saved me from a joyless life as a Mennonite spinster. (I was never going to marry a Mennonite man and raise a child in that joyless faith.) I praise God for making me a dancer and giving me a way out.

It wasn't no straight-and-narrow path but I did the best I could and now, looking back, I would not have done anything different. After all, I made some great friends, like my dear mentor Rose LaRose, my longtime booking agent Dave Cohn and, of course, my best dancing buddies, Storm and Chesty. Of course I'll always cherish my many admirers (especially those men in power who made me feel good about myself) and I'll always have a special sweet spot for Jim, that nice young man who saw me perform when he was still a boy and who later followed me in his red jalopy from town to town, whenever his studies permitted. I still have his letters and a copy of every article and interview he ever wrote about me.

I'd tried to reach him before we were all meant to gather for the same departing flight but it hadn't work out. I was anxious to meet his family. I just hoped the surprise wouldn't kill him.

James Andersen

A notable critic began his review of a certain Broadway comedy with these words: "Friends, family, lovers all have their place in a man's life ... but never in the same room at the same time." Standing beside my daughter Molly, I recalled that discomforting truth as I watched Sondra's fast approach: a tiny threat ... a growing menace ... a looming catastrophe.

Two things saved me; two things I'd learned through recent, hard-won experience. One: No one was actually threatening me. Two: Those I loved best were least likely to hurt me.

And so, knowing that fast-approaching Sondra had always been honest, uncomplicated and unfailingly nice, I expected more of the same — and was rewarded for my faith. After greeting me with a warm handshake and a quick hug, she turned and addressed our group: "Hello everyone. I'm Sondra Lou Churcher, a recently retired burlesk dancer. James has seen many of my shows and interviewed me many times. Over the years we've become friends."

Grateful (and relieved) for her tact, I was more determined than ever to live the rest of my life as my most authentic self. I just had to get through the next two flights and survive my reconnection with Francine.

Francine Rose

The airport was not far but there was a lot of traffic, which gave me plenty time to consider what my life might be like when I returned home.

I imagined getting into a cab at Kennedy Airport, then realizing I had no address to tell the driver. (I'd given up my apartment on Twelfth Street and been tossed from Gloria's townhouse on Minetta Street.) For the first time in my life, I was homeless. I couldn't afford to stay in a hotel, even a cheap one, for more than a few nights. I didn't have any friends close enough to ask. I supposed I'd have to discuss my situation with Jim but the idea of talking to him while he occupied the high ground, turned my stomach.

I took a deep breath. I knew not to take my reversals personally but I also knew the time had come to save myself. No one was responsible for me. And I wasn't responsible for anyone else — now that Molly was an adult. Cold and cruel but that's life.

Those had been my thoughts on arriving at Kigali Airport. Inside the main terminal I recognized Auguste and Debora in the mid-distance, wearing their hospital whites; Albert and Augusta beside them, holding hands. A few feet away were two other couples: Felix and Dativa; Molly and Mark. It seemed everyone had a partner but me.

Off to the side, I saw James and a woman I didn't at first recognize: upper-middle-aged; average height; top-heavy; dyed black hair, teased high. James saw me approaching and waved. The other woman turned quickly to see me, her unmistakable chest heaving like a pitched bale.

With false confidence I approached quickly but right before I reached the point of conversational hailing, I was intercepted by Molly.

"Mom, how are you!" While everyone in our circle watched, she squeezed me tight, kissed my cheek, laid her head on my shoulder.

Over my other shoulder, Mark and I locked eyes. In a double flash I saw him as Jim's prey and Molly's pal. Though unremarkable looking, I swear I could have picked him out in a crowd.

By then I also recognized the woman standing beside Jim. I knew who she was because I knew Jim's secret. At some point (many years ago, before Molly was born), Jim was still doing his best to keep our marriage a triangular thing: me, men (primarily Larry) and Busty (though I wasn't then aware of her existence and wouldn't learn her real name until years later). To my knowledge, Jim never had sex with Busty. His relationship with her was much deeper and stranger. I'm pretty sure he never explored those depths to discover his own true self. At his core he's a cowardly S.O.B.

As I grew closer to Larry as a friend (I don't think either of us really wanted more than that), we began incrementally sharing our vague same-sex affinities, solidifying in our respective minds and hearts just how natural, even inveterate, those feelings were. Eventually, we both were able to name it and, thus, to own it.

During this time Larry also shared with me Jim's history with Busty Evans, beginning with an adorable recounting of himself and Jim as innocent young teens, hiding in the midnight shadows outside a Catskills casino, snatching glimpses of a super-mammaried stripper through a partially covered window. Ironically (and comically), Larry and I both confessed to being jealous of Busty's ability to inspire Jim in ways neither of us could.

Some years later, I discovered a folder of Busty Evans photos secreted in the back shadows of Jim's bedroom closet. (I wasn't snooping. I'd actually been spring-cleaning, knowing Jim would never do it himself.) A year or two later (when I'd next felt the need to sweep and clean), I discovered a second folder, a collection of homo porn. I told Larry about it, just as I had with the Busty Evans folder. Though he claimed never to have seen either folder, he said there were no pictures of himself or Jim in the collection or of anyone else Jim knew personally. He insisted that all the homo pictures were projections of Jim's fantasy life, though I don't know how he could have been so sure.

It was years into our marriage before I openly accused Jim of dishonest homosexuality. Before we married, we'd discussed our sexuality at length and decided that we were straight but open to other possibilities. We were both lying. We just didn't know it. For a long while we each kept our gayness a secret from ourselves, each other and the public. Thing is, we grew older, made strides, achieved clarities — but on different wavelengths and timetables. That makes sense. We're not the same person. (Marriage doesn't dissolve or even soften individuality. At least, it shouldn't.) But when I began writing about women's issues and started reevaluating my own sexuality (especially as a public persona), I expected Jim to do the same. I now see that was unfair. He wasn't ready.

Meanwhile, my housewifery complaints against his lazy selfishness became more strident, even threatening. Our raging arguments, which for years seemed to spiral from Molly's accident, now seemed to rise from an even deeper well of emotional complaint. My best weapon (at least, my sharpest and cruelest) was screaming out his failure to announce himself as gay, calling him *coward* and *fraud*. I said the denial of his urges was a denial of his truest self. I accused him of committing existential suicide. To his credit (at least, in his defense), he declared that his unfinished magnum opus *(Ecce Homo / The Beholding)* would one day be a public and spirited avowal of his most personal beliefs. He asked me to respect the timing of his life choices. This seemed reasonable, until it didn't. With the passing of the years, I increasingly suspected that his work in progress had permanently stalled (if it had ever actually existed, which, for me, was a real thing, as I'd never seen any evidence that he was working on the book).

From my point of view, the coup de grâce to our marriage was my falling in lust with Gloria Applebaum. Her welcoming business offer, her welcoming bed, her welcoming respect for all aspects of me was what drove me from Twelfth Street to Minetta Street.

Sondra Lou Churcher

Of course I knew it was Jim's wife, Francine Rose, who was marching toward us in the terminal. I'd been expecting her. Besides, I'd seen pictures of her through the years.

Though curious to meet her, I wasn't sure how I felt about her. Jim had never spoken of her in terms of love. I knew he respected and admired her but I'd never sensed that he loved her. I also never understood why he liked me so much. Through the years we'd made some joking guesses but we never really got down to the heart of the matter.

Molly X

Before boarding, I wondered: *Who should I sit with?* If I sat alone with Mark, then Dad, Mom and Sondra would likely sit together in a three-person row and I couldn't imagine any combination of that threesome remaining happily composed.

As it turned out, Frankie decided the situation by taking Sondra's arm as we readied to board. "I've heard so much about you," I heard my mother say. "Why don't see we sit together and chat?"

Mark Goldstone

Truth is, only one seating option appealed to me. I didn't want to sit with Molly and hear her blather on about her silly poetry. I didn't want to sit with Jim and risk hearing his huddled confidences. (Having been separated for nearly two weeks, I appreciated the professional distance that had been reestablished between us — and wanted to keep it that way.)

Lucky me, as soon as Francine had grabbed Sondra's arm, Jim approached Molly and said, "Come here, sweetie, let's sit together and catch up." Given that Felix and Dativa were joined at the hip, that left me as the outlier. Which suited me just fine. I had a ream of notes to review and working alone is what I do best.

James Andersen

I assumed Frankie had strong-armed Sondra with the intention of acquiring information that could compromise my integrity. I think she lived for such opportunities. I mean, she hadn't even greeted me. Not even a nod in my direction. She might even have blown past Molly if her only child hadn't thrown herself into her arms for an infusion of maternal sustenance.

Meanwhile, I reached out to Molly, hoping her love and companionship would shield me from Frankie's expected mockery. I also wanted to let her know that Mark had decided to move back with his parents in order to save money and that I thought it was a great idea. Molly surprised me by saying that she wanted to get a job so she could share an apartment with some girlfriends while she continued her studies. She never mentioned Mark.

Francine Rose

I'd read all of Jim's interviews with Busty that were collected in the folder that contained her photos. They weren't bad. But, not surprising, they all suffered from the limitations of Jim's male point of view. Sondra Lou Churcher deserved better. After an hour together, I asked if she'd let me interview her for a national women's magazine. She hemmed and hawed. She said she was ready to leave that life behind and return to her husband ... her gardening ... and her church bingo. I asked if she'd ever been interviewed by another woman and she said no. I suggested that she owed it to herself ... and to all her dancer friends ... and to all the women who might be interested in her story, to do one final interview — with another woman.

Molly X

During those three seconds my head rested on her shoulder, Mom asked how I was doing in the same voice she might have asked, Did you have a nice breakfast? ... Maybe she didn't know that international commandos had just snatched me from a mountain cabin, where I'd been in police custody, awaiting trial for the murder of the world's leading gorilla scientist — a woman, no less.

Had she asked me a single, sincere question, I would have answered her honestly. Had she asked me to sit with her, I would have shared all. I'm not sure why she didn't. Maybe she thought I preferred to sit with Mark. (She still hadn't met him, having paid no attention to him whatsoever before marching off with Sondra. But at that point I thought: *Just as well.*)

For a split second I thought she might sit with Dad, which would have been nice, but she avoided him like the Dengue Fever.

Instead, she headed straight for the stripper lady. Knowing Mom as I did, I figured she'd explore any opportunity to torture Dad. Or maybe she thought the stripper lady might be a good subject for another feminist article.

While the seating arrangements were being decided, Mark moved off by himself, which didn't surprise me as we'd been emotionally separating for a while.

As it turned out, I paired with my dad, which was fine with me.

James Andersen

Sitting with my beautiful Molly, I let go my worries about what Frankie might be getting out of Sondra. I realized I couldn't be hurt if I didn't care — and I no longer did. I was a snake in the process of sloughing off its old skin.

I listened to Molly sing of her youthful independence and her new calling: poetry. I reminded her that Calliope — one of the nine sister goddesses known as the Muses — was the patron saint of epic poetry. She liked that.

She asked me about my writing. I began speaking about all the articles I would be writing for Larry and *The Times* but she said, "No, not that. Your personal writing." I was so touched that she remembered. Along with Larry and Frankie, she was the only other person on planet Earth who knew about my magnum opus: *Ecce Homo / The Beholding.* I told her a little about it for the first time, finally coming clean about my sexual orientation. She just nodded and listened, as if she'd known all along. Then she offered these words of encouragement: "I think you should tell The New School. I mean, it bills itself as a bastion of progressivism, so

I bet they'd support your outing. Besides, it might drive even more students to your classes. I'm sure they'd like that."

The idea of announcing my work ahead of its publication inspired me, though I was concerned what Larry would think. People knew we were life-long friends and might reasonably suppose that he were also gay. I didn't want to do anything that might upset him. I couldn't afford to do anything that might upset him. Still, I had to live my life honestly and he should appreciate that as much as anyone. Then it occurred to me that my self-serving announcement would pressure Larry the way Frankie had pressured me.

I imagined Frankie learning of my intention and saying, "It's about time!" Which made me think that my public declaration would largely defang her anger towards me. Hell, with Molly grown and seemingly focused on a new career of teaching and writing poetry, Frankie and I might be running out of things to fight about. With that, it occurred to me that we might actually be able to live together again. With Mark gone and Molly looking for her own place, the huge apartment felt ridiculously spacious for a single occupant. Sharing the cost would be a boon for us both.

Francine Rose

Professionally, I felt secure. Larry loved the half-dozen articles I'd written about raped and maimed Rwandan females: how they coped and (in a couple of cases) even triumphed. Gloria loved almost all my essay ideas that had been the result of my research in Kigali. She also loved my proposal for an essay about the murdered gorilla scientist (who'd battled outlaws and poachers to preserve her brave scientific inquiry) and my proposal to write about the famed aging dancer whose retirement embodied the dying breath of American burlesque — and the end of that particular sexist voyeurism.

Despite these solid professional prospects, I felt

displaced. I needed a place to live. The only thing I regretted about my trip to Rwanda was that my absence had left me vulnerable to the usurping advances of an even more beautiful, academically credentialed, internationally respected feminist, who swaggered about like Zorro's sister; someone with a rapier mind and a rapier wit; someone younger, faster, better — every older woman's replacement nightmare.

I hadn't been there to defend myself. I hadn't been home (like some people), warming my delicate feet before the salon's blazing hearth. I'm the one who'd bravely volunteered for the feminist front lines in war-torn Rwanda to write cutting-edge copy that just might save millions of women's lives.

Gloria did not hold all the trump cards. In addition to my stories of the gorilla scientist and the queen of burlesque, I had the grand prospect of writing my own magnum opus: *Athena to Zelda, Women of Wonder*. Most importantly, I had the satisfaction of doing it all on my own, with my head held high. A single, proud, unbowed woman.

Felix Kwizera

Somehow, in the terminal, it seemed more comfortable for Dativa and me to stand a little apart from our white friends. This did not make us sad or angry. It is what it is, we thought, and we both agreed that the larger situation seemed to be getting better, though slowly.

Regarding our African adventure, I was, all in all, satisfied and hopeful. I did not find my mother alive but I did find my other momma who'd nursed me as a babe and child and who knew the fates of my parents. I was lucky to learn what I did from her lips. Also, I no longer yearned for Rwanda. It was the place of my birth but I no longer saw it as my home. America (more specifically, New York), even with its drugs, race-hate and gangs, was my home. I would make my way there. I would be a success. I now had a lot of contacts and references to help me. As soon as I was settled professionally, Dativa and I would marry.

Dativa Natukunda

Felix and I discussed our plans. We spoke confidentially and as equals. He told me he would one day buy me a gold and diamond wedding ring but I said no. It's true, I told him, I'd always wanted one — but no more. Now, I only wanted his mother's bone and shell ring. I liked the story it told. When we married, I told him, I would move the ring from my engaged finger to my married finger.

My nanny couple welcomed me back. They were very warm and wanted to hear all about my trip. When I told them about some of the terrible things we saw — and finally shared with them my own orphan history — they both cried. They even hugged me.

The wife was pregnant again. They asked — almost like begging — for me to continue as the family nanny. They gave me a big raise just for coming back and promised an even bigger raise for me to watch their two children.

I was very happy. I thought: *Now I only need my own child to feel complete.* Felix and I decided that we'd name the baby *Felix* or *Felicia*.

Debora Karekezi

We were sorry and not sorry to see our friends go. Our time with them had been both instructive and disruptive. They had their ways and we had ours, and even with common goals there were bound to be disagreements.

But all things turned out blessedly well. The Americans returned to New York while Albert and Augusta remained on our home soil, which was a good thing. Before the arrival of the Americans, Augusta and Albert knew just enough about America to imagine that their lives would be improved and happier if they transplanted there. Thank God they discovered mutual love and nationalistic commitment; otherwise, they might have lived misspent lives of sullen disappointment.

As for my husband's disappointment in having only one child — and that one a girl — it had largely been ameliorated by his grooming young Albert to be his professional protégé. Sadly, when Auguste learned that Albert had kept secrets to contest his professional authority, my husband's long-nurtured dream crashed suddenly. I'd never seen him so disappointed and sad.

Mercifully, another revelation saved the day. When Albert asked for a private meeting in our home, Auguste was prepared to hear the young man's confession and to offer forgiveness — tied to a series of professional penances. But life did not work out that way. Instead of a confession, Auguste heard Albert's declaration of love. "I love your daughter, Sir, and wish with all my heart to marry her."

Auguste was still processing that thrilling news when Albert confessed the particulars of his professional sins. When Auguste knew the whole story of Albert's sacrifice to help Felix find his mother, he forgave Albert all his transgressions. After all, so much cleverness and intelligence, supported by such stalwart principles, were very rare and would be needed to save lives and repair our broken nation. Further, Auguste was willing to concede that we all have secrets and that the keeper is usually best suited to decide the time and place of their revealing.

THE END

More Fiction from EnvelopeBooks

The Green Man | Dan Jones
After humiliating a fellow inquisitor at a trumped-up witch trial in Northern Italy, Brother Jacobus of Vienna is intrigued by rumours of strange events in Northern England. In defiance of the cardinals in Avignon, Jacobus travels to Berwick where he finds a land in disarray, beset by Scottish raiders, eccentric Franciscan friars and talk of demons in the woods. Can he solve the mystery and keep his faith and reason intact?

Mrs Woodbine's Prejudices | Michael Ladner
Prof. Arthur Lash, born Artur Lasch in pre-war Austria, takes his American wife and their three sons back to Vienna, in 1960, to see how well his father is rebuilding the life that was interrupted by Nazi Germany's annexation of Austria in 1938. For Arthur, the journey helps him re-establish his links with the city he was brought up in; for the rest of his family, other emotions are awoken—all watched over by Mrs. Woodbine, the needy, disregarded but loyal family nanny.

Belle Nash and the Bath Soufflé | William Keeling Esq.
In the first volume of *The Gay Street Chronicles*, bachelor Belle Nash attempts to navigate bigotry and corruption in 1830s Bath without compromising his boyfriend, the nephew of Immanuel Kant, or his best friend, the widow of Bath's greatest lawyer. Intrigue and whimsy overflow after—horror!—a soufflé fails to rise.

A Sin of Omission | Marguerite Poland
An emotionally intense novel, set in 1870s South Africa at a time of rising anti-colonial resistance. The book examines the tragedy of a promising black preacher, hand-picked for training in England as a missionary, only to be neglected by the Church he loves. Winner of the 2021 *Sunday Times* CNA 'Book of the Year' Award in South Africa.

The Train House on Lobengula Street | Fatima Kara

An anguished, folksy and life-affirming novel, set within the Indian community in Bulawayo, Rhodesia, from the 1940s to the 1960s, about the capacity of women to gain the same advantages as men in the modern world while remaining faithful to traditional Muslim values. Affectionate and passionate.

Mustard Seed Itinerary | Robert Mullen

Po Cheng falls into a dream and finds himself on the road to the imperial Chinese capital. Once there he rises to the heights of the civil service, then discovers that in addition to the ladders that helped him ascend, there are snakes facilitating his fall. Carrollian satire at its best.

Frances Creighton: Found and Lost | Kirby Porter

Love demands trust, but trust is a lot to ask for a victim of abuse. Having been bullied in Belfast as a boy, at his school and at his church, Michael Roberts suppresses his childhood pains until the death of a girlfriend years later forces him to revisit lost memories.

Belle Nash and the Bath Circus | William Keeling Esq.

In Volume Two of *The Gay Street Chronicles*, bachelor Belle Nash returns to Regency Bath from Grenada, inspired by a new love that leads him into various pretences that may compromise the ambitions of black circus impresario Pablo Fanque.

Lagos, Life and Sexual Distraction | Tunde Ososanya

Twelve short stories, mostly focused on the struggle to survive in Lagos, Nigeria's commercial capital, illustrate the tensions that exist between the generations, between the sexes and between the country's different social classes and ethnicities.

The Attraction of Cuba | Chris Hilton

Chris Hilton went to Cuba to escape the boredom of everyday life and to make money, only to be entranced by the beauty of the country and of Yamilia, a street girl who brought him love and laughter but who could not help him from falling into an inevitable downward spiral.

Princess Brainy | Stephen Games

Princess Raine couldn't help being hated for being clever, but it didn't help that her mother (the Queen) was modern and made her father (the King) ban the fairies. So what was Raine meant to do when disaster came to Rainland and the rivers dried up? Accept her fate or get sacrificed to the revolution?

The Hopeful Traveller | Janina David

A collection of short stories about—and told by—single women who have put the past behind them but are still looking for their anchor in the present. It includes bitter-sweet accounts of the freedoms of postwar life, of foreign travel, of the rekindling of old friendships and of the search for new ones.

A Girl's Own War | K.J. Kelly

Flt. Lieut. Oliver Carmichael and Baron Julius von Stulpnagel had been living together in Berlin, trying to sell forged paintings. Why are they now in run-down Ballingore, in wartime neutral Ireland in 1940, and how will ex-convent-girl Mary Collins and her devoted red-headed sidekick Niamh Slattery play into their hands? Hilarious Irish farce.

Non-fiction from EnvelopeBooks

A Question of Paternity | David Tereshchuk

TV reporter David Tereshchuk has traveled the world questioning the perpetrators of injustice and their victims, but could never prise one answer from his own mother: who his father was. Her evasion set him off on a life of insecurity and alcoholism. And a quest.

The West and the Rest | Ian Ross

Having worked in the oil and tobacco industries, Ian Ross argues that trade is objectively more creative than democracy in bridging cultural divisions. Where diplomats are held back by caution and principle, business executives are incentivised to be adaptable, forward-looking, unprejudiced and trusting. An eye-opener.

A Road to Extinction | Jonathan Lawley

When Britain colonised the Andamans in 1857, the welfare of its African pygmy inhabitants was of no concern. Nine tribes died out. Dr Lawley now assesses the survival prospects for the three remaining tribes and weighs up the legacy of his grandfather, a former colonial administrator

Wembley Speaks: A Year in the Life of a London Suburb

How do very different people talk to each other, react to each other, give and ask for advice, conciliate, commiserate and laugh? In a modern reconstruction of Mayhew's landmark 19th-century social study, EnvelopeBooks turns to the *Nextdoor* social-media networking app to observe an ethnically diverse community engaging with itself on day-to-day issues. A priceless archive.

Lost Levant: A Journey of Ideas | Rupert de Borchgrave

In the last millennium, cultural innovation has moved inexorably westwards, leaving us with too small a grasp of the turmoil out of which our own civilisation grew. In 2003 Rupert de Borchgrave set off on a journey of ideas that took him to the much-disputed grounds where many of the possibilities and problems that shape us now were formed.

Artist Spy Prisoner | George Tomaziu

Artist George Tomaziu was imprisoned and tortured for monitoring Nazi troop movements through Bucharest during the Second World War but imagined that his heroism would be recognised if Romania ever became free. He was terribly mistaken. Three years after the war ended he was imprisoned again—this time for thirteen years.

Why My Wife Had To Die | Brian Verity

There is no known cure for Huntington's disease, a wasting condition that sufferers acquire from a parent. In this painful account, the author vents his rage at society, lawmakers, health services and the Church for not grasping the need, as he sees it, to legalise compulsory sterilisation and assisted dying.

The Martyrdom of Ahmad Shawkat | Michael Goldfarb

When Gulf War II broke out in 2003, Ahmad Shawkat became guide and translator to NPR-reporter Michael Goldfarb. After the fall of Saddam, Ahmad set up a cultural magazine, published eleven issues and was killed for publicly decrying Islamic terror. This is his story.

From Bedales to the Boche | Robert Best

Bedales, the progressive boarding school founded by J.H. Badley in 1893, instilled values that sustained many of its pupils for the rest of their lives. Robert Best recalls its influence on him as an enthusiastic army recruit in 1914 and, from 1916, in the Royal Flying Corps.

My Modern Movement | Robert Best

London's Festival of Britain in 1951 marked the belief that Modern design was visually, morally and commercially superior. Robert Best, the UK's leading lighting manufacturer, thinks the dice were loaded. This is his memoir.

Postmark Africa | Michael Holman

Made an Amnesty Prisoner of Conscience while he was under house arrest as a student in Rhodesia, the author went on to document Africa's emergence from colonialism as Africa Editor of the *Financial Times*. This book is a must-read introduction to Africa's dreams of independence.

Printed in Great Britain
by Amazon

62721893R00133